ALL

"Exceptional…Shearin has proven herself to be an expert storyteller with the enviable ability to provide both humor and jaw-dropping action."

—*RT Book Reviews*

"*All Spell Breaks Loose* not only lived up to my expectations but was even BETTER!"

—*Dangerous Romance*

CON & CONJURE

"Tons of action and adventure but it also has a bit of romance and humor…All of the characters are excellent…The complexities of the world that Ms. Shearin has developed are fabulous."

—*Night Owl Reviews*

"Action packed and fast paced, this was a fabulous read."

—*Fresh Fiction*

"*Con & Conjure* is a great addition to a wonderful series, and I'm looking forward to *All Spell Breaks Loose* and whatever else [Shearin writes] with high anticipation."

—*Dear Author*

BEWITCHED & BETRAYED

"Once again, Ms. Shearin has given her readers a book that you don't want to put down. With Raine, the adventures never end."

—*Night Owl Reviews*

"*Bewitched & Betrayed* might just be the best in the series so far!… an amazingly exciting fourth installment that really tugs at the heart strings."

—*Ink and Paper*

"If you're new to Shearin's work, and you enjoy fantasy interspersed with an enticing romance, a little bit of humor, and a whole lot of grade-A action, this is the series for you."

—*Lurv a la Mode*

The Trouble with Demons

"The book reads more like an urban fantasy with pirates and sharp wit and humor. I found the mix quite refreshing. Lisa Shearin's fun, action-packed writing style gives this world life and vibrancy."

—*Fresh Fiction*

"Lisa Shearin represents that much needed voice in fantasy that combines practiced craft and a wicked sense of humor."

—*Bitten by Books*

"The brisk pace and increasingly complex character development propel the story on a rollercoaster ride through demons, goblins, elves, and mages while maintaining a satisfying level of romantic attention…that will leave readers chomping at the bit for more."

—*Monsters and Critics*

"This book has the action starting as soon as you start the story and it keeps going right to the end…All of the characters are interesting, from the naked demon queen to the Guardians guarding Raine. All have a purpose and it comes across with clarity and detail."

—*Night Owl Reviews*

Armed & Magical

"Fresh, original, and fall-out-of-your-chair funny, Lisa Shearin's *Armed & Magical* combines deft characterization, snarky dialogue, and nonstop action—plus a yummy hint of romance—to create one of the best reads of the year. This book is a bona fide winner, the series a keeper, and Shearin a definite star on the rise."

—*Linnea Sinclair, RITA Award-winning author of* Rebels and Lovers

"An exciting, catch-me-if-you-can, lightning-fast-paced tale of magic and evil filled with goblins, elves, mages, and a hint of love interest that will leave fantasy readers anxiously awaiting Raine's next adventure."

—Monsters and Critics

"The kind of book you hope to find when you go to the bookstore. It takes you away to a world of danger, magic, and adventure, and it does so with dazzling wit and clever humor. It's gritty, funny, and sexy—a wonderful addition to the urban fantasy genre. I absolutely loved it. From now on Lisa Shearin is on my auto-buy list!"

—Ilona Andrews, #1 New York Times bestselling author
of Magic Shifts

"Armed & Magical, like its predecessor, is an enchanting read from the very first page. I absolutely loved it. Shearin weaves a web of magic with a dash of romance that thoroughly snares the reader. She's definitely an author to watch!"

—Anya Bast, New York Times bestselling author
of Embrace of the Damned

MAGIC LOST, TROUBLE FOUND

"Take a witty, kick-ass heroine and put her in a vividly realized fantasy world where the stakes are high, and you've got a fun, page-turning read in Magic Lost, Trouble Found. I can't wait to read more of Raine Benares's adventures."

—Shanna Swendson, author of Don't Hex with Texas

"A wonderful fantasy tale full of different races and myths and legends [that] are drawn so perfectly readers will believe they actually exist. Raine is a strong female, a leader who wants to do the right thing even when she isn't sure what that is…Lisa Shearin has the magic touch."

—Midwest Book Review

"Shearin serves up an imaginative fantasy…The strong, well-executed story line and characters, along with a nice twist to the 'object of unspeakable power' theme, make for an enjoyable, fast-paced read."

—Monsters and Critics

"Lisa Shearin turns expectation on its ear and gives us a different kind of urban fantasy with *Magic Lost, Trouble Found*. For once, the urban is as fantastic as the fantasy, as Shearin presents an otherworld city peopled with beautiful goblins, piratical elves, and hardly a human to be found. Littered with entertaining characters and a protagonist whose self-serving lifestyle is compromised only by her loyalty to her friends, Magic Lost is an absolutely enjoyable read. I look forward to the next one!"

—*C. E. Murphy, author of* Raven Calls

"Nicely done. I actively enjoyed the characters and their banter."

—*Critical Mass*

"Fun, fascinating, and loaded with excitement! *Magic Lost, Trouble Found* is a top-notch read of magic, mayhem, and some of the most charming elves and goblins I've ever encountered. Enthralling characters and a thrilling plot…I now need to cast a spell on Ms. Shearin to ensure there's a sequel."

—*Linnea Sinclair, RITA Award–winning author of* Rebels and Lovers

RUINS
&
REVENGE

RUINS
&
REVENGE

A RAINE BENARES WORLD NOVEL

LISA SHEARIN

NLA Digital, LLC
1732 Wazee Street, Suite 207
Denver, CO 80202

Production Manager: Lori Bennett
Cover art and design: Aleta Rafton
Interior design: Angie Hodapp

ISBN 978-1-62051-266-1

"Wisdom consists of knowing how to distinguish the nature of trouble, and in choosing the lesser evil."

The Prince
Niccolò Machiavelli

1

I knew that saving the world wasn't going to be easy, but I would have appreciated fewer personnel issues.

Though I had only myself to blame.

My strike team consisted of seven goblins—and one elf. An elf who wasn't known for playing well with others, especially when most of those others were not only goblins, but powerful mages.

And I'd been the one who had brought him on board.

Like I said: my problem, my fault, my job to find a solution.

I stood on the beach watching our three sentry dragons being saddled and loaded for departure. Captain Calik Bakari of the Rheskilian Royal Fighter Squadron and two of his best pilots were overseeing every detail. The dragons were their mounts, but only Calik would be piloting his dragon on the journey inland. The other two would be flown by myself and another member of my team.

The two pilots weren't happy about that, and they were making no secret of it.

I didn't blame them, but our plans had changed.

We now had two additional team members—my son Talon, and the elf pirate captain Phaelan Benares.

Calik crossed the rocky beach to where I waited for the lecture I knew was coming.

"The ladies will be ready when you are," he said. "Vendin and Kasit are not."

I sighed. "Dasant and I are more than capable—"

"They know that, but understand that we're close to our dragons. We're going into danger, meaning their girls are going into danger—and they're staying here. Your qualifications aren't in question. That they're not going is the problem. A big one."

"Talon is going as a power boost for Agata, and extra firepower for the team. Bane isn't going anywhere with his broken leg, so our team is down a tomb robber and demolitions expert. Phaelan can fill his boots and then some. There're bound to be booby traps in Nidaar set against mage and magical null. Being magic users, the rest of us would set them off merely by proximity. Plus, Phaelan's a null who knows his way around traps."

Calik held up his hands. "Hey, I don't need convincing, and neither do they. What they are is worried."

"I understand."

"They're soldiers, and you're in charge of this mission. They're good at taking orders—but there's no regulation that tells them they have to like them. They'll just pace a rut in the beach until we get back. We're leaving within two hours?"

"We are."

"We'll be ready." He went back to where the dragons and pilots waited.

There were two other reasons I wanted to take Phaelan with us, but Calik wasn't a magic user, and his acceptance and understanding would only go so far. His job was to fly Sapphira to the mountain said to contain the city of Nidaar, then take care of her and the other two sentry dragons while we found the Heart of Nidaar. He didn't need to know any other details.

My team did. And to get them to accept the elf pirate as part of our team, I had to convince them we needed him.

Phaelan Benares wasn't particularly fond of magic, even less of powerful practitioners. Though Phaelan's feelings would probably be better described as distrust—on the extreme end of the spectrum. All of the goblins going inland were in the top five percent of the strongest mages in the Seven Kingdoms. When your mission was to keep an evil goblin military brotherhood and their alien invader allies from getting their hands on an artifact that could command the power of the earth and seas to destroy all life, you needed the best and baddest on your side. Basically, we'd crossed an ocean to piss off our archenemies by swiping a bauble that was their last chance at power. And a chance to put an end to the Khrynsani made it more than worth the trip.

Our adversaries knew we were here. One of our expedition's ships had been blown up before we'd ever left the goblin capital of Regor. At the voyage's halfway point, we'd been attacked by phantom ships manned by crews of demons and the dead. And once we were within sight of the continent of Aquas, Khrynsani and Sythsaurian weather wizards had conjured a storm to sink our small fleet.

We'd survived and arrived.

But I didn't delude myself. This was where the real danger started.

It had taken four weeks to get here. We had to find Nidaar and accomplish our mission—to keep the Khrynsani and their alien allies from obtaining the Heart—as quickly as possible.

What my goblin team wasn't quite grasping was why an elf pirate captain with no magic was a necessary addition. Telling them "because I said so" might end the discussion, but it wouldn't make the problem go away.

That was the drawback to commanding a strike team mostly made up of your childhood friends.

My name is Tamnais Nathrach. I'm the chief mage for the goblin royal house of Mal'Salin, a duke and chancellor to the new king, that king's heir until he produced his own, and a nearly rehabilitated practitioner of black magic.

Now I can add *leader of an expedition to hopefully save the Seven Kingdoms* to that list.

Surprisingly, Phaelan had come to me and volunteered. Even more surprising—approaching shocking, actually—was that I had agreed with him.

I'd accepted Phaelan's offer not only because I now knew him to be courageous and resourceful. My team had witnessed that bravery firsthand in Phaelan's command of the *Kraken* during the attack of the giant waves, which would make his inclusion easier to accept. But I had a more personal reason.

My intuition told me he would be needed. And I'd learned through past unpleasant experience that I ignored my gut feelings at my peril.

Most people have what can be called intuition, instinct, premonition, a hunch. Some listen when that little voice starts talking, others don't. I wasn't clairvoyant, I couldn't see the future, but on occasion my little voice has been known to give me a shove in a particular direction. It told me we needed Phaelan Benares, and if it was steering me wrong, it would be the first time. I wasn't about to take the risk of telling it no.

I had just learned another reason. A reason that confirmed my instincts.

I wore a piece of the Heart of Nidaar in a ring. The team's gem mage, Agata Azul, wore another tiny nugget in a pendant. She was one of the top gem mages in the Seven Kingdoms, and I had sought her out to use her prodigious gift to help us locate the Heart. During the four-week voyage, Agata had bonded with the Heart's fragment. That bond had saved our fleet when an unknown entity had activated the Heart against us, causing an earthquake and giant waves to destroy our ships. Agata had reached through the fragment to the Heart itself and—with a magical power boost from Talon—had calmed it, stopping the earthquake and saving all our lives.

The earthquake and the giant waves we had experienced were but a fraction of what the Heart of Nidaar was capable of. Nine hundred years ago, a group of Khrynsani dark mages found and gained access to the city of Nidaar and its Heart. Their clumsy attempts to activate and test the stone's power had resulted in a series of earthquakes that laid waste to hundreds of miles of Aquas's eastern coast, draining every lake and river, turning a green paradise full of life into a barren wasteland.

We didn't know whether the Khrynsani had taken control of the stone again, or whether it had been activated by the Cha'Nidaar, the keepers of the Heart who were last seen nine hundred years ago, still determined to protect themselves and the stone. Or—like another stone of my recent acquaintance—had the Heart of Nidaar become sentient and was it now capable of protecting itself from any who traveled to Aquas's shores?

I wasn't the only one whose intuition was telling them that we would need Phaelan before this was all over. Agata had told me she was certain that somehow and in some way, Phaelan Benares's presence would be critical to the success of our mission.

The stone in her pendant had seconded that motion.

Who was I to argue with a woman *and* her jewelry?

That was good enough for me.

Hopefully, it would be good enough for my team.

Phaelan wouldn't exactly be welcomed with open arms, but he would be accepted—for my sake. My team trusted me with their lives, but even my word would only go so far. The rest was up to Phaelan. Not only could he not screw up, he couldn't make even one, small mistake.

And he knew it.

Time for a team meeting.

Elsu Lenmana squinted against the late-afternoon sun and up at the escarpment towering hundreds of feet above our heads, a relic of the earthquake set off centuries before when the Khrynsani activated the Heart of Nidaar.

"That was some earthquake," Elsu said.

Our team sharpshooter had a flair for understatement, a characteristic that carried over to her magic. Her gift enabled her to focus immense power with pinpoint accuracy and complete silence. Magic made noise. Elsu Lenmana's magic did not. She didn't need to get close to her chosen target. If she could see it, she could shoot it. Elsu could generate a needle of fire that could cut through solid rock—or anything else that got in her way.

Goblins were tall and leanly muscled. Elsu was smaller than average, curvy, and soft. Or so she appeared to a casual observer, and Elsu attracted her share of observers— casual and those with intent. She was more than capable of encouraging attention if needed for a distraction, or discouraging attention—or breathing—permanently.

"An earthquake caused by a stone whose new best friend— our team gem mage—feels certain an elf pirate captain needs to come with us," she added.

Dasant chuckled. "Don't forget that opinion was confirmed by her pendant—a piece of that earthquake-causing stone."

"Like that makes it sound better."

The big goblin tossed me a quick grin, then made a show of thinking it over, complete with frown and furrowed brow. "You have to admit it sounds more reasonable than 'Tam's gut told him so.'"

If Elsu's magic was a silent arrow to the heart, Dasant Kele's was a deck-clearing cannon blast. What he lacked in finesse, he more than made up for with sheer destructive power. If something needed destroying, simply point Das in the right direction and he'd take it from there. Cheerfully.

I gave them a crooked grin. "On behalf of my gut, I'm offended. The next time it tries to warn me and save your doubting lives, I'll keep that information to myself. Like that mountain troll ambush outside Dunmor, or that cave full of *not*-hibernating bukas, or—"

"Yes, we've all been grateful for your clairvoyant intestines," drawled a voice from behind me.

As always, I hadn't heard Malik's approach, even on a rock-strewn beach. Preternaturally silent even for a goblin, it was said that Death himself envied Malik Chiali's stealth in approaching his victims—or his friends. Malik was an equal opportunity creeper. He also didn't suffer fools easily or gladly, and felt that the majority of the goblin population fell into the fool category. He was one of the most intelligent people I had ever known, and my friend had little patience with those less brilliant than himself, which meant nearly everyone.

"What are they warning us about this time?" he asked.

"They're saying to take Phaelan Benares with us," Dasant told him.

The only reaction that earned from Malik was an arched eyebrow. "Would this be in reference to Captain Benares's swashbuckling derring-do?" he asked me.

"No."

"His devil-may-care disregard for danger?"

"No."

"His belief that the streets of Nidaar are paved with gold?"

I shook my head. "Jash told him they're not. He enjoyed breaking that news way too much."

Malik spread his hands. "Then Tamnais, my friend, I am at a loss."

"It was Tam's gut *and* Agata's shard," Elsu told him. "Apparently it thrummed when Phaelan asked Tam to go with us."

There went the eyebrow again. "Thrummed?"

"Thrummed," I said. "Agata's description. It happened when Phaelan asked to go with us, and again when I agreed."

"When you *and* your gut agreed," Dasant chimed in.

"Yes, me and my gut. Agata told me she has experienced the same response from other stones of power. It's an affirmation."

Malik shrugged. "Then so be it. Far be it from me to dispute Tamnais's viscera *and* opinionated jewelry."

"Also, Bane's in no shape to go anywhere," I said.

Bane Ahiga wasn't happy and neither was I, but you had to play the cards you were dealt. Bane's cards had gotten him a broken leg in the attack on a pair of Nebian frigates. He was up and moving around, albeit slowly and with the aid of a cane. Without our fleet's first-rate healers, he'd still be in bed. Because of their work, he was walking and getting stronger every day, but he wasn't strong enough or fast enough for what we had to do.

He would be staying behind, working with Kesyn Badru, my teacher and mage heavyweight, as a two-man battlemagic security force for the ships. If we were successful in our quest, we needed a way to get home. If we failed, either we wouldn't need a way home or the goblins and elves on the ships soon wouldn't have a home to go to.

Bane had met with Phaelan and deemed him qualified for the mission. Bane didn't give approval lightly. In fact, he'd never deemed anyone to be even remotely close to his level of demolitions expertise.

That said a lot about Phaelan's skill. I just wasn't sure if what it said was a good thing.

"Phaelan's done a lot of tomb robbing and demolitions in his time," I told them.

"Bane's also a mage."

I smiled slowly. "And Phaelan's a null."

That won me a few slow grins and nods of grudging approval.

They knew what I was saying. A null was a person who had no magic at all. If you had valuables you wanted to keep, you protected them with physical measures such as locks, and magical means, such as wards or spells. If you could afford it, you did both. This ensured that a thief who was also a mage would set off alarms and often fatal countermeasures if they got too close to a vault, or wherever you kept your valuables. Magic could be sensed. It wasn't difficult. What *was* difficult for any magic user was to tamp down their magic so it couldn't be detected at all. Most, me included, could hold it down for less than a minute. That wouldn't be long enough to get into a vault. That's where a null who was also a talented thief came in handy.

A null and thief such as Phaelan Benares.

In addition, the Khrynsani would be looking and listening for goblins. Not listening with their ears, but with their magical senses. An elf registered differently than a goblin; an elf null would register as background noise, if at all.

One thing I wasn't going to tell my team was to behave with Phaelan. Every man and woman on my team, regardless of race, had better be able to take care of themselves. Phaelan would be no exception. My team had spent four weeks at sea on ships captained by his siblings. I was sure they'd heard plenty of stories. They knew what they needed to know. Phaelan was more than capable of taking care of himself. If one of my people took teasing one step too far, they'd find that out for themselves.

I took every mission seriously, and I felt the same way about my entertainment.

Elsu was watching me. She smiled very slightly. "Sounds like we're taking an elf."

2

We would be traveling light, and that included food and water.

No goblin liked field rations, but I would gladly give up gourmet dining to have a week's worth of food that fit in a small pouch at my waist. I could fight or run for my life and not be weighted down. While the taste left much to be desired, you felt full after eating it, and your strength never lagged. As far as I was concerned, when you were in the desert, you couldn't ask for more than that.

Water was more difficult. We each could carry only one waterskin; fortunately, one of our team members had a gift that kept on giving. Water, that is.

Count Jash Masloc was a mage and my best friend. He controlled a microportal to a mountain stream outside of Dragalon. It was just large enough to get a small bucket or a waterskin through for refilling. Each dragon would have a collapsible leather bucket strapped to her saddle. The stream had never run dry. Jash's stash had come in handy many times, but it would be life-saving over the next few days. He was also our team tracker. Jash could sense life signs. If there was an ambush ahead—or we neared a lost civilization living inside a mountain—he would know about it.

We'd sent Indigo, one of our firedrakes, to the top of the escarpment as a lookout. The images sent back to us via the spy gem he wore on a harness showed an empty landscape. Empty of an ambush, at least. There were plenty of rocks. I knew full well that just because we couldn't see any threats didn't mean they weren't lying in wait for us. Hopefully, Jash wouldn't earn his keep that quickly.

The sun was setting beyond the mountains that were our destination, but it was already dark on the rocky beach at the foot of the escarpment. We were dressed for flight and protection from the desert winds in close-fitting leather with minimal seams, though I was certain sand would find a way in. It always did. Personal comfort wasn't our priority.

I'd had goggles made that would darken to protect goblin eyes during the day and clear after dark to maximize our superior night vision. I'd had Bane bespell a pair for Phaelan to allow the elf to see as well in the dark as a goblin. The goggles fit closely around our eyes to protect against blowing sand.

We were as ready as we were going to be.

Our three sentry dragons each carried two saddles: one for a single rider and a second that would accommodate two.

The two-seat saddles would be positioned behind the wings, with the single saddles mounted at the base of the dragons' necks. The three lightest team members would ride there. That would be Agata, Elsu, and Talon. Since we had the two pieces of the Heart, Agata and I would fly together, along with Phaelan, on Mithryn. Elsu would fly with Dasant and Malik on Amaranth. And Talon would fly with Calik and Jash on Sapphira.

Elsu was an experienced flier, Agata was unfazed by most anything, but Talon was eyeing Sapphira with trepidation.

I came up beside Talon, but kept my voice down. "What's the problem?"

"Not flying. It's flying up front."

"The lightest fly up front."

"Talk about incentive to gain weight."

"Calik will be right behind you."

Talon snorted. "And you'll have Phaelan behind you."

"Hopefully not screaming in my ear."

Phaelan had only one previous flight under his belt and made no secret of the fact he'd hoped it would be his last. Right now, he was standing in front of Mithryn, out of her biting range, but perfectly inside her turn-to-ash zone. A frozen grimace that I think he intended to be a smile was locked on his face.

I strolled over.

"I take it you're trying to make friends?" I asked him.

"I wanted to properly introduce myself."

I grinned. "Oh, she remembers who you are. Not only are sentry dragons very intelligent, they have long memories. You were less than polite last month in the warehouse before we set sail. All three dragons were right there when you said you weren't having any overgrown, fire-breathing lizards on your ship."

Mithryn narrowed her red eyes and rumbled deep in her chest.

"And you just reminded her again," he said without moving, including his lips. He tried smiling again. "I believe the lady and I may have gotten off on the wrong foot."

I leaned toward Mithryn. "He means he was rude."

"I think she knows that."

"Oh, I *know* she knows that."

Phaelan straightened his flight leathers. "I want to apologize."

"Then you should be talking to her, not me."

Phaelan cleared his throat and took a single step forward—a single, highly nervous, step forward.

"Madam, my behavior was boorish and inexcusable, and was based on unfamiliarity and ignorance on my part. I hope you can find it in your heart to forgive me and…uh, and not drop me to a messy death over this godforsaken continent."

"At least he's honest about his motivation," I told Mithryn.

The dragon snorted in a blast of sulfuric smoke. That it was in Phaelan's direction was merely a coincidence.

Maybe.

Phaelan held firm as long as he could, but his eyes started to water as he was forced to turn away, coughing. "Is that a yes?" he rasped.

"Dragons value actions over potentially empty words," I told him.

"Wise."

"They are. Think of it this way—your legs will be strapped in, so while she's probably tempted to do a couple of barrel rolls just for fun, Agata and I will also be her passengers. Mithryn likes us. Our fighter squadrons choose female dragons over males because they're more focused.

The males are too easily distracted. That means these ladies are professionals and know how to act like it. Not to mention, Mithryn knows you're carrying Nebian black powder and a few of Bane's toys."

"Nope."

"Nope, what?"

"Nope, I'm not carrying any of Bane's toys. Bane checked my demolition gear and approved. Me going instead of him is bad enough, he didn't want to give up his goody bag, too."

Flying with Phaelan behind me was going to be nerve-racking enough without knowing precisely what he was carrying in his pack.

Think positive thoughts, Tam.

"Well, between liking us, and you carrying explosives, Mithryn will behave."

Phaelan flashed a grin. "I'll take it."

I tried to smile. "See, you can be wise, too."

"Good, because I'm starting to think the wise thing to do is stay right here."

"Mithryn will—"

"This isn't about the dragon," Phaelan said. "It's about the rock. What's this I hear about Agata's pendant liking me? I've got news—I don't like *it,* and I'm not going to sweet-talk it into changing its mind."

"It would not change anything if you did," Agata said from behind him.

Phaelan didn't jump at Agata Azul coming up behind him on silent feet. He clearly wanted to, but he'd made admirable progress in adjusting to goblin stealth. On some level, I think he might even have sensed Agata behind him.

"And it didn't indicate like or dislike," she continued. "Merely approval of your presence on this mission."

"Yeah, so it can kill me."

"I beg your pardon?"

Phaelan saw the shard hanging outside of Agata's leather armor, raised both hands and took a step back. "Kill me, get me in its crosshairs, destroy my life. I'm a Benares. Bad things happen when rocks with names attach themselves to us."

Agata frowned in confusion. "It was a benign reaction. I sensed no animosity. In fact, the shard responds to me in precisely the same way as it did to you earlier."

"And it likes you? For a painless, non-evil reason?"

"Yes."

The tension eased from Phaelan's shoulders, but didn't completely go away. It was all we could reasonably expect right now.

"You can't blame me." Phaelan's eyes flicked nervously to the shard. "That rock on the end of your necklace came from the Heart of Nidaar, right?"

Agata nodded. "That is correct."

"That thing's mother tried to kill all of us. What if that little nugget wants to take us home to mama so she can finish the job?"

I had to admit that was a good question. And especially astute coming from Phaelan.

"Stones of power do not attack on their own volition," Agata assured him. "At least this one doesn't," she added, as much to me as to Phaelan.

Agata knew my experience with the Saghred had made me want to avoid contact with stones of power at any cost.

But in this instance, I had no choice. The Heart of Nidaar had to be found and kept out of Khrynsani hands. No one was more qualified to hunt down Khrynsani than I was. During the voyage to Aquas, Agata had gone out of her way to allay my fears by assuring me that most gems were benevolent and their magic beneficial.

"The Heart was being wielded by a person or persons," Agata was saying, "either defensively due to fear of us, or with malicious intent against us." She stepped forward and placed a hand lightly on Phaelan's arm. His tension lessened a little more at her touch. She had done the same to me more than once. It had worked then and was working for Phaelan now. "It's our job to put a stop to both."

Agata Azul, calmer of earthquakes and jittery pirates— and nervous goblin mages. A truly gifted lady.

"But I'm not a gem mage," Phaelan's gaze was curious now, and aimed at the pendant—and Agata's chest. "What can I do?"

"For one, our target isn't where you're looking," I said pointedly. "It's up there, across a desert, and somewhere inside those mountains. We'll need every advantage we can get. You and Talon are officially advantages, perhaps even weapons. I never leave behind weapons I might need."

"And your team agrees?"

"We do."

Jash.

In addition to being my best friend and second-in-command, Jash Masloc was a cheerful teaser of a certain elf pirate captain.

He glanced at Phaelan's flight armor. They wore the same

size, so he'd given the elf one of his own sets. I'd had all of our armor bespelled so it would blend with the terrain we'd be crossing by changing color like a chameleon.

"Sorry it's not your usual crimson," Jash noted.

Phaelan turned his arms this way and that. "But it is sleek and flexible." An instant later, he had drawn one of the curved swords slung across his back, tossing it lightly from one hand to the other, with a meaningful look at Jash. "And not one leathery creak. I approve."

"We goblins pride ourselves on our stealth," Jash said. "Our armor is made accordingly." The words weren't there, but the intent was, and I knew Jash's intent. Yet another goblin trait other races found off-putting. If Jash turned his intent into action and attempted to sneak up on Phaelan, even in jest, the joke would not be well received.

He and Phaelan had locked eyes. I read them both. Jash was teasing, mostly. Phaelan was saying to bring it.

I stepped between the two of them. "Gentlemen, and I am using that term lightly right now, I need—and *will have*—cooperation, not confrontation, between each member of this team. If that is going to be a problem for either one of you, change your attitude. Now."

Jash and Phaelan's eyes had remained locked while I spoke.

After a brief hesitation, Jash extended his hand. "I started this the day we sailed, so it should fall to me to apologize. Sometimes my idea of good, clean fun isn't the same as others'. If I have delivered insult, it was not intended."

Phaelan shook his hand. "I assure you, if you'd crossed my line, you would know." One side of his mouth tipped up in a crooked grin. "I can also assure you that I'll always give as good as I get, and then some."

Jash's answering grin was an exact match.

Great. Now it was a competition.

They wouldn't kill each other, but the bickering and barbs to come might drive me to kill them.

I draped an arm around their necks, giving a quick squeeze to make my point. "Just be sure neither one of you crosses *my* line. Understand?"

"Understood," they said in unison.

At least they said it together. For now, I'd take what I could get.

3

Agata, Jash, and I took Mithryn to the top of the escarpment.

Agata's connection with the Heart of Nidaar via her pendant had saved our lives once. Now it was time for the little shard to help save the lives of everyone in the Seven Kingdoms by showing us the way to its home.

Indigo's scouting flight had shown no ambushes waiting for us. It wasn't that I didn't trust what we'd seen via the spy gem in Indy's harness, but there was more to black magic than met the eye. I knew what the Khrynsani were capable of, and that included being able to conceal themselves in plain sight. The Sythsaurians were still largely an unknown variable, but their magic, like themselves, was completely alien.

Jash was there to sense the unseeable.

However, Jash's gift involved being able to sense that something was alive. The Sythsaurians had two legs and two arms, but did they have heartbeats, blood flow, and body temperature on par with goblins, elves, or humans? We knew their magic was powerful, but how powerful? Powerful enough to cloak themselves beyond what a mage of Jash's skill could sense? I had no doubt we'd find out the answers to those questions over the coming days, but I didn't want our first mistake to be fatal. So as a precaution, Agata would remain veiled and shielded on Mithryn until we were absolutely certain there was no danger. She was too valuable to the mission to needlessly risk her safety.

When sticking your head over the top of a cliff in a hostile environment, a little caution could go a long way toward a longer life. Once Agata had determined our direction, the others would join us. She needed an accurate reading, and seven goblin mages and a nervous elf pirate would kick up more psychic noise than anyone, regardless of how talented, could be expected to work around.

Our shielded heads rose over the edge of the escarpment, and then the rest of us, and we remained in one piece. Just because no one waited to separate our heads from our shoulders wasn't reason enough to lower our defenses or paranoia. Both were equally valuable survival tools.

Mithryn touched down on a vast plain of rock almost gingerly, as if she expected the ground to crumble beneath her claws. We weren't about to let down our guard, but we all at least started breathing again.

We stayed still, silent, and cloaked, with Mithryn ready to dive over the side of the escarpment if anything that wasn't us so much as blinked.

"Nothing," Jash said quietly from the saddle behind me.

I trusted Jash's assessments.

But caution outvoted trust as I slid silently from Mithryn's back, shields and veil still firmly in place.

Jash did the same.

I used every sense I had—magical and mundane—as I scanned as far as my eyes could see.

Not a trace of life.

I glanced at Jash. He nodded, and we dropped our shields and veil.

We were safe.

At least for the next five minutes.

The view via Indigo's spy gem hadn't done the sunset justice.

Magnificent was the only word that could even come close to describing it, and even that fell short. We stood there, gaping at the beauty of the copper and golden glow of the sun's rays against the plain of broken rock stretching to the haze in the distance that was the mountain range, our destination.

Jash shook his head in wonder—or dismay. "Not one stone standing on top of another."

"No obstacles means we can fly in low and fast."

My friend chuckled. "Phaelan's gonna love that." He squinted. "How far away are those canyons?"

"The first one is just past the halfway point," I told him.

"That's a lot of desert to cross to get to any kind of cover."

Behind us, Agata cleared her throat. Loudly.

I knew I'd forgotten something.

Mithryn was still veiled, so it was disconcerting to see Agata drop her shield and veils and slide down the dragon's flank to land solidly on the ground.

I murmured a few words and Mithryn winked into view.

Agata stood perfectly still for nearly a minute, staring at the mountains in the distance. "They look so close."

"Four days by foot," I said. "All night and then some by dragon."

"That's not nearly close enough." She indicated my right hand. "I need your ring now."

I slid the ring off and passed it to her.

The ring and pendant had been gifts to my ancestor, Kansbar Nathrach, from Baeseria, the queen of Nidaar, for revealing the Khrynsani plot to steal the Heart.

While our goal was to find the Heart of Nidaar, I held a secondary hope that the Cha'Nidaar still lived in the city. Kansbar's story had ended in suicide, the result of psychic rape inflicted by his Khrynsani interrogators. I very much wanted to meet the people who had helped him—the ancient golden-skinned cousins of my silver-skinned race.

Agata had removed her gloves and slid the ring onto her index finger, turning the stone around to face inward. The gem mage then knelt, placing her hands flat on the ground, fingers spread and pointing to the west, toward the mountains.

Jash and I waited.

We neither spoke nor moved, and had stilled our magic to ensure that nothing would interfere with what Agata was attempting to do—establish contact with the Heart of Nidaar to give us the stone's exact location and our flight path.

A vibration came up through the soles of my boots. A vibration that quickly turned to a rumble, as if the land itself were growling.

Mithryn shifted uneasily. Agata remained kneeling with

her eyes closed in concentration, so I forced myself to remain still. I quickly held up a hand to tell Jash to do the same.

Agata slowly rubbed the rocky ground with both hands, speaking soothing words I couldn't make out. I didn't need to know what they were. They weren't meant for me. I wasn't the one getting angry. However, I did have the market cornered on scared—for Agata. I wondered if stones of power could hold a grudge. Agata and Talon had stopped it from killing us all when we arrived at Aquas. Now, we weren't off the coast in ships. We were standing on the land it called home. I wasn't exactly feeling welcome, but I wasn't the one who'd thwarted its attack.

Agata opened her eyes. The rumbling stopped.

"Well," she began, "It's not what I would call happy that we're here."

I remained absolutely still. "I got that impression."

"I'm still getting that impression," Jash said. "As in, I'm still feeling a shaking."

"That's you," I told him.

"Oh. Well, you can hardly blame me."

I didn't. We had to find the Heart of Nidaar, and not only did the Heart probably not want to be found, it didn't even want us walking on the continent it had claimed for its own.

Agata still had her hands flat on the ground. "I would compare it to a growl."

"Do you still say someone was at the controls when the Heart caused that monster wave?" I asked.

"Normally, I'd say yes, but—"

"This isn't normal."

"No, it most definitely is not."

"Kansbar didn't mention anything about the Heart being sentient."

Agata stood. "I'm not getting open hostility, more like a warning. The Heart is so attuned to Aquas that it can sense those who don't belong standing or walking on its surface. I think it's not having a more violent reaction because we carry pieces of it in the pendant and ring. It may be confused as to how pieces of itself came to be outside of the city. Whenever we land, I should dismount first. Hopefully that will prevent the Heart from striking with an actual earthquake."

"At least we'll be flying and not walking," Jash noted. "Mithryn, my love, have I told you how beautiful you are today and every day?"

The dragon gave him a flat look.

"Did you get a direction?" I asked Agata.

"See those two really tall mountains to the left?"

"Yes."

"And the slightly smaller one in between?"

"Yes."

"That's the one. Or the best I can tell with this growling. It should get clearer the closer we get."

"Should."

Agata shrugged. "Gem magic isn't an exact science."

Jash squinted against the setting sun. "How far would you say that is?" he asked me.

"If we fly all night, we should be close by sunrise. Barring any interruptions—or eruptions."

"Barring those."

We all knew this would be the easy part. The difficulty and danger would come once we were underground and closer to the Heart.

I suspected that Sandrina Ghalfari had been able to track our fleet through me. We had both signed our names in blood to the front page of Rudra Muralin's record of Kansbar's torture. That had done more than enable us to read the words on the pages; it had linked us on some level, the same level that had allowed Sarad Nukpana to infest my dreams. We'd all signed and read the book. Yet, I couldn't locate Sandrina. I didn't know why. Perhaps, since Sandrina and the interrogation record were both using Khrynsani magic, she was immune from tracking by non-Khrynsani forces.

There were entirely too many questions and not nearly enough answers, or even logical reasons.

If Sandrina had already reached and gained control of the Heart, she'd also be able to track us using the shards in our possession. I'd taken to warding myself. Agata and I had agreed to do the same to the shards once we started our flight inland.

"Will warding the shards affect the Heart's ability to perceive us as friendlies?" I asked her.

"I will still be able to correct our flight path as needed," Agata said. "And I would imagine the Heart will still be able to sense the shards."

Jash shifted uneasily. "Is that a good or a bad thing?"

"Yes."

"I shouldn't have asked."

"I would advise that the crews stay on the ships as much as possible," Agata told me. "The Heart's influence lessens over water."

"So 'less influence' is what stirred up that mammoth wave?"

Agata tried a smile. It didn't quite make it. "Less is relative."

"What's to stop it from kicking up another wave once we're gone?"

"We—and any Khrynsani or Sythsaurians—will keep it occupied with our presence. I believe the Heart will save its strength for what it sees as a more immediate threat."

"And since we have two pieces of it, the Heart likes us?" Jash ventured.

"I wouldn't go that far. However, I don't think the Heart will destroy us outright until it has more information."

"So we don't make any sudden or aggressive moves."

"I wouldn't advise it."

I had a pleasant thought. "And if the Khrynsani have yet to reach the Heart and don't have a piece of the stone with which to soothe or at least confuse it …"

Agata's smile made it this time. "Let's just say I wouldn't want to be anywhere near them right now."

4

The Heart of Nidaar had growled at us. It'd thrown rocks at my team.

There had been a bit of an avalanche while we were gone.

The rest of the team weren't where we'd left them. They were mounted up with Sapphira and Amaranth hovering over the water about twenty yards from the beach.

Seeing the slabs of cliff that'd landed entirely too close to where they'd been, I would've taken to the air, too.

"Oops," Agata muttered from her saddle in front of me as Mithryn coasted down to the beach.

"What the hell did you do up there?" Dasant bellowed over the water.

"Think the Heart's finished throwing things?" I asked Agata.

She tossed a glance back up at the cliff. "If something's already loose it'll still fall, but I think the Heart's finished—for the moment."

"Long enough for all of us to land for a few minutes?"

"Your guess is as good as mine, but probably."

I signaled for Dasant and Calik to land on the beach, but to stay as close to the water and as far from the escarpment as possible. We landed, and Jash and Phaelan quickly switched dragons. Since Phaelan had only ridden a dragon once—and since I'd been the one who had insisted on bringing him—we'd decided that he'd be on Mithryn with me. While they switched dragons, Agata and I told everyone what had happened topside.

Phaelan hated magic, but right now he looked like a man who wanted nothing more than to be able to levitate.

"So the entire continent is possessed?" he asked.

"I wouldn't call it 'possessed,'" Agata said. "More like protective. It knows we're here. However, since we have the shards, it's not acting openly against us."

Elsu snorted. "It's not trying to kill *you*. Us, it tried to squash. We barely got airborne in time."

"We won't be touching down until close to dawn," I told her. "No landing, hopefully no problems."

"So, once we land, how are we supposed to find and get into the city?" Malik asked. "Walk politely?"

"I'll take Mithryn on point, and Agata will fine-tune our direction as we go—and see if she can talk the Heart into believing that we mean it no harm."

Our mission was to prevent the Khrynsani and Sythsaurians from getting their hands on the Heart of Nidaar. If they obtained it as a power source, the portals to the Sythsaurians' world would open, allowing vast armies to pour into the Seven Kingdoms. Every option was on the table to keep them from the Heart, including destroying it. The Saghred had to be emptied of souls before it could be smashed to bits. The Heart of Nidaar was self-sustaining, no souls needed for fuel. The Saghred had been the size of a man's fist, but the Heart of Nidaar was said to be considerably larger—and embedded inside of a mountain. Even if it could be destroyed, we might not be able to get close enough to do it. But we wouldn't know that for certain until we found it.

We veiled ourselves and the three sentry dragons before we rose above the top of the escarpment. Veils were a quiet magic, and we were highly adept mages. Even so, those who would be hunting us were equally as skilled. The earthquake nine hundred years before had left behind a landscape that looked like mountain ranges in miniature. It would have been a slow and dangerous passage on foot, but our dragons skimmed over the jagged peaks, leaving only a few feet between us and them. It was too close for Phaelan's comfort.

While everyone on the team had flight experience with sentry dragons, Dasant and I had logged the most time in the pilot's saddle. Sentry dragons preferred the pilots they'd trained with, but they would adapt to other hands at the reins. They just needed to be experienced hands, or shenanigans would follow.

Sapphira had her pilot/partner Calik at the reins. They would fly as one. Mithryn and Amaranth would likely try and pull a fast one, but it'd merely be a test of our piloting ability rather than actual mutiny. These were three of the best sentry dragons in the Rheskilian squadron. They were professionals and knew how to act like it. They were also highly intelligent and mischievous. The girls would push our boundaries, but once we proved ourselves qualified to hold their reins, all hijinks would end.

Mithryn was out in front with Sapphira and Amaranth behind and to the left and right, Amaranth slightly higher, with Sapphira a little lower. We were all on alert for any form of attack.

Our flight positions weren't merely defensive.

The area between the coast and the mountain range that was only a distant haze had been mapped, but only in the most rudimentary sense. Landmarks had been marked that were either helpful in orientation or dangerous and to be avoided.

The most recent maps had been made three hundred years ago, the time of the last official expedition to Aquas. The land could have changed since then. No one knew whether the Heart had caused other earthquakes, or whether the land, once disturbed, had continued to shift and settle.

Since marking corrections on a map while flying was impossible at best, suicidal at worst, each dragon had a spy gem mounted on her chest harness. Mithryn's gem faced forward, Amaranth's was aimed straight down, and Sapphira's gem was angled to catch the rear view. Once we'd returned home, combining the views would provide an invaluable source of mapping information for future explorers.

I was counting on the map I had memorized still being somewhat accurate.

I was counting even more on Agata Azul's skill.

Our ship's healer had cleared both Agata and Talon for

travel. Flight had been do-able; traveling to Nidaar on foot would have been impossible for both of them. They'd nearly drowned in the Heart's attack on our ships, and while the healer had declared their lungs free of seawater, they had both taken a beating. We all wore filters over our mouths and noses that connected to our helmets, not only to keep dust from getting into our lungs, but to warm our breath in the night air. Deserts might be hot during the day, but the temperatures dropped rapidly at night. Talon and Agata needed to be protected from both dust and cold as much as possible.

The sun had sunk beyond the horizon, but the last rays still illuminated the peaks of the mountain range in their glow, turning the land we flew over from gold and copper to brown and black.

We had been airborne for only an hour. We would not stop until we reached our destination, the base of a mountain whose peak cut a ragged gash across the twilight sky.

We didn't know what we were going to find and what condition it would be in when we found it. The Heart was in perfect working order. But what about Nidaar? The Cha'Nidaar had never been seen again after my ancestor's encounter. Without a population, the city would not have been maintained.

We'd be playing this one as we went along, with our primary goal being to keep the Khrynsani from getting anywhere near it.

However, there was one thing we knew we'd be encountering once we got close to the mountains.

A maze of deep canyons.

The Heart had cracked the land like a giant spiderweb, radiating outward from the mountain range. The earthquakes had caused massive splits in the ground, forming rifts and canyons, revealing entrances to dozens of cave networks, any of which could be dead ends.

The weather wizard attack seemed to confirm that the Khrynsani and Sythsaurians had a head start. I had read every book and document, and memorized every map that was in the Khrynsani temple library. But what if the Khrynsani had access to other sources of information? Better, more accurate sources?

The maps didn't show what was beyond the mountains. The Khrynsani hadn't cared to know. What they wanted was inside one mountain. Kansbar Nathrach's party had landed fifty miles south of our location. I had the coordinates from Rudra Muralin's torture of my ancestor. I knew the mountain they had camped at the foot of. But they had been blindfolded when the Cha'Nidaar had taken them deep inside the mountains to the hidden city, walking for at least half a day. Some of it could have been backtracking to confuse them, but Kansbar hadn't known, and as a result, neither did I. When he was taken out of the city, he had been blindfolded again, the blindfold removed only when he was on the surface, presumably far away from Nidaar.

The Cha'Nidaar had told my ancestor that they wanted to be left alone. Their queen had told Kansbar that they would never be found again. So far, the Cha'Nidaar had made good on that promise.

The information in all the books I'd read seemed to have come from the same, ancient source. The most revealing had come from Rudra Muralin's record of my ancestor's torture, and even that was severely lacking.

Supposedly, the Cha'Nidaar were goblins much like

ourselves who left Rheskilia about fifteen hundred years ago for an unknown reason. Some sources said it was due to political differences, others social, and still other religious. We goblins were a contentious lot; it could have been all three and a few more piled on besides.

Regardless, they had set out for the west, to Aquas, a continent as shrouded in mystery then as it was now.

The language that goblins spoke then was as far removed from what was spoken now as it was possible to be. The records of the Goblin language from that time were as confusing as they were sparse. I had attempted to locate an expert in ancient Goblin languages, but there were none to be found, which was hardly surprising considering Sathrik's penchant for imprisoning and executing not only those who disagreed with him, but also those with higher intellectual capabilities than himself. Of all the Mal'Salin kings, Sathrik had ranked toward the bottom in terms of intellectual curiosity. He had gladly turned over his thinking to Sarad Nukpana. That had been his fatal mistake.

Nidaar was deep inside a mountain. There would not be any trails for us to follow. All we had were knots of intersecting canyons, at least one of which opened into a network of tunnels that led into the interior of the mountains.

It would be up to Agata Azul to lead us through the maze to enter the city of Nidaar.

And up to me and the rest of us to protect her while she did.

5

We were still a few hours' flight away from the base of the mountain range as the sky had just begun to lighten at our backs.

We had all spent the night keenly alert to any physical movement on the ground or magical movement against our senses. I didn't want to stop until we'd reached our destination, but we needed a rest before we got any closer. The nearer to the mountain that contained Nidaar, the greater the probability of danger.

I scanned the ground for a place to land.

I didn't choose it.

It chose me.

Directly below was the same scorched and blighted landscape we'd flown over all night. Though the closer we flew to the mountain range, the more broken the ground was, which made sense. The closer to the Heart, the cause of the earthquakes, the greater the destruction. Looming over a relatively flat expanse were the remains of a plateau. One side had collapsed in a tumble of broken rocks, leaving a sharp outcropping behind, though from this angle, it looked more like a cliff.

An all-too-familiar cliff.

I'd been there before. Not in person, but in my dreams.

The dreams I had shared with Sarad Nukpana.

I'd never determined whether my subconscious had chosen the location for our conversations—or was it Sarad's doing?

If Sarad had somehow influenced it, and here I was in the exact location of that dream…

My mind thought "trap"; my gut said unpleasant co-incidence.

Normally, I'd go with my gut, though when dealing with Sarad Nukpana, there was no such thing as a coincidence.

I banked Mithryn toward it for a flyover to see the surrounding land from a cliff-top viewpoint.

Yes. This was it.

I scanned for any sign or remnant of magic. Nothing. I did it again. Still nothing. All I could see was rocky desolation.

I signaled to the others that we were going in.

I chose a spot to set us down. It was clear enough to land, and there was not a living soul to be seen. I'd felt Mithryn's stomach growling beneath me for the past hour. No doubt she'd love to find a living soul—with meat attached.

The ladies had eaten yesterday morning. Sentry dragons

could go for nearly two weeks between meals, though unless you wanted to fly on a hungry dragon, putting them on any kind of diet was ill advised. They were highly trained, but to them, goblins were highly tasty.

I wouldn't mind feeding them a couple of crunchy Khrynsani.

Sentry dragons could land nearly anywhere. Used as they were in the military and law enforcement, they were accustomed to landing while being shot at. The dragon would simply incinerate their attacker, land, and get down to business.

However, that approach wasn't nearly as effective when the offensive party was the ground itself.

As she was the dragon carrying the lady in charge of persuading the Heart of Nidaar to behave, Mithryn landed first.

Or at least she tried.

The instant she touched down, the ground began to growl. Agata was right. It was an excellent word to describe it.

I indicated with my legs to Mithryn that she was not to take off again.

The dragon turned her long neck and gave me a side-eye and a rumbling growl of her own.

"Yes," I told her. "I'm sure."

She had landed gently, and even politely. The ground didn't open and swallow us, and the shaking decreased to a faint vibration. It wasn't a warm welcome by any stretch of the imagination, but I'd take it. It wasn't like we had a choice.

I waved for Calik and Dasant to bring Sapphira and Amaranth down.

When their claws touched rock, the dragons received the same welcome and, like Mithryn, they were not amused.

"Let me see what I can do about this." Agata threw her right leg over Mithryn's neck and slid down her shoulder to land on the ground—and not feet first.

I winced in sympathy.

"Okay, my legs aren't working," she called up to me.

That was going to be the challenge for all of us.

I had ridden all night on many occasions, but all of those times had been on a horse. Sentry dragons were considerably larger. And we had been flying at a speed far beyond that of the swiftest horse. And while our legs had been strapped down to prevent falling off, basic survival instincts made those not familiar with travel by dragon clench their legs to ensure they didn't end up as a greasy spot on the desert floor.

My team knew not to do that. However, I'd forgotten to mention it to Agata, Talon, and Phaelan.

My bad. Though in my defense, I'd had a lot on my mind.

But better late than never. "You might want to take it—"

Talon hit the ground, gasped, and emitted a pained squeak.

"Easy," I finished.

And Talon and Phaelan would have an additional source of pain that Agata would not. Again, a detail I should have mentioned.

Phaelan flopped over Mithryn's flank to the ground. When he could breathe again, his words blistered the air blue. They were in Elvish. Even if we didn't all understand the language, we would have gotten the gist.

Jash laughed. A laugh that went up a few octaves the instant his boots hit the sand, then he made his own verbal contributions. In Goblin. Again, no translation necessary.

The rest of us gingerly dismounted.

"Stretch, get a drink and a bite to eat, and take care of anything that needs doing," I told them. "We take off in twenty minutes."

I walked over to where Jash was standing bent over with his hands on his knees. He blew out his breath in a pained hiss as he slowly straightened up.

"Tell me why I'm here again?" he asked me.

"Keep anyone from sneaking up on us, and to use that water-filled microportal of yours."

"Right now, I'm not sure those are good enough reasons." He put his hands to his back and stretched, resulting in several large pops. "I'm too old for this crap."

"You're not even thirty, and you're younger than me."

"Like I said, too old."

"Well, it's not much farther," I told him. "At least the flying part."

"Then it'll be dank, dark tunnels. Oh joy."

I lowered my voice and tilted my head. "That cliff?"

"Yeah?"

"That's the one from my dreams."

"With Sarad?"

"Those are the ones."

"Why the whispering? Everybody knows about them."

"I don't know. Something about it feels wrong."

"You had dreams. Sarad Nukpana was in them. That's plenty enough wrong for anyone."

"That's not it."

"Then what is it?"

"It feels as if I've been here before—and not in a dream."

I hesitated. I knew of only one way to describe what I'd felt when I'd seen the cliff. When you had a history of delving into black magic, there wasn't much that could creep you out, but this did.

"And not in this life," I finished.

"Kansbar?" Jash asked quietly.

I nodded once. "As little as I like it, it's the only other option I can come up with."

"You think it came from signing your name in blood in Rudra's book?"

"Perhaps. It may have helped trigger it. Rudra tore into Kansbar's memories, but there wasn't this kind of detail. It's like recalling a memory—*my* memory—of a place I've never been before."

"Okay, that is spooky."

"Yeah."

A mage's name was powerful. Our blood was even more so. Using both was asking for every kind of trouble. The vilest of curses could be worked with the blood signature of a rival mage. I'd heard of a mage using a blood-locked book to kill all his rivals—all of whom had read it by signing their names in their blood.

I'd signed my name in that book because I had to know what Kansbar had seen and experienced. It'd been risky as hell, but to learn as much as I could about what we'd be facing, I'd had no choice but to take that risk.

I had the small book on me, shielded in a protective canvas sleeve beneath my chest armor. I had finished reading it, but I wasn't about to go anywhere without it—or let it go anywhere without me. For the book to fall into the wrong hands could be fatal. See previous statement regarding a mage killing all who had read a certain blood-locked book.

I had discovered in short order that one of the consequences of signing my name in blood on the same page as Sarad Nukpana was a dream link. As distasteful as having Sarad visit me in my dreams was, it had the benefit of allowing me to trick information out of him.

I had yet to have Sandrina Ghalfari visit me in my sleep, but that didn't mean that she couldn't. Perhaps she preferred to take advantage of a more strategic connection—tracking and finding me while I was awake. I could shield my physical body and ward my mind, but the connection granted by a blood-linked book went deeper, beyond any ability to shield or ward.

I'd known that, too.

Jash was silent for a few moments. "You're twisting the ring."

I glanced down at my hands. My left hand was busily turning the ring on my right hand.

"You think the rock had anything to do with you 'remembering' this place?" he asked.

"It is a power source," I said. "And there's never been an opportunity to determine what all they're capable of."

"Like storing memories? Kansbar wore the ring and the pendant from the time he left Nidaar until he reached the coast. The land was still shaking with quakes and aftershocks. I imagine he saw all kinds of memorable things, things he would've loved to have forgotten." He paused. "Stones of power can bond with their wearer."

"You don't have to remind me."

"I think we can say that the Saghred was a special case. You're not feeling manipulated, are you?"

"No."

"Though it wouldn't be a bad thing if the rock nudged you in the general direction of its mother."

I gazed up at the top of the cliff. I needed to go up there. If the Heart's shard in my ring was nudging me or activating Kansbar's memories stored inside, I needed to give it every chance to tap those memories.

6

Jash went to water the dragons, and I searched for a way to get to the top of the cliff. On the west side, rocks had slid into more or less a natural stairway. That would get me most of the way up. I'd figure out the rest when I got there.

Agata approached from our landing site, the wind catching her desert cloak. "Mind if I tag along? I need to get a more accurate reading on our direction."

As we climbed, I shared what I had told Jash, and his theories.

"If that was the case," she said, "it stands to reason that I would be having flashes of Kansbar's memory as well. Unless it is somehow tied to a blood relationship."

"Kansbar never fathered children, so I couldn't be a direct descendant."

Agata shrugged. "You're both Nathrachs. Perhaps a direct relation isn't necessary."

As we neared the top, there were enough hand- and footholds to get us the rest of the way. I went first and did a quick scan of the surrounding land with my mortal senses and with magic. The feeling that I'd been here before was even stronger. The light was entirely different. It was dawn now, and had been midday then.

There were no signs of life of any kind, but that didn't mean it wasn't beautiful, breathtakingly so.

The sun was just beginning to rise over the eastern horizon, spreading its first rays across the land we'd spent the night flying over, the light alternating between a rosy glow where the rising sun highlighted the landscape, with the areas behind rock formations still hidden in shadow and darkness.

"It's clear," I said, holding out my hand to assist Agata the rest of the way.

Agata rolled her eyes, but she took my hand, and I pulled her up. She turned, and when she saw the sun rising over the Sea of Kenyon over a hundred miles to the east, and the land between us and the sea stretched out at our feet, her dark eyes sparkled in wonder and delight.

We stood in silence, taking it all in. I noticed that Agata's hand was still in mine, small and warm.

As soon as I noticed, Agata realized it as well, and slipped her hand from mine, quickly walking to where she could see our landing site.

"There's one major difference between us that you don't seem to have considered," she said.

I did a confused double-take. "Excuse me?"

"A difference between us. The reason you're possibly experiencing flashbacks from Kansbar and I'm not, even though we're both wearing pieces of the Heart."

Oh, that difference.

"While we both carry a piece of the Heart given to Kansbar," Agata continued, "you signed your name in blood on the first page of Rudra Muralin's book. I didn't. Rudra had direct access to Kansbar's memories. I'm not familiar with how these things work, but listening to you read, I didn't get much of a visual of what Aquas looked like. I'm assuming Rudra only wrote down what he felt would be useful in finding Nidaar. He didn't describe this cliff in his book, but he must have seen it in Kansbar's memories."

"So signing my name got me more than simply the words on the page."

Agata spread her hands. "Like I said, I don't know how these things work. Is that possible?"

"It's not impossible. It is, however, an extremely unpleasant thought."

"I'll not disagree with you there." She took off the necklace. "Your ring, please."

I slipped it off my finger and slid it onto the fourth finger of her outstretched left hand.

"Let's get this done." Agata knelt on the ground and pressed her hands into the loose pebbles.

It didn't take long for her to confirm that we were still going in the right direction. The good news was that the mountain was less than an hour's flight ahead. The bad news was that it looked exactly like every other mountain in the range, and none of them had any obvious entrances. The

Khrynsani had never found a way into the mountain in their hundreds of years of expeditions.

For all we knew, our time had run out.

As I stood there, the sunlight glinted on the desert floor to the south.

Glinted?

I put my hand on Agata's shoulder, holding her where she was. "Veil and stay down."

She looked up at me, and for once didn't question.

It was too late for me to duck, so I veiled *and* shielded.

The glint didn't move but it also didn't belong here—and neither did the dark patches on the ground nearby.

We needed to get a close look at that, much closer.

Getting down from the cliff went a lot faster than climbing up.

The possibility of spotting signs of pursuit was a powerful motivator.

We had brought Indigo with us for scouting.

Talon tugged the hood off and sent the little firedrake flying into the dawn sky with a lift from his wrist. Once again, Indy was wearing a harness with a spy crystal.

As the firedrake climbed in the air, his color changed to match the sky around him, and he nearly vanished. Only the faint beating of his wings betrayed his position. Once he found a wind current, he would go into a glide, becoming essentially invisible to anyone below, including us.

Talon's pale eyes were locked on Indy's position with unblinking, complete concentration.

Malik was equally intent on the small crystal ball clutched

in his hand, seeing what the crystal on the firedrake's chest was recording.

In the crystal ball, we watched the drake's view of our small encampment as he flew higher, gaining altitude, until we were specks on the ground and the dunes and rocks spread in an endless sea to the south and east.

When Indy reached the area where I had seen what looked to be bodies, the drake's prey drive kicked in and he descended for a closer look.

Details came into gruesome focus.

I would be lying if I said I wasn't glad to see that the dead, dismembered, and partially eaten bodies were Khrynsani and Sythsaurian. As far as my team was concerned, the only good Khrynsani was a dead Khrynsani. And since the Sythsaurians were their allies in our destruction, dead lizard men were a sight for sore eyes as well.

Malik was smiling down at the carnage reflected in his crystal ball. "Beautiful work. A trifle haphazard, but well done."

The black I had seen from the cliff was both cloth and blood.

Jash looked like he couldn't believe what he was seeing. "They wore those heavy black robes of theirs in the desert?"

Elsu chuckled. "Idiots."

"Evil idiots," Jash added.

Malik continued to smile fondly at the crystal-confined tableau. "Yes, but they're our evil idiots." His smile broadened into a grin. "Or at least these were."

I headed toward Mithryn. "Saddle up, we need to get a closer look."

⊷⊶

Whatever had killed and partially eaten the goblins and lizard men was long gone. That didn't mean we weren't alert for their return. Three fire-breathing sentry dragons should be able to handle anything that tried to take a bite out of us, but I thought my caution was well-founded.

Whatever had done this clearly preferred goblin meat.

Phaelan had his sword out and used the tip to raise the cloak of one of the dead Sythsaurians.

"There's a lot left of this one," the elf noted. "Lizards must not taste good."

Indigo jumped down from his perch on Talon's shoulder and hopped over to sniff the body. He quickly pulled back in what I could only call revulsion.

"They must taste really nasty," Talon noted. "Even Indy doesn't want anything to do with them, and he'll eat anything."

The black robes, a lot of blood, and various bits and pieces were all that was left of the Khrynsani.

There was more blood than could have been contained in the relatively intact bodies that we found. However, there were pieces of others, and signs of still more having been dragged away.

"Eat some now, take a few home for later?" Malik mused.

The ground was hard and not conducive to footprints, but there was more than enough blood to show us the size of the predators who'd done this.

I knelt to get a closer look at one print. It was twice the size of my hand—with claws that punched into the soil where blood had soaked into it.

There were signs that at least the Khrynsani had tried to defend themselves. In addition to the stink of disemboweled bodies we smelled the acrid sting of fire magic. Charred streaks marked the rock, and where it had struck sand, glass had formed from the intense heat.

"Eight Khrynsani and five Sythsaurians from what I can tell," Malik said.

I stood. "Judging from the scraps of robes, at least some of those were senior mages. Whatever these things are, they're either impervious to magic—which is unlikely—or the attack was so sudden they didn't have a chance to properly defend themselves."

"The mages burnt a lot of rock and sand," Agata noted. "But there're no dead attackers to show for it." She glanced over at Sapphira's feet. "Is it me, or do those tracks kind of look like Saffie's?"

Dasant stood from where he had been examining one of the dead-and-tasted-but-not-eaten Sythsaurians. "I'd say from the bite radius on this one's torso, plus the size and depth of those claw prints, we're talking about a beastie that's at least in the dragon family, though thankfully not a fire-breather. The distance between the front and back feet would put these things at well over a dozen feet long and several hundred pounds."

"There's no sign of dragons or horses," Agata pointed out. "How did the Khrynsani get here? And why here?"

I felt a sudden chill that had nothing to do with cold.

My dream.

Agata noticed and instantly knew the reason. "Sarad knows of this place, and so do the Khrynsani. If there is a portal—"

"I don't sense any portal magic here," Jash said.

I'd surveyed the area around where the attack had taken place. "There are no footprints other than in this area."

Jash shrugged. "Maybe the lizards handled the transportation. We already know their magic feels different. Some of that residual magic could be from a portal."

"Over here!" Talon called.

I ran to where he stood.

Blood and scraps of Khrynsani robes trailed off the edge of a six-foot-wide crack in the ground that extended some twenty feet in either direction.

Talon's voice was subdued. "Like Malik said, eat some here, leave some for later. Can you see the bottom?"

I carefully leaned forward. "No."

Without another word, we started backed away from the opening. Talon stumbled on a small rock, sending it tumbling over the edge. It bounced its way down, and down, and down. I didn't hear it hit bottom.

Anyone that fell—or was dragged—down there, if they survived, wouldn't be coming out the way they came in.

The others had come up behind us.

"This could be one reason why some of those Khrynsani expeditions never came home," I said.

"I'm having a disturbing thought," Elsu said.

"Only one?" Jash was starting to look queasy. The stench was getting to him.

"These dragon things, they're big, so they eat a lot. They're obviously not going without. What are they eating? It may look like nothing lives out here, but it's apparent that looks are deceiving."

"And they're coming from underground," Malik added. "Precisely where we need to go. Oh joy."

Dasant's lip curled in distaste at a bloody smear left when one of the Khrynsani was dragged underground. "And they've got a taste for goblins."

"Glad I'm not a goblin," Phaelan muttered.

Jash grinned. "If they've never had elf, you'll probably be a delicacy."

I barely heard any of them.

The sun was up, the sky brightening to what promised to be a cloudless blue.

Except in the distance to the south.

What had looked like the dusky haze of a predawn sky was a rapidly expanding darkness.

This was bad.

"Incoming. Due south," I said.

"Another storm?" Agata asked.

Phaelan raised his spyglass. "I don't think so. That's like no storm cloud I've ever seen."

"That's not rain," Malik told us all. "That's sand, and it's headed right for us."

7

The roiling sand was a dark wall coming from the south. I didn't know about sandstorms on Aquas, but I'd heard of one in the Nebian Desert that lasted for nearly a week.

We didn't have a week.

And if we got caught in that storm, our time was over.

"Any chance this is the Khrynsani weather wizard's doing?" I asked Agata.

She shook her head. "I'm not sensing any magic or malevolence behind it."

"Just Mother Nature's welcome to Nidaar," Malik said. "Marvelous."

Calik was creatively swearing. "Sand at that velocity will blast the skin right off the dragons' wings."

"We'd be screwed, too," Phaelan muttered from the saddle behind me.

Both were true. Though we riders were leather-clad, helmeted, and goggled, our three sentry dragons were about as vulnerable as it was possible to be. Their wings were fibrous skin stretched between long, thin bones. It wouldn't take much blowing sand to permanently damage a dragon's wings. Any attempt at flight during the height of this storm would shred their wings completely.

I swung into the saddle. "According to the maps, there should be some small canyons ahead large enough to land in."

And we just might have company when we got there.

The Khrynsani and Sythsaurians were here. We'd just seen proof. There was one thing I knew from distinctly unpleasant past experience: finding dead Khrynsani meant there were three times as many live ones lying in wait for you.

Let the games begin.

Kansbar had said that the mountains above and around Nidaar had been undamaged by the Heart-spawned earthquakes, meaning that the Heart of Nidaar hadn't destroyed its own home. However, that need to protect ended at the base of the mountain range.

The force of the quakes had torn the land apart, forming deep canyons that radiated out from the mountains to a distance of approximately ten miles. The canyons narrowed to fissures for nearly another ten miles.

We needed the shelter of one of those deep canyons, and we needed it now.

The good news was that while searching for shelter, we were getting closer to Nidaar's mountain. The bad news was that the sandstorm was moving faster than our dragons could fly.

The morning sun was now obscured in an eerie twilight. It was as if the storm was spreading from the south to wrap around behind us, herding us toward the mountains. It was the direction we needed to go, but if we didn't find shelter soon, we'd die before we ever reached our destination.

We were no longer flying together, but had put a couple hundred yards between us to give us a better chance of finding a shelter that would meet our needs.

I guided Mithryn lower.

With the wind speeds increasing, we were almost out of time.

We needed a canyon wide enough to accommodate a dragon's wingspan, but narrow and twisty enough for adequate protection. A straight canyon would simply concentrate the sand and wind into a narrow space.

None of us would survive that.

A sudden gust of wind buffeted Mithryn's wings, bobbling us from side to side. Agata reacted by crouching lower in her saddle to cut wind resistance.

Phaelan's reaction was more verbal.

Then I saw it.

In the distance was what looked like an opening in the rocky ground that met our shelter needs.

I wasn't the only one to spot it. With a shrill cry to alert her sisters, Mithryn dived for the widest part of the gash, determined that she would fit.

I agreed with her, but pulled back on the reins to slow her approach to a speed less terrifying to those of us on her back.

Phaelan didn't agree with her at all.

At least his screams were manly.

Mithryn had to tuck in her pinions to fit, and fit she did, but barely.

The other sentry dragons followed suit—without any screaming from their passengers.

The sun was up, but the canyon was still pitch dark. Even my goblin eyes were hard-pressed to make out any details of the rock walls that rose on either side of us. Sentry dragons were cave dwellers. Whether it was too dark to see your hand in front of your face, or high noon, they would find their way.

I reached out with all my senses. No sign of magic, which hopefully meant no mages. Since we had yet to experience one of the Sythsaurian mages up close, their ability to obscure any sign of their magic was still an unknown.

Mithryn touched down on the canyon floor and folded her wings against her sides. Amaranth and Sapphira landed nearby.

In the saddle in front of me, Agata went perfectly still.

I leaned forward. "What?"

"No tremors."

When we were closer to the Heart of Nidaar than we had ever been, the stone went silent.

"I can't see that being a bad thing right now," I said.

"Me, either."

"Well, I can't see *anything*," Phaelan said from behind me.

"Saffie, give us some light," Calik said from nearby.

She obliged, sending out a modest-sized gout of flame.

Whatever had eaten those Khrynsani and Sythsaurians lived below the surface. We were now below the surface. We didn't know what those creatures were, but we did know that some of the Khrynsani's top mages had gotten themselves eaten. It's been my experience that fire will cause monsters to at least pause before they ate you.

Saffie's blast showed walls that widened toward the canyon floor like the bottom of a pyramid. That would give the dragons enough room to take off again once the storm had passed. They might need to turn sideways to clear the top of the canyon walls, but that wouldn't be an issue for our nimble sentries.

Everyone quickly dismounted, shielded, and conjured lightglobes. If there was anything down here with us that wanted to kill and/or eat us, we didn't have time to waste trying to hide from it. Right now, that sandstorm was scarier than a mystery monster.

Calik nimbly dismounted from Sapphira. "Let's find cover for the dragons."

I leapt from my saddle and sent my lightglobe along the ground directly in front of me—ground that wasn't dirt.

"It's a floor," Agata said, her voice awestruck.

The floor stretched from one wall to the other and as far as Sapphira's fire blast had extended. It wasn't ornate, just perfectly smooth and level—without any seams whatsoever.

"All of this was once covered," Agata continued, sliding down Mithryn's flank. This time I was there to catch her.

"Notice how the walls are smooth up to at least fifty feet," she continued, "and curved inward. The quake must have collapsed the ceiling and opened it to the surface."

"She's right," Elsu said. "This has been hand carved. Nothing fancy, but nice work."

It wasn't a canyon at all. It hadn't been worn by water or opened as a result of one of Aquas's earthquakes. What was open to the sky had once been covered by sandstone. The broken rock lying in piles on the canyon's floor proved it—as did the intact façade.

I pushed more of my will into the lightglobe hovering above my open hand, both brightening its light and expanding its range.

And illuminated a wonder.

"Holy crap," Talon managed.

I stared. We all did. It was all I could do.

Carved into the canyon's wall was the façade of a building: a temple, from the sheer size of it. A pair of giant doors were standing open, doors that were easily three times my height with an opening wide enough to accommodate a sentry dragon.

Agata stepped up beside me.

"Ever seen anything like this?"

"Never."

I reached out with my magical senses and scanned for any hint of danger. "Jash? Is there—"

"Not a soul."

"Then how about—"

"And no soulless monsters, either."

Dasant tossed his supply pack over his shoulder. "Since nobody's home, boss, may I suggest we invite ourselves in?"

8

After a quick inspection of the interior, we got the dragons inside to safety.

The ceiling soared above our heads, allowing our sentry dragons to stretch to their full height, working out the kinks and sore muscles that had come with flying all night. There was also ample room for extending their wings for the same purpose. Jash activated his microportal to get fresh water for all of us, but especially the dragons. Once they were full, the ladies carefully folded their wings and settled down for a much-deserved rest.

Elsu used her booted foot to slide her pack against a nearby wall. "The girls have the right idea. We're not going anywhere anytime soon."

"Agreed," I said. "Let's get some rest while we can. We'll

need it." Talon had started to wander off to explore. "That especially means you and Agata."

I expected an argument, but Talon didn't give me one. Apparently fatigue won out over curiosity. Agata had already found a place to rest. Calik was busy checking the dragons for any injuries.

The rest of us separated to explore our temporary home. How temporary remained to be seen. The sandstorm outside showed us no signs of abating; in fact, it sounded like it was increasing in intensity.

We were alert, but I didn't feel any danger, and Jash didn't sense any signs of life except for ourselves.

When we completed the circuit, we returned to where the others waited.

"Any sign of Khrynsani?" Talon asked anyone who might know.

"They've got a special stink all their own, no magic needed," Jash told him. "It doesn't matter how long they've been out of their temple; they can't get rid of that nasty temple incense smell. All my nose is smelling right now is dust."

"How about Sythsaurians?"

"Haven't had the misfortune of standing downwind of one, but I know what their magic feels like. They're not here, either."

Jash had said no one was at home, but someone had built all this long ago, and the fact that it was now abandoned invoked quiet, if not reverence.

It was easily four times the size of the throne room in the Mal'Salin palace, and that was ridiculously large, intended to instill awe and fear in all who walked through its doors.

"We found this place just in time," Agata said quietly.

We'd left the temple doors partially open, but had shielded the open space to keep out the sand—and any unwanted guests/predators. However, shields didn't block out sound. The sandstorm's winds howled down the length of the canyon.

Standing in the temple doorway, Calik had to tilt his head all the way back to see the canyon rim. "Taking off again might not be as simple."

Phaelan barked a laugh. "Getting in here was simple?"

Calik shrugged. "You steer a ship over giant waves; I dive a dragon into a hole in the ground. When it comes time to get airborne again, the girls will need enough room for a full wing extension. However, they are excellent jumpers and climbers. They can scale these walls with no problem."

"No problem for them," Phaelan retorted.

Malik chuckled. "We'd have to sedate Captain Benares and tie him in his saddle."

"Talon didn't scream on the way down," Calik said.

"Because I couldn't breathe." Talon slowly turned in a circle. "Why is there one way in and no way out?"

There were no hallways, doors, or stairs leading anywhere else. It was strange, to say the least, and had all of us on edge.

"No clue," Jash replied for all of us. "But that means only one place to post a guard." He grinned and held up his bucket. "I'm back on water duty, so someone else is going to have to pull the first guard rotation."

"I'll do it," Dasant said around a bite of jerky. "I caught a couple of short naps while we were flying."

Phaelan stared in disbelief. "You *slept*? You're a pilot!"

Dasant shrugged. "When you fly a lot, it gets kind of

boring after a while. Amaranth knows what she's doing. She doesn't need me to tell her to stay in formation."

"I'll back you up," Elsu said, "in case you get bored and fall asleep again."

Rest was needed, but we were all too keyed up.

Our survey of the room hadn't offered up many clues about what this building had been used for. Any details that may have remained on the floors and walls were obscured by sand that had been blown in through the open doors. Judging from the amount of sand inside, those doors had been open for years, perhaps even centuries.

We weren't alone in this desert waste. I could feel it. Jash had yet to sense that we were being followed. He was right; we weren't being followed. The Khrynsani were already here. We'd seen the proof only an hour ago. Perhaps others were seeking shelter from the storm as we were, in a similar structure nearby.

We had discovered a trough-like pool carved against an interior wall to the left of the doors. Jash had used his microportal to refill our water skins, and was now refilling the trough for the dragons. Magic of any kind made noise, even briefly opening a small portal. I had no doubt there were people listening for us, so the less magic we used, the better. However, warding the doors and replenishing our water supply was necessary and worth the risk.

"Do you think this is—or was—part of Nidaar?" Talon asked.

"I can't see it being anything else," I told him. "But there must be more to it than this. Who would excavate something this extensive and leave it a dead end?"

"And why?" Agata added. She looked around, then held out her hand. "Let me have your ring. I want to try something."

I gave it to her. "Get a better fix on the Heart and perhaps another way out of here?"

Her lips quirked in a brief smile. "Kesyn was wrong. The obvious doesn't always elude you."

I felt her gently push her will into the stones, and both began to flicker, then softly glow. She went to the nearest wall and began a slow circuit of the chamber. I followed at enough of a distance so my magic wouldn't interfere. Malik joined me.

Agata slowed further once she reached the back wall, holding the pendant in one hand and the ring in the other, continually pushing her power through both.

The stones' light suddenly went from a glow to what I could only call an excited sparkle.

The wall responded.

Roughly five feet above our heads, two round, shield-sized areas of the wall began to shimmer beneath their coating of dust.

"What is that?" Malik breathed from beside me.

The others quickly joined us.

"Whatever it is, the sand's covering it," I said.

Agata turned to me, her dark eyes sparkling with excitement much like the stones she carried. "Can dragons blow air as well as fire?"

"That they can," Calik replied.

We put on our goggles and covered our lower faces. Between the sulfuric breath and flying sand, breathing was a challenge. We ended up retreating to the entrance while the sand and dust settled.

What was revealed was worth any discomfort—as well as our all-night flight.

The outside doors may have succumbed to the elements long ago, but these were perfectly preserved. The doors were easily twice our height, but narrow. Each door was no more than three feet wide, and unlike the surrounding walls, each appeared to be carved from a single slab of obsidian.

I sent a lightglobe up to one of two pale disks that had been set into the doors. They were over a foot across, and when the globe's light struck it, the disk's interior flickered like flames.

Encircling each disk was what looked like a serpentine golden dragon.

The disks were identical to the pendant the Cha'Nidaar queen had given my ancestor—the one Agata Azul now wore.

Malik swore softly. "Is that—"

"Yes, it just might be."

An entrance to Nidaar.

9

"Who knew dragons were so useful? First a bellows, and now a ladder." Phaelan stood looking up at the huge glowing disks.

Sapphira was standing on her hind legs in front of the doors with her long neck extended as far up as it would go.

Agata was perched on top of the dragon's head, inches from one of the stone disks.

One of Jash's buckets full of water was hooked on Saffie's left horn, and Agata was cleaning the disks and golden dragons of centuries of grime.

Talon was busy beneath Sapphira doing the same with the door itself. When I'd asked why, Talon said he was curious about something. He was focused, so I didn't ask any more questions. Talon had good instincts; there could be something important under all that dust.

When one of the disk's dragon frames had been cleaned, Sapphira had begun warily sniffing at it.

The sentry dragon wasn't sure how she felt about all this. I was.

The two huge disks could be the beginning of an even bigger problem.

I'd assumed that the stone that comprised the Heart of Nidaar would be extremely rare, limited only to the Heart itself and a few smaller pieces, like those in the ring and pendant.

The city of Nidaar was supposed to lie beneath the mountain that was still to the west of us, meaning that these doors probably marked the outermost reaches of the city. To use two slabs of the stone as decoration on doors far from the central city meant that it wasn't nearly as rare as I'd believed.

Was Agata's skill up to the challenge of locating the Heart itself amongst who knew how many large specimens? Or could we possibly end up on a wild goose chase inside of a mountain?

Talon had finished cleaning a large section of the door, exposing obsidian so finely polished that it was essentially a black mirror. He was running his hands over the door, just above the surface, his concentration intense and complete.

My son showing that kind of interest in a mirror of any kind made me uneasy in ways I never thought possible.

"This could be a functioning mirror, if there was another to link it to," Talon said. "Have you ever heard of the Cha'Nidaar having mirror mages?"

"I don't know," I replied quickly. "They would have had what the goblins of that age did."

"There were no mirror mages among the goblins of that

period," Agata called down to us. "That magic was limited to the elves."

I definitely wanted to change the subject away from mirrors.

"What have you found?" I asked her.

She had finished clearing the disks of dust. Now she came down from her draconic stepladder and stepped up to the doors, hands extended palms out. "No magical locks, no wards, nothing primed to throw me across the room." She glanced at me. "Permission to push?"

I'd already checked it and likewise had detected nothing. There was no sign of any kind of lock.

"Be my guest," I told her.

She pushed.

The door didn't budge.

It also didn't strike back, so it was kind of a win.

Agata pushed again, leaning into it with all her weight, which, to be honest, wasn't really all that much.

Nothing.

Dasant stepped past her. "Let me try."

Agata smirked. "Don't hurt yourself."

Dasant was big for a goblin. When the doors didn't so much as creak, he redoubled his efforts and added a grunt.

"And yet the doors remain unimpressed," Malik commented dryly. "How dare they?"

I detected a flicker from where the two doors met. "Stop," I said.

Dasant stepped back. "What's wrong?"

"I saw it, too," Agata said. She glanced at me. "Do you think?"

I again passed her my ring. "Only one way to find out."

Agata quickly wrapped the pendant's chain around her fingers, hanging the pendant so it rested in her palm. She put my ring on a finger of her other hand. She paused for a few moments, pushing her will into the stones.

And pushed against the door.

Nothing.

That was concerning.

"Maybe if you don't push," I suggested. "Just touch the stones to the doors. Let them do the work."

She did.

And the door didn't.

Agata handed my ring back to me with an exasperated sigh. "I'm all out of ideas. I think some food and a little sleep will do me some good."

I slid it back on my finger. "I think we all need—"

Agata stumbled over a rock, and I caught her with one arm, catching myself with the other hand against the door as more rocks shifted under my own feet.

The stone in my ring blazed to life when my hand touched the door.

Agata got her balance and stepped away from me, breaking contact.

Only my hand, with its glowing ring, remained on the door.

"You're doing that," Agata said with something akin to awe. "Are you sure you don't have any gem magic?"

"I'm sure."

"Push the door open," she said.

I did.

Easily.

And found myself the focus of my team's attention.

I grabbed the door and stopped it from opening further. We had no idea what was on the other side. Until we did, it was enemy territory.

"I have no clue how I did that," I told them.

Dasant clapped me on the shoulder. "We know."

I motioned for Talon, Phaelan, and even Agata to get to the far sides of the doors. Agata and Talon shielded Phaelan.

My team got our defensive magic ready to let fly. Dasant moved to the opposite door.

I nodded, and we pushed in unison, the doors opening easily and in complete silence, as if they had been used only yesterday.

And my mere touch had unlocked them.

We didn't need light to sense the sheer size of the chamber beyond.

"Any unfriendlies?" I asked Jash.

"Not a one."

"Calik, would you have Sapphira do the honors and put a little light on the subject?"

"She'd love to, sir."

"Just enough to get a look," I cautioned. "We wouldn't want to torch anything important."

Sapphira breathed an almost dainty fireball.

The room was narrower than the chamber at our backs, more like a large corridor than a room. And unlike the temple's soaring ceiling, this one barely extended beyond the height of the doors. At the other end waited an unassuming door. One door, not a double, and closed.

"Well, the dragons won't be going any farther," I noted.

"And they're perfectly fine with that," Calik said. "And so am I. The ladies and I will be nice and cozy right where we are."

The floor was something else altogether.

Only a light coating of dust covered the tiles; some weren't much bigger than my foot, others were the circumference of one of Sapphira's claws or even larger. The tiles were both square and rectangle, and had no discernable pattern.

"There must be hundreds of them," Agata murmured.

Careful not to cross the threshold, Phaelan knelt and blew the dust away from the tile at his feet, revealing an unfamiliar engraved symbol.

The elf sat back, surveying the vast expanse of tiles between us and the plain door at the far end. "Would Sapphira be willing to do a little light housekeeping?"

Within moments, with Calik's guidance, Sapphira's exhales had cleared every tile.

And every tile had a different symbol.

Malik cleared his throat. "Is anyone else grateful we opted for prudence?"

Each symbol was different, but one element was the same. In the center of the tiles that made up the room's threshold was something we all recognized.

A skull.

"Now that's what I call a welcome mat," Elsu muttered.

"Could this be the entrance to a tomb, perhaps?" Malik wondered aloud. "It could explain the skulls."

"Or it could be a warning," I said.

"I believe that is a safe assumption," Malik replied.

Phaelan glanced from the floor to the ceiling. "The ceiling tiles don't have markings, but they match the floor tile sizes exactly. That's never good." Then he scanned the floor, his dark eyes darting back and forth.

I looked out over the expanse, trying to see what he was seeing. "What is it?"

"They're different shapes—and colors. There's a pattern; it just can't be seen from floor level. I need a boost."

"Saffie's ready and able," Calik told him with a smile.

"Yeah, I thought you'd say something like that." The elf pirate blew out his breath. "Without risks, there are no rewards."

With a gleam in her yellow eye, Sapphira lowered her head.

Phaelan hesitated. "She's not going to—"

"Do anything unprofessional," Calik finished for him.

Without another word, Phaelan climbed to a perch just behind the dragon's head and gripped one of her horns for balance. To her credit, Sapphira was a perfect lady as she lifted the elf to give him a better view of the floor.

Phaelan surveyed the tiles. "It's a snake." He paused. "Looks kind of familiar."

Every goblin froze.

Dasant swore.

Malik nodded. "My sentiment exactly."

I stepped over to Sapphira. "Calik, bring him down. We need confirmation."

Calik had paled. It wasn't only my team who suspected what we were looking at.

The pilot said a few words in Goblin, the dragon lowered

her head, and Phaelan gratefully jumped down. I took his place. Sapphira smoothly raised her head, giving me a clear look at a symbol none of us wanted to find here.

I whispered a single word. It was one of the foulest words in our language, but it described perfectly what lay between us and the only way we had into Nidaar.

The serpent seal of the Brotherhood of the Khrynsani.

10

"Are you sure?" Phaelan asked when I'd told them. "Don't
a lot of evil secret societies use snakes as their club mascot?"

"Yes," Malik said, "but not like this one. It's definitely
Khrynsani, albeit an older version."

"How old?"

"The Khrynsani have been around for over two thousand
years."

"And the Cha'Nidaar, these gold goblins, when did they
get here?"

"Estimates put it at between twelve to fifteen hundred
years ago," I replied. "The Cha'Nidaar had no love for the
Khrynsani. Perhaps this could be a warning to any who got
this far. Though tilework this intricate, and of the emblem
of your archenemy…it's unexpected. As unexpected as it

would be if I put a Khrynsani seal on my front door. I simply wouldn't do it."

Or as unexpected as if I opened a magically locked door with a touch—and power I didn't know I had.

"So, what does finding a Khrynsani serpent here mean?" Talon asked.

"Nothing good."

"Meaning it would be ill-advised to casually stroll toward yonder door," Malik said. "Considering the suspicious stains on a few of the tiles toward the center of the room, we will want to take our time."

Elsu stood on tiptoe to get a better look. "Stains?"

"The bloody smears that are all that's left of the last poor bastards who tried."

"You sure it's blood?" Elsu asked.

Dasant snorted.

"You're right. Stupid question. Malik knows blood."

"And those are marble tiles," Malik added. "Unless they're properly sealed and maintained, when blood sinks in, *nothing*—magic or mundane—will get it out."

Phaelan grinned and clapped his hands once, rubbing them together in unabashed glee. "Booby traps! *Now* we're having fun."

Phaelan's tomb-robbing experience was one of the reasons I wanted him with us, but the degree to which he was enjoying himself was more than mildly disturbing.

"An outer entrance to a city wouldn't have the approach completely covered in booby-trapped tiles," Malik said.

"It would if they didn't want anyone getting in," Phaelan countered.

My eyes roamed the floor, looking for any clue as to which tiles weren't safe—aside from the blood-smeared ones, that is. "The queen told Kansbar that they would never be found again."

"We found them," Phaelan said.

"We found two rooms; we haven't found them. And we're not in the city."

"It also doesn't appear that anyone else has had any better luck," Malik noted.

"Jash, are you sensing any signs of life?" I asked.

"Nothing."

"Agata, anything from the Heart?"

She pointed across the booby-trapped room to the unassuming door. "That way."

"The snake goes all the way from this door to that one," Phaelan said. "I think we can safely eliminate taking that path."

"Is there enough room in front of the door for all of us?" Elsu asked.

"The same amount that we're standing on now," I told her.

"Anyone wondering if we're making much about nothing?" Talon asked. "The bloodstains are all on the white tiles. Just stay off—"

Malik pointed to a smeared gray tile. "Except that one."

"Oh."

"In my experience," Phaelan said without taking his dark eyes off the tiles, "if a pattern as detailed and potentially important to a culture or cult as that snake extends from here to where we need to go in a winding path of sorts, the way to pass without getting squished lies in the history of the symbol and how these people perceived it, combined with—"

He stopped, sensing we were all staring at him. "What?"

"Nothing," I told him. "Merely absorbing your knowledge."

"Combined with what was physically possible for those who had to pass through on a regular basis," the elf pirate continued. "Unless you wanted to lose your people, big jumps would be ill-advised." He glanced around at my team. "So, who's the ancient Khrynsani expert?"

Malik's expression went from surprised amusement at Phaelan's articulateness and perception to resignation. "That would be me." He took a breath. "This particular symbol dates back to the Khrynsani's founding, when they were more concerned with gaining knowledge than world domination."

Talon's brow went up. "You mean they weren't always evil?"

"There were some evil individuals as members, but as an organization, the Khrynsani was academic rather than military." He gave a humorless smile. "Remember that it's not knowledge itself that is evil, but the uses to which it is put."

"The Cha'Nidaar left Rheskilia, came here, and have been protecting the Heart of Nidaar ever since," Agata said. "Could the reason they left be conflict with or persecution by the early Khrynsani when they changed their mission?"

Malik pondered. "The time the Cha'Nidaar were said to have arrived here roughly coincides with the ascension of Domin Sulat, who is recognized by modern Khrynsani as the first leader of the order as it stands today. So, that is entirely possible. And each segment of the Khrynsani serpent represents a tenet of Khrynsani belief."

"Which ones would the Cha'Nidaar have agreed with?" Phaelan asked.

Malik's eyes glittered with the challenge. "Or thumbed their noses at, if the architect of this deadly game had a dark sense of humor."

"Unfortunately, none of the bloody tiles are part of the serpent," Elsu said. "So, no help there."

"There are twenty-one tenets," Malik said. "I can see the first two. However, both can be interpreted as relatively benign, meaning we would need to choose which one the Cha'Nidaar would have agreed with—or disdained more."

The tail of the Khrynsani serpent began one long stride across several white tiles from the doors' threshold. None of those tiles were bloodied. The triangular tile representing the serpent's tail had no symbol. The next two did—and they were side by side. Therein lay a potentially deadly choice.

"I can't see a people who protect a source of power rather than exploit it treating Khrynsani tenets lightly," I told him. "If they needed to cross this room on a regular basis, I would think they would have chosen symbols that reinforced their beliefs. They would want to avoid contact with the symbols which were counter to that."

Malik nodded slowly. "That makes sense. However, it doesn't answer my question."

"And whoever's blood that is out there, did it belong to mages or nulls?" Phaelan asked.

"It doesn't matter," Malik said, securing his gear bag across his back. "I have to be the one to go. You don't know the symbols and their meanings. They are complex, and a few look very similar but have opposing meanings. I can discern the difference; you could not. It is I who must take the risk."

"Lightglobe or torch?" Dasant asked him.

"A torch might be the safer choice. The less magic used,

the better. If it doesn't like mages, I'll discover that soon enough."

"Which one of the first two tiles will you take?" I asked him.

"I'll start with the tail. It's a comfortable stride. The next two would not be." Malik grinned. "I can see the Cha'Nidaar wanting to step on the tail of the Khrynsani serpent. As to the next two tiles that are side by side, I'll go with the right tile."

"Why the right?"

"Because it was written by Greid Renu, who eventually became Domin Sulat's second-in-command—and then strangled him." Malik flashed a grin. "I've always admired his work ethic."

I nodded, then smiled tightly. "Good luck, my friend."

Malik nimbly stepped from the threshold to the serpent's tail without incident.

He paused then, shining the small torch across the two tiles at his feet. I saw him take a deep breath before stepping forward with his right foot, and when nothing happened, following with his left.

Malik proceeded smoothly until he reached the middle of the room—the area where the bloody tiles were. Malik shone his torch on the next few tiles, then straightened.

"I have a bit of a dilemma," he called back to us. "The next five tiles have no symbols. The sixth has one; however, there should be two tenets that come before it."

"Have they been worn away by age?" I asked.

Malik turned to face us. "There are no symbols there to have been worn down. It appears those two tenets were never inscribed."

Dasant muttered a curse.

"You said it," Elsu agreed.

Phaelan stepped to the edge of the booby-trapped floor. "You've taken every third tile, right?"

"Correct," Malik said.

"The sixth tile—the next one that has a symbol—is that a 'good' tenet?"

"Yes."

"Are the two that were omitted also 'good'?"

"One is more moral than the other, but neither could ever be called good."

Now it was Phaelan's turn to swear.

"I see no alternative than to jump to the sixth tile," Malik said. "Though it appears that option was tried by one of the previous contestants, and from the red smear on the tile next to the one I would be targeting, he overshot his landing."

"But you won't," I told him firmly. "That's an easy distance for you, Malik. Leave your pack where it is, we'll pick it up on the way over."

"Or if you don't mind possibly sacrificing your pack, you can toss it to that tile as a test," Agata suggested.

"If I'm wrong, I won't be needing my pack."

"Will there be enough room for you to land with your pack there?" I asked.

"Let's just say I'm motivated to be light on my feet."

Dasant glanced at me. "Boss, should we have a retrieval spell ready…you know, just in case?"

Phaelan's brow furrowed. "Retrieval?"

"I'd reach out and grab Malik with magic and yank him back here."

"Doesn't sound comfortable."

"It's not."

"But it's better than being flattened."

"No magic," Malik called. "I'm getting the feeling that would not be welcome here. The tiles haven't moved, but when I step on them, they are vibrating."

I frowned. "Like the ground outside?"

"Essentially."

"Then let's not make it angrier."

"Agreed." Malik carefully removed his pack's straps from his shoulders. "The pack goes first. That way, I get my test—hopefully successful—and my pack isn't in anyone's way when the rest of you come across."

No one spoke, moved, or even breathed as Malik got his pack in precisely the right grip to distribute the weight as evenly as possible. He turned to the side, his feet in a fencer's ready position, and tossed the pack.

It landed exactly in the center of the tile.

Dasant cleared his throat. "Uh, boss, I just had a really bad thought." His voice was the barest whisper. "I hate to bring this up, but what if Malik's pack was too light to set off the trap?"

Malik spoke without turning. "Das, you bastard, I heard that."

"Sorry, but it's a viable concern."

"Yes, it's viable. It also does not help."

He jumped.

And landed.

And remained unsquished.

Malik nimbly—and very quickly—crossed the rest of the

floor without stopping, arriving on the other side alive and whole.

He shouldered his pack, turned to us, and grinned in challenge. "I think Das should go next."

11

Das crossed without incident, followed by Elsu, Jash, and Agata.

Phaelan was about to go, with Talon next, Indigo flying across after him, and me crossing last. Indigo would remain with us. We didn't know what to expect in the caves and once we reached the subterranean city. Indigo might become an invaluable member of the team.

All those who had already crossed had felt the vibration in the tiles beneath their feet, but it hadn't gotten any worse. I'd take that as a good sign.

As a pirate and expert swordsman, Phaelan was used to keeping his balance and even fighting with a pitching deck beneath his feet. Vibrating tiles probably didn't even register.

Talon had been a dancer. He was as nimble as a thief sprinting across a city roofline.

He leapt with graceful power across the blank tiles in the middle of the room, landing perfectly where everyone else had.

The tile exploded upward, propelling Talon into the air.

Indigo squawked loudly and I sprinted across the floor, only half looking where I was stepping.

Talon curled into a ball in mid-air, turning once, twice, and three times, then landed squarely and safely on the next safe tile.

I slid to a stop, the toes of my boots on a white tile. I pinwheeled with my arms, rocking back on my heels.

The white tile didn't react.

"What the hell?" I yelled.

Malik's eyes were wide and Phaelan was white as a sheet. Looked like my two booby-trap experts hadn't been expecting that.

And here I was out in the middle of the floor, one leap from the trick tile, not knowing if the next one I stepped on would be my last.

As fast as it had tossed Talon, the trick tile, capping a thick metal pole, lowered back into its mounting.

My mind raced. Could it have been set to not react for six people, with the seventh to cross setting it off?

"You might want to avoid that tile," Dasant suggested.

"You think?"

He winced. "Actually, you might want to avoid any of them. Too bad you can't levitate."

"Yes, that is too bad. Does anyone have any *practical* solutions?"

Phaelan barked a humorless laugh. "How are you at tightrope walking?"

I opened my mouth to retort, then closed it again, an idea

coming to me. "The tiles are activated by pressure, a certain amount of weight. What if I stepped on the exact place where four tiles meet? The corner, and only with the ball of my foot?"

Phaelan mulled that over, then began to nod. "If you could keep your balance, there wouldn't be enough of your weight on any one tile to trigger the trap." He added a smile to his nodding. "It could work."

Agata had her arms crossed, hugging herself. "Or it could trigger the first one you stepped on."

"Do you have a better suggestion?" I asked it gently and completely without sarcasm, which, considering that my knees were about to knock together, was nothing short of a miracle.

"You know I don't."

I slid my pack from my shoulders, leaving it on the tile. "If I make it across, screw caution, we'll use a retrieval spell on it."

Indigo had flown across to where Talon stood safely on the other side.

"Indy can fetch it," Talon said.

My boots were flexible, made for running and agility. They hadn't let me down yet. I hoped this wouldn't be both the first and last time.

"Stick to the corners of every third tile," Malik cautioned me.

I flexed my feet. "Let's get this over with."

There were approximately thirty more tiles to cross, meaning I'd be taking ten more steps, any of which could drop me through the floor to whatever death awaited below, fling me into the air to land on a trap tile, or send death to skewer me from above. My imagination treated me to a rapid-fire vision of all the ways I could die, giving special emphasis to what my mortal remains would look like as a result of each.

I told my imagination to shut up.

I'd often been grateful for long legs, but never more so than now. I carefully placed the toe of my boot on the exact spot where the supposed "good" tile intersected with three other unknowns. While being careful and precise, I was also moving as fast as goblinly possible.

I not only arrived at my destination, I was also in one piece.

There was no reaction from any of the tiles, the ceiling, or the walls around us.

I started breathing again.

And so did Talon and Agata.

Indigo darted out, plucked my pack from the floor, and sped back to us. He didn't want to be out there, either.

"Tam," Calik called across the room. "How long do you want me to wait?"

We had previously discussed three days, but that had been when we thought we'd be closer to Nidaar's mountain before entering the city. While assured that this was some sort of outer gate, I had no idea how much farther we had to go.

"Let's stick with three days," I said, glancing around at my team.

They nodded.

I had one of the firedrakes' spy gems. They could also be used for short-distance communication. I didn't know of an instance when they had been used to communicate between the surface and deep inside a mountain, but I'd always been of the opinion that if you pushed enough magic into a thing, it would work. Each member of the team carried a smaller version, the size of a large marble.

"Are you sure?" Calik asked.

"Positive," I told him. "Take care of yourself and the ladies. And if you need to leave, do it."

The dragon pilot laughed. "Tam, I've got three hyper-protective, fire-breathing dragons. I'll never be safer in my life. Just make sure that you come back—all of you."

"That's the plan."

12

I turned toward the single door that had been our objective. It was made of plain wood, with an iron frame and hinges. With the exception of Elsu, we were all taller than it was.

"I tried it," Malik said. "It's locked, and there are no wards."

Dasant shrugged. "If it worked once, boss…"

I held my hands out toward the door, palms forward, doing a quick scan of my own. Malik wouldn't blame me for checking after him; he would have done the same, and quite often had. We'd discovered the unpleasant way that what was unwarded for one could be deadly for another.

Not one tingle. The door was clean.

And highly suspicious.

The opening would be wide enough to admit only one

person at a time, and that person would have to stoop to get through. It was a perfect ambush point.

There was no knob, ring, or handle.

"Everyone against the walls," I said. Not that it would do any good if something on the other side was waiting to introduce our insides to our outsides. The floor behind us was no longer safe. We couldn't go back. Forward was our only option. When our mission was complete, we would have to find another way out.

I carefully put my hand where a handle should have been and slowly pushed.

It opened into darkness with a grating creak of hinges.

We all winced. Phaelan and Dasant mouthed their respective favorite curses.

So much for sneaking into Nidaar.

I reached out with my magic and quickly scanned through the door. There was no discernable barrier that would be triggered by shielded and cloaked mages stepping through.

I glanced at Jash, my brow raised in unspoken question.

He shook his head.

Nothing alive waiting on the other side. Though we'd discovered the dead could be even worse.

"I'll go first," I said. "Wait here."

I shielded, cloaked, and stepped into darkness.

To a goblin's eyes, there are varying degrees of darkness, far beyond what an elf or human can distinguish.

Below me, the blackness was deeper, telling me that where I stood was a ledge. Above me was lighter, with the reason gradually becoming apparent.

Strands hanging from the cavern's vaults began to glow

with a brightness that defied their delicacy, illuminating a space even larger than I had sensed. I hadn't seen the phenomenon before, but I'd heard of it. The luminescent strands were created by cave spiders. Small and clever, the creatures had adapted to live in the darkness by making their own light. Any life that found its way into a cave was instinctively attracted to them. Bright drops stood out along the length of each strand. As the spiders spun their traps, they secreted a sticky substance so that any prey that made contact would be stuck and unable to escape. Fortunately, they were too small to be of any danger to us.

The webs' light was faint, but it was enough to show me that the shelf of rock where I stood was big enough of accommodate all of us. A rough-hewn stair curved against the wall to the left, giving us a way down to the cavern floor. We would be forced to go single file, and would be completely exposed with our backs literally to the wall. I couldn't see the floor of the cavern, but we had no choice.

I ducked back to where my team waited and told them what I'd seen.

"Phaelan, use your night-vision goggles to get down the stairs, and watch your step," I told him. "Depending on what we find there, it's up to you to determine if you want to keep them on or off."

The elf pulled the goggles up to his eyes from where they'd hung around his neck. "I'll take them off if I can. Peripheral vision sucks in these things."

I nodded. "Then let's move. I'll take point with Jash second to tell me if there's anything in that cavern that wants us dead."

"I might duck first and tell on the way down."

"Just as long as you make it obvious."

Dasant chuckled. "His girly squeal always works."

Jash fired back with a crooked grin. "If it ain't broke, I'm not fixing it."

"Okay, people," I said. "Keep it quick and quiet. Let's move out." I glanced at the door, our last contact with the surface. "And the last one through, close the door."

The cavern floor was farther down than it had appeared. As we descended, less light from the webs made their way down to us. There was a single "oof" from Phaelan when he bumped into Malik, but other than that, the elf pirate didn't misstep or make any noise. I had to admit I was impressed.

It took us at least half an hour to reach the bottom.

Jash moved in close, speaking in the barest whisper. "Still no life. We need to risk a lightglobe."

I kept my own voice down. "Agreed. I'll do it."

I conjured the tiniest point of light, no larger than the drops along the cave spiders' web strands, and sent it darting away from us into the darkness, increasing its brightness when it was far enough away not to expose us any more than we already were.

As it brightened, it showed an enormous chamber with stalagmites rising from the cavern floor to form towering monoliths, or fusing with others to form curtains of stone. Between them wound a path that was no more than six feet wide. The stairs we had just descended had been carved out of a wall that curved around to give us no choice but to take the path where it led.

"You think they want us to go that way?" Elsu asked.

"I'm not opposed to being given obvious directions," Malik said. "However, I harbor an extreme dislike of being herded."

He left "like sheep to the slaughter" unsaid, but we all knew what he meant. Malik had said it before, and it had turned out to be all too accurate on more than one occasion.

I appreciated his omission.

"The Heart is in that direction as well," Agata said.

"Since Jash says we're alone, drop your cloaks and shields. Save your magic reserves for later. Hopefully we won't need it, at least for a while. As soon as we find a defendable area, we'll stop and rest."

We had been steadily descending through the cavern for the past hour, keeping our lightglobe out in front of us. I'd expected the temperature to go down, not up. My experience with caves, tunnels, and mines had been cold, damp, and miserable. This was still uncomfortably damp, but the cold had been replaced by heat and humidity. A slight breeze blew from up ahead, bringing with it a hint of the mossy undergrowth of a forest floor. Considering how far beneath the surface we were, that was impossible, though my nose was telling me otherwise.

"I thought caves were supposed to be cool," Phaelan said. "It feels like the Daith Swamp down here."

"There's never been a survey of these mountains," Agata told him. "With all the seismic activity, I wouldn't be surprised if this mountain was a semi-dormant volcano."

"Wonderful. Yet another way we could die down here."

I ran the back of my hand across my eyes. Sweat. I had wanted nothing more than to take off my helmet, flight leathers, and everything underneath, and take a dip in the pool we'd just passed.

Until I'd seen the worms that lived there. We'd thought they were reeds, until Phaelan tossed in a piece of jerky.

Worms.

Hungry worms.

With teeth.

"Does everything down here want to kill us?" Dasant asked.

Malik slapped at an insect on the side of his face. His hand came away bloody. "No, they just want to eat us. Whether we're still alive or not does not concern them."

"The Khrynsani don't want to eat us."

"But their green, scaly friends might."

Minutes later we encountered the last thing we wanted to see—other than giant, man-eating insects.

A dead end.

It hadn't been a dead end until recently. However, when in a cavern, "recently" was relative. The rockfall blocking our way could have happened a few years ago, or a few millennia ago. When it happened didn't matter. That it was in our way now did.

"Can we blast it?" Dasant asked.

"I would strongly advise against it," Agata said, surveying the structure of the small mountain of rocks. "We don't know how thick it is on the other side, or how stable the roof is here. We could easily bring it down on top of us." She summoned a lightglobe. "I need to check the walls on either side."

I nodded and told the others to take a break, as I followed Agata at a distance that wouldn't interfere with her magic. Some of the worms in that pool could have land-dwelling cousins.

Agata stopped and removed her pendant, placing it flat against the wall, her attitude one of intense listening. "I'm getting the same strength of signal as before, and the wall is thin here." She shone her lightglobe on the rock above our heads. "And the rock above us is more substantial."

The others had joined us. Dasant shouldered his way to the front. "Then one good kick should do the—"

"Not that thin," Agata said.

"Ma'am, you underestimate my motivation."

"And you mistake the stability of the roof over our heads. I said it's stable. Not necessarily impact-proof. A couple of your 'good kicks' could bury us all."

Elsu elbowed Dasant aside. "I've got this one. Will cutting an opening less than waist high and just wide enough to squeeze through be too disruptive?"

The gem mage considered that for a moment. "It shouldn't be."

"*Shouldn't be* versus *buried alive*," Malik mused. "Sounds like we have a winner."

We all cleared out of the way so Elsu could go to work. She used a small rock to outline where she planned to cut. "Does that work?"

"Das might lose some skin," Jash noted. "But a couple of good kicks should pop him out the other side."

"How thick is it?" Elsu asked.

Agata held up her hand, indicating the distance from

her wrist to the tip of her longest finger. "It's this thick from the floor to just above my knees. Then it thins out to about this deep." She held up her little finger. "We need surgical precision here."

"That's what you're going to get," Elsu told her. She handed Agata a small, pointed rock. "Scratch an outline of the shallow part."

Agata did.

Elsu nodded in approval. "I can work with that. And if we grease up Das, we might manage to get him through."

Dasant gave her a look. "Very funny."

"Why thank you. I was only going for mildly amusing." Elsu removed her gloves. "I need everyone to move back."

We did as told.

Elsu raised her right hand, palm facing the wall she was about to obliterate. Within moments a needle-fine beam of red light shot from the center of her palm. When the beam struck the upper part of Agata's outline, the rock began to disintegrate in a cloud of dust. It took nearly half an hour, but Elsu's skill carved us a way through to the other side.

We squirmed through, to find ourselves in a continuation of the same cave. About twenty yards to our left lay the other half of the rockfall. It was huge. It would have taken weeks to have tunneled through, if it could have been done at all.

"Good work, Elsu," I heard Dasant whisper.

We walked for hours before finding a small cave that not only offered protection, but had a stream nearby with fish large enough to make them worth cooking. We weren't about to pass up a dinner of something other than dry field rations. Phaelan and Jash volunteered to catch dinner, and Malik volunteered to stand guard and critique their fishing skills. I was surprised Malik didn't go for an involuntary swim.

The fish that they caught were freakish-looking, eyeless and pale as ghosts, but we were hungry. Elsu had conjured a fire that was smokeless, but provided both heat and a way to cook the fish. She wasn't a firemage, but if it could be done with fire of any kind, Elsu was the one who could do it. Indigo had left his perch on Talon's right shoulder and had taken it upon himself to guard the cooking fish. Elsu was rewarding his heroic efforts with bits of fish from the prongs.

Agata pulled me aside out of hearing of the others. "I could have kept going. We don't have time to stop."

"We also don't have time for our gem mage to collapse," I told her. "You and Talon nearly drowned less than forty-eight hours ago. We've flown all night, and walked for nearly half a day." I sat on a rock and rested my back against the wall. "I don't know about you, but my legs are aching from being on a dragon all night, sprinting for my life across a booby-trapped floor, and trudging through a dark cave. All of us need to take a break. We don't know what's ahead, but we know what was behind us—Khrynsani, Sythsaurians, and something big and mean enough to kill all of them. If we run into any of those, we need to be rested."

Agata glanced back at the others sitting around the fire and lowered her voice further. "I just don't want to be the one holding us up."

"You're not." I stepped closer. "If there had been any choice, I would have left you and Talon with the ships."

Agata bristled. "I didn't come all—"

I held up a hand. "In an ideal world, the two of you would still be in bed and under a doctor's care. Nothing in our world is ideal right now, and unless we're the first ones to find the Heart, things will get worse and not get better ever again. We have no choice but to have you with us. We need you. I need you. But all of us need rest. You never pass up the chance for sleep, food, and water when you get it. Who knows when or if it'll happen again."

Agata's hand strayed to the disk pendant. "If we must stop, I'll make good use of the time."

"To rest."

"That too. We're still being given no choice of which direction to go. That can't last much longer. When we have options, I want to ensure we're closing in on the Heart."

"Eat first and lie down for a while. Then try to make contact."

Agata gazed at me, her expression unreadable. I thought for a moment she was going to argue with me, but then she turned and without another word went to where she'd left her pack, and Elsu handed her a plate with a portion of today's catch.

After our meal, Dasant and Elsu took up guard positions. I'd expected sleep to elude me, but I think I was out before my head hit my pack.

13

I was dreaming.

I knew I was dreaming, but I couldn't wake up.

I hated it when that happened.

At least I wasn't on the edge of a cliff with Sarad Nukpana.

I was in a room unlike any I had ever seen. A room I had never been in, but yet one I remembered.

The center of the Cha'Nidaar people. A gathering place.

The throne room.

The floor was made of the white tile we'd encountered in the booby-trapped room, though here I didn't get a sense of any of them being a danger. There were sconces mounted on all four walls, set with flickering dragon egg–sized gems— the same stone as the Heart of Nidaar. I hoped this was a figment of my over-tired imagination and not the reality. If it wasn't, Agata was going to have her work cut out for her in pinpointing the Heart's location.

Then there was the throne itself.

It was carved from a single piece of Heartstone.

"Yes. You remember."

I froze. The voice wasn't speaking a language that I should have understood. It was a version of Goblin, but one that had not been heard in thousands of years. Yet I understood it perfectly, even though I had not heard it with my ears.

The words had appeared in my mind.

Unlike in my dream with Sarad Nukpana, I had not tried to draw a weapon. I knew I would not have one, nor did I try to summon magic. To attempt such an act in this place and before this individual would be the height of rudeness, not to mention ineffective.

I slowly turned and beheld the woman I instinctively knew I would see before me.

Baeseria, the queen of Nidaar.

She was tall, slender, and ageless. Her skin was as burnished gold, and her long hair straight and the purest white, as were her robes. A simple gold crown rested on her brow and was set with a single, flickering Heartstone.

The stone in my ring glowed in response.

Baeseria smiled, wistful yet oddly warm. "I know you cannot be Kansbar Nathrach, yet you favor him."

I bowed. "He was a distant ancestor, Your Majesty."

I was caked with cave dust and desert sand, but I was a representative of the goblin king and my people. Some of those people had brought the ultimate betrayal to this land. My best manners were called for, even in a dream.

"I sensed when you landed on our shores, and knew that the ring and pendant had come home. I thought that it might be Kansbar returning."

"No, ma'am, that wouldn't be possible."

"An honorable man. Do you know if he had a good life?"

"No, Your Majesty. He did not."

"Khrynsani." She didn't ask it as a question.

"Yes."

"You are very much like him. As to him being a distant ancestor, distance isn't always measured in years or even centuries. True power is in the blood. You are of Kansbar's blood. The gift you possess is the same, passed down through your line."

"Gift, Your Majesty?"

A hint of a smile passed over Baeseria's lips. "It is no coincidence that you—and your son—have journeyed to our shores and found your way into the outer reaches of our home."

"So Nidaar still exists."

"It does."

"And your people?"

The smile faded. "You will discover this for yourself."

"Why have you…" I gestured in the general direction of my head.

"Come to you in a dream? Because you must be warned."

"But it is your people and the Heart that are in danger. We—"

The queen waved her hand, cutting me off. "The danger is not to us. It is to you, to any who come here. You must turn around, you must take your people, your loved ones, and leave while you still can. If you—"

Tongues of flame, like those inside the Heartstones, rose up between me and the Nidaarian queen, sweeping her words away and blocking her from my sight.

The tile beneath my feet opened, and I dropped into icy darkness, tumbling down, falling faster and faster. Hands reached out from the darkness, grabbing me…

Jash was shaking me awake.

My head was still resting on my pack, but it felt like I'd gone a couple of rounds with the nearest rock. I groaned and swatted at my friend, who wasn't going to be that for much longer if he didn't stop.

"Are you all right?" Jash asked. "You look like crap."

It was all I could do to get my eyes open. "Good morning to you, too."

"Seriously, Tam. You don't look good. Didn't you get any sleep?"

"I slept. I even dreamed."

"It wasn't Sarad, was it?"

I tried to sit up, wincing with the effort. "No. Queen Baeseria."

I now had the undivided attention of the entire team.

I squinted toward Elsu's fire and quickly looked away. Way too bright. I couldn't see the pot of coffee brewing there, but I could sure smell it.

"If one of you would put me out of my misery and get me a cup of that, I'll tell you all about it."

Elsu poured me a cup, and I accepted it with abnormally cold hands.

I dropped into icy darkness, tumbling down, falling faster...

I shook my head to clear it and groaned.

"Movement is bad," I whispered.

The coffee was too hot to drink, but a burned tongue was a small price to get that sensation out of my head.

After I'd downed half a cup, I felt up to telling them what had happened.

"Do you think it was real?" Talon asked when I'd finished.

I nodded, slowly. "There was a vague description of Baeseria's throne room in Rudra's book. What I experienced was far too detailed."

"Do you believe that was the same Baeseria who met your ancestor?" Agata asked.

"It wouldn't be the first time that contact with a stone of power lengthened a lifespan. So yes, I believe it's entirely possible."

"With a throne carved from a solid block of the Heartstone." Agata leaned back against the cave wall and briefly closed her eyes. "I'm looking for a specific piece of hay in what's turning out to be a very large haystack. Can't any part of this be simple?"

Malik knelt next to her. "Magus Azul, Tamnais knows what is at stake here. We all do. The fate of the Seven Kingdoms is in our hands."

Dasant cleared his throat. "Uh, Mal, I don't think you're helping here."

"Give me a chance to finish, and I will."

Dasant raised his hands. "Far be it from me to interrupt one of your pep talks."

"Magus Azul," Malik continued. "Tamnais brought only the very best on this mission. You included. If he did not believe you capable of finding that piece of hay in a haystack, I assure you, you would not be here."

Agata tried for a smile. "Thank you, Malik."

"Most of all," I began, "the throne doesn't have the power to cause earthquakes. The Heart does. You'll be able to tell the difference."

Phaelan took several deep gulps from a cup that I suspected had more than coffee in it. "And now we're in danger from some unknown killer who will take down anyone who gets too close to the rock."

"Not just anyone," Agata said. "Anyone other than the Cha'Nidaar."

The elf shrugged. "They protect the thing. It has to like them."

"Not necessarily," I said. "Remember the Saghred?"

"I'd rather not."

"It thought nothing of consuming those devoted to it," I said. "Food was food. When it hungered, it would take whoever was available. The Heart is self-sustaining. Baeseria only warned of danger; she didn't mention the Heart. The danger was to *all* who came here, regardless of their motives."

"I'd say the things that butchered and ate that squad of Khrynsani and Sythsaurians would be a danger to anyone," Elsu said.

I shook my head. "I think it was something else."

"There's something worse than Khrynsani, lizard men, or

the monsters who ate—or at least tasted—them," Malik said. "I, for one, am positively giddy with anticipation. Anyone else?"

Silence.

Malik took Dasant's place on guard duty so the big mage could at least take a nap. Though he was probably hoping to have his curiosity satisfied if something worse than goblin-eating monsters happened by. Jash joined him.

I'd slept for less than an hour, but I wasn't anxious to try for more. I was still groggy from my dream experience, plus I had guard duty of my own.

Since we were now in the Nidaarian cave system, Agata wanted to conduct a more in-depth ritual to pinpoint the Heart.

She cleared a space near the front of the cave, dusting away sand and debris until she had an area of smooth rock. She used a piece of white chalk mixed with silver dust to draw a ritual circle roughly six feet across, giving herself enough room to sit with space to ward against interference from the presence of the rest of us. I'd given her my ring to strengthen the signal as much as possible, and we had all moved away and behind her, stilling our own magic so as not to distract from any possibility of direct contact with the Heart.

She completed the circle, then sat cross-legged, placing the items she would need before her. She selected a small silver knife and pricked her finger, squeezing the tip to get a single drop of blood, and used it to seal the circle. Agata removed the pendant from around her neck and bowed her head over her open hand. With the same knife, she carefully cut her palm, waiting until enough blood had pooled, then laid the pendant in her bloody palm, placing her other hand that was wearing my ring over it, enclosing the pendant completely.

She sat utterly still for nearly half an hour, eyes closed, her brow furrowing and shoulders tensing as she searched.

I kept my emotions as quiet as my magic, not wanting to add to the difficulty she was obviously having.

I was having difficulty of another kind.

Staying awake.

When Agata finally opened her eyes and broke whatever contact she had made, we all remained quiet as she bandaged her hand and cleaned the pendant, hanging its chain back around her neck. Only when she had broken her ritual circle did we release the holds we'd had on our own magics.

She turned, her dark eyes finding mine, her frustration apparent.

"Did you find it?" I asked.

"Yes and no. Yes, I believe I found the Heart, but I also found similar signatures between us and it. So no, I couldn't get an exact fix. You wouldn't want to take another nap and ask the queen for directions, would you?"

I smiled. "If she contacts me again, I guarantee that will be the first topic of discussion. In the meantime, we'll go in the direction of the strongest signature. And if that leads us to the throne room, perhaps we can speak to Baeseria in person."

Jash suddenly appeared from where he'd been standing guard at the entrance to our cave. "I smell Khrynsani."

14

Agata scrambled to her feet, swearing under her breath. "It's my fault. I tried to be quiet, but I wasn't getting enough information, so I said screw it, and pushed hard."

"Not a chance," Jash told her. "*I* sensed *them*. They haven't sensed us. Something's keeping them busy in a bad way, but it's not in looking for us."

Malik grinned. "Shall we see what we can do to further ruin their day?"

In moments, everyone was geared up and ready to move.

I pulled my blades where I could get to them fast. "Jash, we'll take point. Das and Elsu back us up. Then Phaelan, Agata, and Talon. Mal, make sure no one comes at us from behind. Let's go."

I had no intention of engaging until I knew what we were

dealing with. The Khrynsani didn't know we were here, and I'd prefer it stayed that way, though my preferences had been getting short shrift lately. I knew what my team was capable of and wasn't concerned about any pack of Khrynsani outfighting them, either with steel or spells. If they had Sythsaurians with them, that could pitch the scales more in their favor, or not. The only magic I'd experienced first-hand was them conjuring and controlling the goblin ghost crew of the *Wraith*. Hand-to-hand combat was an unknown.

Phaelan was good in a fight with mortal weapons. He'd even brought a weapon of a type I'd never seen before. Phaelan called it a shoulder cannon. It was a metal tube about the length of his arm with a mounting stock that fit on top of his shoulder. He had a pouch of ammunition for it slung across his chest. Inside was a padded box that protected the plum-sized pouches from water and sudden impact. I strongly suspected the contents were Nebian black powder. I suspected because I didn't want to ask and have my concerns confirmed. Nebian black powder was one of the most powerful explosives known. It could also be extremely unstable when subjected to the wrong conditions. Kind of like a certain elf pirate captain. Instead of cannonballs, Phaelan said it was built to use any fist-sized stone. He'd brought some with him, and with all the rocks around, he'd be able to quickly scavenge for more.

I didn't like traveling with Nebian black powder, but as our team's demolitions expert and the only magical null, Phaelan might be the only one able to get anywhere near the Heart, so those pouches of highly unstable powder might mean the difference between success and failure, life for the Seven Kingdoms or death. As lethal as I knew Phaelan and his accoutrements to be, I still wanted to keep him in the middle of the pack. Raine would never forgive me if anything happened to her cousin, whom she loved like a brother.

Talon was as much of an unknown as any Sythsaurians we might run into. He had power to spare, but he was just discovering what he was capable of. That made for hesitation or false starts, which could be deadly to him or any one of us.

Agata we simply could not lose. We would be blind down here searching for the Heart without her to guide us.

Jash suddenly ducked inside a roughly circular jumble of boulders. The rest of us followed suit and froze. I listened with all my senses, magical and mundane.

Jash was right.

Khrynsani.

Beneath what I knew to be the magical stench of Khrynsani was a familiar, oily presence.

Sythsaurians.

Jash glanced at me and grimaced.

That confirmed the presence of the lizard men. I would've loved to have been wrong. Taking on Khrynsani had always been enjoyable in a getting-to-slaughter-your-sworn-enemy kind of way. The addition of possibly even more powerful opponents took all the fun out of what we were about to do.

My mind raced. If we could get past them undetected, we'd get to keep our advantage of secrecy. The Khrynsani and Sythsaurians knew we had arrived in Aquas, but they did not yet know that we were here under the mountain. We all had the same goal, though. If we didn't take them on here, we'd be doing it later, without the element of surprise. If it were only me and my team, there'd be no question of our strategy—take them out now so we wouldn't have to watch our backs for them later.

But it wasn't only my team. I had Talon and Agata, and even Phaelan to think about. Yes, Agata had shown her nerve and fighting skills back in Regor, but see previous statement regarding mission failure if anything happened to her. I loved a good fight as much as the rest of my team, a fight that didn't have me needing to protect anyone.

I gestured for Malik to scout ahead. Jash had confirmed the enemy; Malik's skill was his preternatural silence and patience. His wards were such that he could have been standing in the midst of those Khrynsani, and none of them would know he was there. And Malik could hold that ward as long as necessary, to the point of putting himself in a trance so deep that his heartbeat slowed so as to be undetectable, all the while maintaining just enough consciousness to hold the ward and continue to hear and see everything that was said.

Malik Chiali had the proverbial nerves of steel.

The Khrynsani would never sense him, let alone see him.

I didn't have the same confidence about the Sythsaurians. Their senses could be entirely different, or they could have devices that hid them from detection.

We waited.

I didn't like waiting, never had.

Fortunately, Malik was back within minutes.

Unfortunately, he was wide-eyed and pale.

"Oh, this isn't good," Dasant muttered.

Malik opened his mouth to report, and a roar split the air behind him.

I snatched Malik behind the boulders and threw out the strongest shields I had, noise be damned.

Whatever it was hit my shields at a run. Hard.

I looked up.

If this thing was in the dragon family, it was a distant, ancient branch. There was intelligence in those yellow eyes, all of it aimed at keeping its belly full, and those eyes were looking at us like we were the tastiest things to come around in some time.

It stood on powerful hind legs and raked my shields with scythe-like claws, sending up sparks. It should have been thrown across the cave. All my shields seemed to do was piss it off. The creature was easily ten feet tall, with scales that looked more like armor. It had rows of serrated teeth, the longest the length of my fingers. I had no desire to get any closer for a more accurate measurement.

It wanted to get much closer.

Its feet were four-toed, like a bird's with each toe ending in a short, hooked claw. The long legs flexed backward, also like a bird's. It had no wings. This thing was built for speed on land, for running down its prey and ripping it to shreds.

I felt Dasant powering up behind me. I moved aside to give him enough room to work.

Dasant flipped his hands up, palms toward his target, and opened up with twin columns of red death, hitting the mutant dragon squarely in the head. It exploded in a gratifying burst of blood, armored flesh, and bone.

A deafening shriek came from right over our heads.

An even taller version of Dasant's victim rose up over the wall of boulders that was all that stood between us and being shredded for this thing's next meal.

We were trapped where we were. We could fight these things as they came at us, but for how long? I assumed these were what was keeping the Khrynsani and Sythsaurians occupied. Or had the wingless dragons already slaughtered them and were now turning their attention on us? If any Khrynsani were left alive, Dasant's display had left no doubt who and where we were. A circle of boulders wasn't a defensible location; it was a bowl now filled with tasty meat morsels. Us.

The beast's neck wasn't long, but it was long enough to reach us.

Not if I reached it first.

"Das!" I hissed, and dived out of the opening between boulders.

Dasant was right on my heels.

When we got a look at the entire creature, we froze for what was only a second, but it would have been sufficient time to get ourselves eaten if any of the beasts had been so inclined.

I could see only the one, but I could smell more.

One crisis at a time, Tam. Take this one, then worry about the next one.

I thought I had enough raw power to take out the creature with one shot, but I knew Dasant did. I shielded us both and he went to work.

Within two heartbeats, bits of monster skull and brain went flying, filling the air with a pink mist. We had to dive out of the way to keep from being hit when the massive body hit the ground.

The things knew we were here, and once the Khrynsani and Sythsaurians didn't have monster troubles of their own, we'd have even more company. The only thing the boulders did for us now was to corral us as prey for whatever happened along. But being out in the open with things that could easily run any of us down was suicide.

That left one course of action.

Cloaks for everyone.

I ran back to the opening, and nearly got myself fried.

I threw my hands up.

Elsu swore and absorbed the green flame that had covered her hands. "Don't do—"

"Grab Agata and cloak," I told her. "Jash, cloak Phaelan. Talon—"

My son had the fingers of one hand around Indigo's jaws, keeping the firedrake quiet. He vanished, his cloak covering Indy as well as himself.

I cloaked myself. "Agata, lead us toward that signal."

I hadn't told any of them to stay quiet, and I didn't need to.

There were Khrynsani nearby. I didn't want to make any noise to attract more creatures that wanted us dead, but at least the Khrynsani didn't want to eat us. I didn't know what their two-legged lizard allies preferred. However, I knew exactly what the things moving in the dark around us wanted. All I had to do was think of a way to ensure it wasn't us.

I smelled what had happened to the Khrynsani before I saw it.

Blood. A whole killing field's worth.

There had been a battle here, but there were no bodies left behind. If some of the dead had been Sythsaurian, they had been taken as well. Maybe the things that lived down here weren't picky eaters like their surface brethren. All that was left was blood and the occasional partial leg or arm. Unlike on the surface, there wasn't any sign that the goblins and lizard men had had enough time to fight back. There was no scorched ground, no stink of black battlemagic in the air.

The attack had been a frenzied slaughter, almost as if the creatures had been defending something.

And they were still nearby.

I wouldn't say it was a stench that hung in the air, but it smelled wrong and felt worse. If I had to assign words to describe it, they would be rage and residual terror. Rocks couldn't feel either one, but I could. I wasn't there yet, but my skin was crawling in the direction of terrified.

Given a choice, I would've much rather had the giant centipedes.

We were being followed.

I tossed a questioning glance at Jash, who raised his closed fist in front of his chest. He opened it, revealing all five fingers, quickly closed it and opened it again.

Ten.

We had ten living breathing things on our trail. Whether Khrynsani, Sythsaurian, or both, we were outnumbered by two. Whether their power was a match for ours remained to be seen. And we would be seeing it. Eventually.

To whoever was following us, we served a purpose. If we got tired of having them tag along, we could always set up an ambush and ask them not-so-nicely to stop. Until then, I felt better knowing the Khrynsani were behind us.

I was more concerned with what was moving in front of us.

The team proceeded lightly and in complete silence.

Except for Phaelan, who occasionally scuffed the ground. Though I had to admit he'd made impressive progress. Knowledge that a pack of Khrynsani was on our tail was a potent motivator. Even Talon had stopped talking.

Jash glided further into the tunnel's depths. We had gone dark. With my goblin night vision, I could still see him. Problem was, the only things down here with us were other goblins— and monsters who didn't need to see to hunt their prey.

"Are the Khrynsani still behind us?" I asked Jash.

My friends nodded. "They stopped when we did. They're not ready to catch up to us. Yet."

Malik snorted. "Why would they want to? We're leading them right where they want to go."

The Khrynsani were keeping their distance, and after what we'd just experienced, I didn't see them in any hurry to overtake us. They'd be content to let us blaze the trail—and take the losses.

15

The cavern was a tumble of boulders, fallen stalactites, and pillars that rose from floor to ceiling, giving the appearance of a maze.

I felt like a mouse in that maze.

Agata led, her steps swift and sure, leading us toward the strongest signal she had sensed during her ritual to connect with the Heart. Jash and I were immediately behind her, defensive spells at the ready. The others followed with Dasant and Malik bringing up the rear.

Claws scrabbled on rock from in front of us.

And behind.

Then silence.

The maze widened out and then disappeared, leaving us exposed.

We weren't attacked.

I knew what the creatures were waiting for.

They wanted us to run. We'd been herded through the maze, and now they wanted us to flee like the prey they thought we were. I heard four separate scratches of claws on the cavern floor, all from different locations. Close, but separated. Definitely a hunting pack—one that had recently fed on Khrynsani. They were satisfied for now. We were the after-dinner entertainment. Yes, they would kill and eat us, but they'd rather play with us first. They hunted as a pack, so stalking was part of the game. The instant we ran, the game was over and the killing would begin.

Those Khrynsani might just have saved our lives.

I nearly smiled. That would be a first. I held up a hand, signaling everyone to stop.

Jash looked at me like I'd lost my mind.

I wasn't sure he was wrong. But I was sure we were dead if we made any sudden moves.

"How much farther?" I asked Agata, keeping my voice low and calm.

Her eyes darted from side to side. I knew what she was seeing. The beasts were stalking us, staying mostly out of sight, giving us occasional glimpses to build our terror to the point where we'd make a break for it.

All part of the game. A game I was determined not to play.

Agata exhaled slowly, calming herself. "On the other side of the cavern." She indicated direction with the slightest nod of her head—and a sardonic snort. "Wherever that is."

Okay, that wasn't what I wanted to hear.

"What's your plan?" she asked me.

"Get out of this alive."

She almost smiled. "That's a goal, not a plan. Try again."

"For starters, we can't run."

"What the hell do you—" Phaelan froze and lowered his voice when hisses came at us from multiple points in the darkness.

"We run, we die," I told him quietly.

"I've got news," the elf shot back in a whisper. "We're dying anyway. It's just gonna take longer and hurt worse."

"It's called buying time."

"I'd rather buy a broadside of cannons."

"They've got bellies full of Khrynsani. They're not hungry. They want to play."

Dasant cleared his throat. "Uh, I don't know about everyone else, but I'm not feeling playful."

"Neither am I," I told him. "At least not for their game. I propose we play one of our own."

Jash was staring vacantly into the distance. "There are more out there."

"Of course there are," Malik muttered.

"Monsters or Khrynsani?" I asked Jash.

"Yes. Four Khrynsani—"

I grinned. "And at least four playful beasts. We're going to play a game," I told my team. "And those Khrynsani are going to be our game pieces. These things hunt by movement and scent, but they prefer movement."

"No shield covers scent," Elsu said. "And between the eight of us, we've got enough scent to attract every beastie down here."

Talon squinted into the darkness, desperately trying to see what Jash was sensing. "We can't outrun those things."

"We don't have to," I told him with a grim smile. "We just have to outrun *them*."

Them. The four Khrynsani hiding behind a stalagmite curtain that curved around on itself, making a small room. It was similar in structure to the boulder formation we had hidden inside. One way in, and if you were pinned in by these creatures, the only way out was into their jaws. A Khrynsani had just popped his head over the top to have a look, instantly attracting the beasts' attention. Clicks and hisses came from the darkness around us as the beasts coordinated their attack.

If we hadn't escaped that circle of boulders when we had, the same would have happened to us. I pushed that thought aside.

"Four Khrynsani and at least four beasts," I murmured. "One serving per customer. Good thing it's Khrynsani and not lizard men—apparently nothing on this continent wants to eat those."

Dasant chuckled. "I don't know how fast those lizard men are, but I know I can outrun a robe-wearing Khrynsani."

"Four tasty distractions coming up," Malik muttered as two more Khrynsani, right on cue, popped their heads up to have a look around.

Idiots. Soon to be ripped-to-shreds idiots.

They saw the beasts the instant the yellow-eyed creatures saw them. One of the Khrynsani emitted an appetizing yelp before they both ducked back out of sight.

Too little, too late.

Prey drives activated.

One of the beasts stalked out of the shadows. It was larger than the others.

Back home, there were giant salamanders in the depths of

Rheskilia's largest silver mine. The females were larger than the males, much larger. Maternal affection was nonexistent. Those that hatched quickly and fled the nest even quicker were deemed strong enough to survive. Any sluggish hatchlings would be immediately consumed by the mother. In her defense, she had guarded her nest day and night for eight weeks, never leaving to feed. The new mothers were hungry, and in their minds, slow hatchlings were good for only one thing.

This was probably the alpha female.

A low rumbling came from her as she lowered her head, leisurely taking in the Khrynsanis' scent, and I could swear the long slit that was her mouth curved into a vulpine smile.

The stalagmite curtain wouldn't prove to be that much of a challenge, but it'd give us a couple of extra seconds to cross the cavern.

I held up a hand, telling everyone to wait. We needed the beasts committed to one meal before another made a run for it.

It didn't take long.

The big female glided with unnerving grace to block the one opening with her body.

A single shriek came from inside.

That was all it took.

The beasts couldn't tear the rest of the stalagmite curtain apart fast enough to get at the tasty Khrynsani morsels inside. One even helpfully tried to make a run for it—and was grabbed by two of the beasts.

Messiness ensued.

I signaled. We ran.

If you're handed a distraction, take it. If that distraction also decreases your enemy's numbers by four, take it *and* be grateful.

My gratitude to the beasts would only last until the next time one tried to eat us. If they didn't bother us, we wouldn't bother them.

I smelled black magic erupting from behind us as the Khrynsani made a desperate last stand. From the sudden burning stench, they had taken out one of the beasts, but while they were destroying one, the other three would be eating them.

"Tunnel," Agata panted. "Just ahead."

The silence behind us was sudden and absolute.

Except for the crunching and squabbling between beasts as they fought over a kill.

We almost made it.

A smaller beast, hunched and scarred, burst out of the dark right in front of us.

A second, and then a third appeared, trumpeting in rage and excitement, surrounding us.

We instinctively circled, going shoulder to shoulder, facing our attackers.

My team unleashed hell.

Good battlefield magic was whatever took out your opponent and ensured they wouldn't get back up. The best battlefield magic not only destroyed your opponent, but struck fear into the hearts, minds, and souls of other enemy combatants, causing them to flee the field in terror.

My team was the best.

However, these enemy combatants weren't capable of terror, only hunger and the thrill of the hunt.

Together, we stood a chance. Separate, we were vulnerable, then dead.

In less than a minute, we had been separated.

I swore and redoubled my efforts.

I risked a glance at Phaelan. With no magic, he was the most vulnerable.

I was wrong.

Jash and Phaelan were working together to deal death with a lethal combination of magic and metal. Jash would strike with his arm-length lightning bolts, branding a jagged, glowing line in the beast's scaly armor, and Phaelan would dart inside the screaming creature's reach and deliver death up close and personal with his twin blades to the vulnerable belly. The elf was moving with near-preternatural speed, risking evisceration himself to get between the beast's legs. A glint against the light of Jash's bolts showed the shields encasing the elf pirate. Jash had shielded him with the best he had, sacrificing some of his own power to protect Phaelan.

Talon was with Agata, using surprisingly subtle magic to maximum lethal effect. Blazing red motes of burning light swarmed like hornets around the beast they faced, searing their way through and burrowing inside wherever they found a chink in the thing's armor.

Indigo was staying well above the beasts' heads, darting with hummingbird speed to aim gouts of fire at their eyes, zipping away before any lashing tails could snap him out of the air.

Agata was using her gem magic to launch rocks at any beast within her sight. Rocks of a size that could bash in their skulls, or at least give them a concussion.

The rest of my team was more than holding their own, but the noise was drawing more beasts out of the darkness.

"Surrounded" quickly became "outnumbered."

We were ten kinds of screwed.

I darted away in an attempt to draw some of the beasts away from my team.

It worked too well.

One of the beasts lunged and snapped its jaws where I had been standing. Cloaks and wards didn't matter with predators that hunted by smell.

I didn't dare call out to my team for fear of drawing even more attention to either myself or them. But all that my silence would get me was being eaten alone.

Unless…

My lips curled in a slow grin.

These things lived in the dark, and I was willing to bet my life they didn't like bright light.

The beast that had just missed me was being cautious. They weren't stupid. It knew I could hurt it, but its prey drive was stronger than any fear it might have been capable of.

I ducked behind a boulder. First its jaws came around the edge of the rock, along with a charnel-house stench to go with the bits of flesh stuck in its serrated teeth. I held my breath to keep myself from gagging. The beast had to be fully committed for this to work. It thought it was about to pick off wounded prey. No danger, an easy goblin meal.

The yellow eye came into sight, narrowing when it saw me, and shaking the ground beneath me with a pleased rumbling growl.

Come on, you ugly bastard.

Its nostrils flared as it inhaled, taking my scent.

I opened my clenched fist and the lightglobe flared like a tiny sun, darting in a collision course with the beast's left eye with a spell that would make it stick. The thing's hide might have been harder than armor, but its eyes were just as vulnerable as any other creature's.

The lightglobe sizzled when it made contact, melting the eye and sticking in place.

The beast screamed in agony.

I ran.

The other creatures couldn't see me, but they'd be able to smell me. I was counting on the wounded one attracting all of their attention. Rheskilia's giant salamanders wouldn't hesitate to slaughter one of their own if they'd been wounded and weakened. I hoped these things had similar base instincts. While they were occupied with their injured pack member, we'd run like hell for the temporary safety of Agata's tunnel.

All in theory.

Five of the beasts ran toward the screaming and thrashing one.

The sixth didn't move. It was larger than the others, and stood straight and tall, tracking me as I ran, even though I was cloaked.

The alpha female. Smart and cunning.

Great. Just what I needed, a strategic thinker.

And then I tripped, landing in a full sprawl on the floor.

She lunged, clearing the distance between us.

I twisted as she snapped her jaws shut where I had just been. I rolled to my feet, summoning and flinging a blazing lightglobe at her eyes. No time to add the sticky spell.

She ducked, and to my amazement swatted it away with her lashing tail.

Then struck at me like a snake.

An explosion tore through the air. Almost in slow motion, the creature fell forward, hitting the ground, the impact force nearly sending all of us to the ground with her.

The beast's entire back was missing, blown away. The dust settled, revealing Phaelan slowly sitting up, bloody and battered, holding his shoulder cannon across his lap, smoke coming from the barrel.

He spat a mouthful of blood. "Kicks harder than I remember."

I ran to where the elf pirate lay sprawled, his lower leg twisted at an unnatural angle.

"Ankle." The elf hissed air in and out from between clenched teeth. "Feels broken." He fumbled in the pouch at his belt for another round. "Go ahead. I'll hold her friends here."

We were separated from the rest of the team by rocks—and more beasts. They had their orders: get to that tunnel.

"I'm not leaving you," I told Phaelan.

"I'll be right behind you."

"Yes, being eaten." I bent, lifted the elf pirate, and tossed him over my shoulder.

At least that was my plan.

Phaelan was shorter than I am, but the weight was still there. I was committed. Unfortunately, the beast was equally committed. Unless I wanted to hand it a double meal, not outrunning him was not an option.

It's true that we goblins are known for our speed and grace. However, we least display those qualities on ground covered in broken, jagged rocks that shifted underfoot under the best conditions. My optimal conditions didn't include a swearing elf pirate slung over one shoulder, with a hungry and highly motivated monster snapping at my heels.

"We've…got…company," Phaelan managed.

"I'm aware of that."

"He has friends."

I didn't dispute that our dash across the cavern floor had attracted more dining companions for our pursuer. I simply put on a burst of speed, which would have worked much better if I hadn't hit a smooth patch of the cavern floor, slick with glowing moss.

I saw it just before my right boot landed right in the middle of it.

The beast that was right on my heels was focused on making us his next meal.

He wasn't watching where he was going, either.

Slimy moss. The great equalizer. Downfall of predator and prey alike.

The beast's triumphant roar rose in pitch to a something resembling a cry of surprise as one powerful leg shot out from under him. Then the other, and with a boom that shook the cavern, the behemoth landed hard on its meaty side, its massive head striking the stone an instant later.

While down, the monster was far from out, but he was stunned.

I'd take it.

I don't know how I stayed on my feet. I had an elf over one shoulder, and my run was more like a barely controlled lurching.

But stay on my feet I did, and when the moss ended, a beautiful expanse of dry, smooth, and non-slimy rock floor began.

Malik and Elsu were just ahead, standing to either side of a goblin-sized opening in the cavern wall. They were beckoning wildly, their eyes at a point entirely too far above my head and entirely too close behind me for any kind of comfort.

I trusted the panic of my friends implicitly, and kept running. I had no clue where the crevice led, but I was pretty sure that what was chasing me wouldn't fit.

We burst through the narrow opening, the frustrated roars of the beasts fading behind us.

16

The fissure was wide enough to fit only if we went one at a time. My shoulders brushed both walls, but I made it through carrying Phaelan.

The narrow entry widened into a small chamber. The rest of the team was there and appeared to be unharmed. It wasn't an ideal situation, but we were safe from at least the beasts for now.

I knelt and set Phaelan down as gently as I could, leaning his back against a wall. "Elsu, I need your healer kit. Jash, water."

While we all carried basic medic kits, Elsu had been entrusted with the more powerful supplies.

Phaelan's eyes were dazed and glassy. He was in danger of going into shock.

"Talon," I called. "Get me a blanket and help me get him out of this armor."

Phaelan's left arm and chest were covered in blood. The vambrace had been ripped completely off, and the overlapping leather covering his chest had been slashed open. His ankle may have been broken, but getting any bleeding under control was my first priority. The elf's upper body was covered in dirt, blood, and bits of flesh that didn't appear to be his. I wouldn't know the extent of the damage until I got him cleaned up.

Several of the chest straps didn't need to be unbuckled, because they'd been sliced through by claws. Once Talon and I got him stripped to the waist, the extent of Phaelan's injuries were apparent. At some point, one of the beast's claws had penetrated the leather armor and the arming jacket beneath, and opened a line across the elf's ribs. Talon bundled the blanket around the parts of Phaelan that weren't presently bleeding. The slash didn't appear to have penetrated the muscle wall, just skin. A fraction of an inch deeper, and Phaelan would have been eviscerated and dead. With her healing skills, Elsu would be able to close the skin without stitches.

Phaelan glanced down at his chest. "Left side. Goes nicely with the left ankle. I do try to be tidy."

"That thing wasn't going for tidy when he ripped into you," I told him. "What happened to your cloak and shield?"

The elf had enough awareness to look sheepish. "I kind of got separated from Jash."

"That wasn't a good thing to do."

Phaelan gazed blearily down at the blood covering his left side. "No, I don't believe it was."

Jash spat a few choice words from behind me. "I told you to stay put."

I assumed he was referring to Phaelan, but I had separated

myself from the team, too, so he could have been angry at either one of us—or both.

"Sorry about messing up your spare leathers," Phaelan told him.

"I have more. Why the hell did you go running off?" Jash was livid.

Phaelan shrugged, and winced in pain. "Tam did."

"That's no excuse. Tam's a battlemage. He's qualified to do stupid things. You're not."

"I'm alive. So it worked."

"Because of Tam."

"True." Phaelan flashed me a grin. "Thanks, Tam."

"You're welcome. And I agree, you shouldn't have gone off on your own."

"I didn't mean to. I'd just finished slicing open a belly, looked up, and there was this big, clawed foot coming down. I rolled, and there I was, separated, armor slashed, and all by my lonesome. It didn't take much."

"Don't do that again," Jash told him. "You're my responsibility."

Phaelan was incredulous. "You told him to *babysit* me?"

"You are the magical null on the team," I said with a perfectly straight face. "It's the responsibility of the mages to protect you when needed."

"See," Jash told him.

I couldn't stop a little smile. "But I didn't specifically order Jash to protect you. Just cloak you. Apparently, he took it on himself to go above and beyond."

Phaelan grinned up at Jash. "Is that so?"

Jash ignored him, but his face was flushed. "You need water, right?" he asked me.

I pressed my lips together against a grin. "That's correct."

Jash went off in a huff to access the water portal.

Other than the ankle, and a nasty gash across his ribs, Phaelan's injuries were superficial. Some of the blood was his, most wasn't. A master healer like Mychael Eiliesor could have mended all of it in minutes with no loss of his own strength. We didn't have a master healer. Elsu was a capable battlefield medic, and so was I. Either one of us could set the ankle and close the wound, but we had no ability to restore Phaelan's strength as a healer of Mychael's skill could easily have done. Phaelan could do that himself with sufficient rest, but that would take time—and a place to rest without risk of being eaten. Time and a safe place to spend it were things we didn't have. I had no doubt Phaelan would force himself to keep up with us, but he couldn't take another attack like the one he'd just sustained. Now I would have to assign Jash specifically to Phaelan. Not that I needed to; Jash had already taken that duty for himself.

Jash returned with the water, and I set him and Elsu to work cleaning and doing what healing she could do to Phaelan's ribs. The elf had yet to have any reaction that could indicate that the beasts' claws were poisonous. At least one thing had gone in our favor.

And just because we hadn't seen or heard any Khrynsani or Sythsaurians, didn't mean they weren't out there. Dasant was standing guard near the entrance.

Thankfully Phaelan's boots laced up, so I wouldn't have to cut his boot off. We had no spares, and considering where we were, going barefoot wasn't an option.

"This is going to hurt," I told Phaelan.

Phaelan took a swig from his flask. "You think?" He saw

my glance at the flask. "Medicinal purposes only. I hurt like hell, but I don't care."

"And if you're holding that flask, you won't take a swing at me in the next minute. Also, screaming would be ill-advised just now. We are trying to hide, you know."

Phaelan arched a brow. "Screaming?"

"Excuse me, making a manly exclamation of discomfort."

I went to work on extracting the ankle from the boot. Other than a couple of sharp breaths, Phaelan was stoic. Once again, I was impressed, not surprised. Dealing with and working despite injuries was a fact of pirate life. Ships wouldn't board and plunder themselves.

"Good news," I told him, examining the bare and bruised ankle, "is that it's not broken. Bad news is that it is a severe sprain."

"In addition to fire, I can channel extreme cold, Captain Benares," Elsu said without looking up from her work on Phaelan's ribs. "Once I'm finished with this, I'll get some cold on it to help with the swelling. Then we'll wrap it and boot you back up."

Phaelan took another swig. "Sounds like a plan."

"We don't have the luxury of much time for you to rest it," I told him, "and you're not going to be able to run on it."

The elf tilted his head back in the direction of the cavern. "If those things get in here, I guarantee you that I *will* run—and probably pass all of you. For me, survival always wins over pain."

The beasts hadn't tried to get in, but we had heard them snuffling around the crack we'd wedged ourselves into. Agata, Talon, and Malik had gone to try to find a way out that didn't involve exiting the way we'd come in.

Jash had delivered the full waterskin, but was back at work trying to wrestle what looked like a tree branch through his portal. With a final grunt, it came through, the effort nearly landing him on his backside.

He saw all of us looking at him. "There must have been a storm up mountain," he said. "Branches and debris end up in the river and get washed downstream."

"Yes," I said, drawing the word out. "That has been known to happen. You've dragged one through because…?"

"Phaelan's going to need help walking. That is unless we all want to take turns carrying him. With a little magic manipulation, this will make a nice staff."

"Magic?" Phaelan asked. "How can—"

"Like this." Jash held out the branch like a quarterstaff. With a small surge of his will, he stripped off the bark and straightened the wood, all in less than a minute. "Give me another few minutes, and I'll have it dry and reinforced." He jerked his head toward the fissure leading out into the cavern. "You'll be able to crack one of those things' skulls and this staff won't break."

Agata ran back into the chamber, her eyes gleaming with excitement. "Come quickly! You have to see this."

17

Agata led me to the back of the cave and into a small niche.
The light from our globes barely extended this far, casting
the space in flickering shadows. I'd expected another fissure.
There wasn't one. I'd also expected to see Talon and Malik.
They weren't here, either.

Agata saw my confusion and concern, and her smile
broadened. "They're down there—and in there."

I looked down. Then stepped closer. I wouldn't have seen
it unless I'd been standing right in front of it.

The opening was less than knee high and barely shoulder
width.

I went down on one knee in front of the opening. "Talon
and Malik—"

"Are in the next chamber," Agata said.

"They are?" My brow creased in worry. "But I can't sense them."

She smiled. "What's inside is shielding us naturally. No magic needed. As long as we're in there, the Khrynsani won't be able to find us. Go on in, and see for yourself."

I looked up at her. "I trust you with my life, but I'd like a little more to go on before I dive into a hole in the ground."

"You don't like surprises, do you?"

"In this place? At this time? No, I don't."

"You're no fun."

"I wouldn't go that far."

"Very well, spoilsport, through there is the strong signal that I've been getting. It's not the Heart, but we must be close."

"*Now* I'm intrigued."

"Would you like to go first, or shall I?"

I tossed a dubious glance at the size of the opening—or lack thereof. Both Talon and Malik were slightly narrower through the shoulder than I was.

"If you can get in, you'll be fine," Agata assured me. "The tube widens a little after that, and tilts slightly down. After about thirty feet more, you'll be in."

"Tube?"

"That's the only way I can describe it. It's smooth as glass."

I knelt and went down the rabbit hole.

Agata was right. The tunnel was rock, but perfectly smooth, almost too smooth to offer purchase. The slight downward slope helped.

I squirmed out and found myself in another world.

I slowly got to my feet and just stood there, awestruck.

We were surrounded by crystals. The walls, ceiling, and even floor were completely covered in glittering crystals. And each one flickered inside with what appeared to be dancing flames.

Crystals made from the same stone as the Heart of Nidaar.

An entire cave covered in them.

I felt rather than saw Agata emerge from the tunnel. I was incapable of taking my eyes from the sight before me.

The room glowed as if lit by thousands of flickering candles.

Agata slowly turned in a circle, cheeks flushed and dark eyes sparkling. "Isn't it magnificent?"

For a gem mage such as herself, being in the presence of so many stones of power must be intoxicating.

"So much for where the Heart of Nidaar came from," I whispered.

I felt the need to speak quietly, as if I was standing on sacred soil—or crystals.

The chamber wasn't large by any means. It was only a little larger than Phaelan's cabin on the *Kraken,* with an even lower ceiling. I could just stand up straight.

Agata was right. I couldn't sense Talon and Malik until I was in the room with them. The crystals' distortion covered all magic—and the life signs of its practitioners.

"It's a geode," Agata said. "The biggest I've ever heard of."

"And it's filled with Heartstones." Talon held a crystal that filled both of his hands, the interior flickering like a campfire. The little firedrake on his shoulder was turning his head this way and that, chirping in curiosity at the strange object. "Agata found the way in, and Indy flew in the hole before I could stop him."

"An intrepid adventurer," Malik said.

"Could this be what you were following?" I quietly asked Agata.

The gem mage was gazing around, her eyes still wide in wonder. "No." Then her eyes refocused on me, her expression becoming uncertain. "However, it does bring up a problem. I'm sensing more geodes like this. They're giving off the same signature as this chamber. There is another signal, one that's beyond any of these in strength, but with all of these chambers so close, it's difficult to get a fix on it."

"Difficult?"

"Difficult as in I haven't been able to yet."

At that moment, she looked younger, more vulnerable. I had to remind myself that she was only a few years older than Talon, though infinitely more experienced in magic.

"I imagine this many stones of power would temporarily overwhelm your senses." I tried to sound reassuring. "You just need to get your bearings is all. I don't know much about gem magic, but I would think smaller stones, regardless of how many, couldn't possibly give off the same signature as a specimen the size of the Heart of Nidaar, right?" I sincerely hoped I was right. If I wasn't, we were beyond screwed.

"No, they shouldn't."

"We have some time," I assured her. "Phaelan needs to rest before he can continue. You need to do the same. Relax and sort through what you're sensing."

"I do have a general direction of the stronger signal. And

yes, I am certain of it." Agata pointed to the other side of the glittering chamber where Malik stood. "That way."

"Uh, through the wall?"

Malik gestured me over. "The wall just looks flat from over there. There's a niche that widens into a short tunnel—a very narrow, short tunnel. It's a way out of here, but it doesn't lead to a place we want to be."

I had a feeling those beasts had been protecting something. Now we knew what.

A nest.

Worse than a nest. A pack nest, as in guarded by the entire pack.

They weren't all here right now, but the number of nests and eggs in each one said loud and clear that the contents of that cave wasn't the work of one female.

It also answered the question of where all those Khrynsani and Sythsaurian bodies had been taken, and probably the ones from the attack on the surface as well. I watched as one of the beasts took a gray-skinned leg from a pile of bloody parts and chewed it up before leaning its long neck over the nest and regurgitating the contents into the mouths of an eagerly mewling clutch of newborns—newborns the size of large dogs. Next, the parent selected a green arm from the pile of remains, and went through the same action of chewing and feeding. The beasts' young devoured the Sythsaurian limb just as quickly as they had the goblin leg.

"The little ones don't seem to be picky eaters," Malik noted dryly. "Perhaps their palates become more sophisticated as they grow."

Bile rose in the back of my throat. "Perhaps."

We drew back from the fissure that led into the monster nursery, its charnel-house stench effectively masking our scents from the occupants. Or so we hoped.

I gestured them back into the chamber of gems. "This could be a problem. Is there any way out of here other than this and the way we came in?"

Malik shook his head.

"Great. So, full-grown monsters waiting for us on one end, baby monsters and overprotective parents on the other. And the direction of the strongest signal is through the nursery, meaning that's the way we have to go."

"As far as I know now, that's correct," Agata said.

"And once we set foot in there, where do we go, how far is it, and is the way out large enough to accommodate all of us at a full run?"

"Except for Phaelan," Talon reminded me. "He won't be running."

"We'll overcome that challenge when we get to it," I said. "I've been in a sea dragon nest before and I survived. A clear escape route then is why I'm alive now." I turned to Agata. "I hate to pressure you, but do you think you can get that information within an hour?"

18

We'd climbed out of the geode chamber and rejoined the others. I'd just finished describing our route and its dangers.

"We can pull Phaelan through," I told Elsu.

The elf had been dozing, but I think "pull Phaelan" woke him up.

He sat up groggily. "Pull Phaelan through where?"

"The next chamber over has our exit, and is the way to the Heart." I didn't repeat that it would also put us in the middle of a monster nursery and in the most danger we'd been in so far. Like I'd told Talon, we'd overcome that challenge when we came to it—though it was increasingly looking like me tossing Phaelan over my shoulder again. Dasant was physically the strongest among us, but if we had a herd of irate monster parents on our heels, I wanted the floor cleared in one blast, and Dasant was the best qualified to do that. "We can just put you on your bedroll and slide you right through the chute into the geode," Jash chimed in. "You don't have a problem with closed-in places, do you?"

Phaelan was instantly and completely awake. "As a matter of fact, I do. A big problem."

Jash winced. "Oh."

"How big a problem?" I asked.

"I'd rather face the things we just ran from."

Elsu was incredulous. "Wait, let me get this straight. You enjoy booby-trapped rooms, and gutting things that want to eat you is fun, but you'll lose it if you have to get cozy with a rock chute."

"That's right."

Dasant shrugged. "Speaking of rocks, we can hit him over the head with one."

"The way forward is the only way out," I told Phaelan.

The elf pirate took out his flask and shook it. It was almost empty. He sighed, looking far too pale. "I didn't bring nearly enough liquor on this trip."

We put Phaelan on his bedroll and with Jash carrying one end and me the other, we carried the elf over to the tunnel. Phaelan's eyes were squeezed shut as tightly as physically possible. His color hadn't improved, but at least he wasn't screaming. The elf was determined to see this through. I didn't tell him that he wouldn't like the geode chamber much more than the chute he had to pass through to get there. I'd deal with that panic attack when Phaelan had it.

I hadn't entirely eliminated Dasant's rock-induced concussion solution.

I attached a rope to Phaelan's armor harness and Jash took it through the tunnel with him. We pulled Phaelan from the cave to the geode, his breath hissing through clenched teeth.

Just because we didn't need to worry about the beasts getting to us in here didn't mean the same would be true for any Khrynsani and Sythsaurians in the vicinity. That being said, they'd have to squirm through from the outer cave where we'd first sought refuge. If a head suddenly popped through the tunnel, Dasant was standing by to lop it off. The more likely possibility was any Khrynsani who found themselves trapped in the monster nursery seeking refuge in the fissure that led to our geode. Their screams would probably give us plenty of warning, and Malik was there ready to give them a warm welcome in their own blood.

Elsu had wrapped Phaelan's foot for the trip through the tunnel, but once we were all in the geode, she'd unwrapped it and had her hands around his ankle, channeling cold into it in an attempt to keep the swelling down. She wanted to wait until we were ready to make a break for it before wrapping it and putting his boot back on.

I was relieved to see that Phaelan took being inside of a geode better than I'd thought. Small rooms were fine, rock chutes were not.

Agata went to the niche that led to the exit from the geode into the monster nursery to give her a clear sensory path to the Heart. Malik left the geode, stationing himself near the nursery entrance. He couldn't sense Agata's efforts, so she was safe from external detection.

I could barely keep my eyes open. I'd lost track of how much time had passed since we'd descended from the surface, but during that time, I'd only had one hour's sleep. The worst danger was still ahead of us. The geode was keeping our magics silent and our presence hidden. There wasn't going to be a better time to sleep than now. It'd probably be the last chance I'd get. Agata didn't need me figuratively looking over her shoulder. If I was asleep, she could relax further, making her work easier. Malik and Dasant were keeping watch and would wake me if I was needed.

My breathing deepened, and I felt myself drifting off.

As I did, the Heartstones in the geode seemed to glow a little brighter.

I was in the throne room again.

But instead of an open space with doors at one end and the throne carved from a solid Heartstone at the other, there was a forest of columns, each covered in the same Heartstone crystals we'd found in the gigantic geode.

I knew the throne was somewhere ahead of me, but I couldn't find it. The crystals' glow was too bright for my goblin eyes. I reached for the goggles around my neck, but like my weapons, they weren't with me here in my dream. I put my hand above my eyes to shield them. It helped, but not enough to help me find my way. A buzzing noise further disoriented me. It was rising to a deafening roar, coming from everywhere and nowhere at once. A wave of dizziness swept over me and I fell to my knees, hands over my ears in a desperate attempt to block the sound.

I started losing consciousness.

"You must not fall asleep."

The voice cut through the noise, familiar, soothing.

Queen Baeseria.

Warm hands slipped over my own and the roaring ceased. My head cleared and I was able to open my eyes and look up.

I was on my knees before the queen of the Cha'Nidaar.

Her hands moved from my ears to the sides of my face, holding me there, her pale eyes intent on my own.

The columns still glowed, and the roar had faded into the background, but its disorienting influence was still there, waiting for the queen to take her hands away. I knew I would be overwhelmed again the instant she did, and this time there would be no hope for me. I would be destroyed.

"And all of your friends along with you," she said. "You ignored my warning."

"Not ignored, Your Majesty." My voice sounded distant, coming from another place. "We have no choice but to continue."

"You always have a choice."

"There are others. Goblins, but not like us."

Her gaze was solemn. "Khrynsani."

"Of course, you've dealt with them before. Last time when my ancestor—"

"And many times before that—and since." The queen's voice was filled with regret. "The Khrynsani are why we are here now."

The booby-trapped tiles. The Khrynsani serpent.

"Yes," she said, reading my thoughts. "But that is an old story, a story that does not need to be retold here and now."

"The Sythsaurians. They are here to take the Heart, to destroy the Seven Kingdoms."

My words did not affect her. "As the Khrynsani would have done so many centuries ago. It is why we are here, why we guard, why we remain." She paused, her eyes sad. "It is why we will always remain."

"But you don't need to," I insisted. "You can—"

"Destroy the Heart? Yes, I am aware of your intentions. It was a solution we have tried ourselves. Tried and failed. The Heart cannot be destroyed, nor can it be taken." She leaned down, her faces inches from my own. "It is safe. You and your friends are not. You must go." She gazed into my eyes, then released my face, straightening to loom over me, her features cold and impassive. "But you will not go. You will fulfill your mission, regardless of the danger, to yourselves, to us all. If you insist upon continuing—"

"I do, Your Majesty."

"You are stubborn and quite trying."

"Yes, ma'am. I have been told that before."

"I hope that against all odds you will live to be told that many more times."

Queen Baeseria faded, and the void was filled by the buzzing that crescendoed to the roar of a million hornets, filling my ears, my head, all of my senses, merciless...

I awoke with a gasp that turned into a whimper as I rolled over, hands cradling my head.

"Me, too," Jash rasped from nearby. "Worst damned hangover I've ever had, and I didn't even get to have the fun of tying it on."

I managed to open my eyes.

The crystals surrounding us were glowing, just as in my dream.

Or was it not a dream, but instead a dire warning?

Then the crystals winked out, their glow gone…

…into us.

I gazed at my hands, now gleaming with a pearlescent sheen, in wonder. "Jash…"

"Tam, your face."

I looked up. My friend's normally gray face was luminous, as if glowing from within.

"Uh, boss…" Dasant said from the tunnel entrance.

I scrambled to my feet, going around a corner to where he stood guard.

The big mage was staring at his glowing hands. "Is this a problem, boss?"

Talon was still asleep, his pale gray face gleaming softly.

"You ignored my warning…regardless of the danger to yourselves—to us all."

"I think we have a problem." I whispered, as much to myself as Dasant.

19

The elf pirate slept, but he wasn't glowing.

Only the goblins had been affected—or infected—by the Heartstones around us.

Agata sat perfectly still, eyes closed, expression serene, concentration complete. She was nearly as oblivious as Phaelan to everything happening around her.

I knelt before her, not touching her. When a mage of her power was in a trance of that depth, any kind of contact was dangerous to both parties. But if there was any possibility that what had happened had been triggered by Agata reaching out to the Heart…

"Agata." I kept my voice calm. The last thing I wanted to do was to startle her. That could also be very bad.

No reaction.

"Agata, wake up." Louder, more forceful.

Nothing.

Screw caution. I wrapped my hands around her upper arms and gave her a shake. "Agata, wake up, now."

She did, with a gasp and full-body shudder, her eyes focused on something far away.

I started to shake her again when her eyes focused on me and she smiled, a beautiful, unspeakably happy and relieved smile.

"Tam, I've found the Heart of Nidaar."

Our skin had stopped glowing within a few minutes. It had stopped because it was absorbed into us.

I felt it. We all did.

I'd felt something more when I'd touched Agata.

A sensation I'd hoped I'd never experience again.

Agata's smile had vanished once she'd seen all of us—and herself. "What happened?"

I told her about my dream, and Baeseria's warning.

"I know exactly where the Heart is," Agata said. "The noise from this geode and the ones nearby have been interfering. While I was trying to tell the difference between the geodes and the Heart, the geode noise faded into the background, and I heard the Heart loud and clear. It was as if my mind completely opened and I sensed every stone of power in this mountain—and beyond."

"Do you think the power coming from the Heart over-rode—"

"No. *I* did it. The power to push the geode's distortion aside came from me, not the Heart."

"I take it you haven't been able to do anything like this before."

"Never. It's one of the most difficult abilities for gem mages to master. *Very* few ever do."

I began to understand. "And within half an hour, you were able to not only find the Heart's exact location, but also communicate with it."

Agata was nodding. "It's spooky. Scary even. I mean, I'm grateful to have the information; I'm just not comfortable with how quickly I got it."

Elsu stood from where she had been working on Phaelan's ankle. "I think I was affected, too. I felt my power go out and into Phaelan—power at a level I shouldn't have. Phaelan, stand up."

The elf raised an eyebrow. "Without an ankle wrap?"

"If I'm right, you won't need it."

"If you're wrong, I'll be back on the floor."

"That's a risk I'm willing to take."

Phaelan shrugged. "You're the doc." He stood unaided, shifting his weight from one foot to the other. "I don't know what you did, but it's as good as new. Better even. My feet had been aching from all that walking. Not anymore. They feel great. *I* feel great." The elf picked up the staff Jash had made for him and tossed it from hand to hand, then gave it a couple of expert spins. "I won't need this for walking, but I never turn down a backup weapon."

"Phaelan wasn't glowing," Jash noted. "Do you think it only affects goblins?" he asked me.

"Either that, or it only affects magic users. Phaelan's a null."

"Hey, if it keeps me from glowing like you guys," the elf said, "I'm grateful for whichever one it was."

"Mal? Das? Did you get a power boost?" I asked them.

"I feel like I just had my best day's sleep in years," Malik said. "And I'm an insomniac. However, my skills are more understated than others. But based on rest alone, I'm ready to take on whatever jumps out at us."

Dasant nodded. "I'm ready and raring to go, too."

"Talon?"

"Like Das said, ready and raring."

Jash glanced uneasily at the Heartstones encasing us all. "Uh, Tam, add me to the list. I know there are more of these giant geodes across that monster nursery from us. One in particular is worrisome."

Agata started. "You can sense the geodes?"

"No, I can sense the Khrynsani and lizard men taking shelter *inside* that geode."

"Khrynsani mages whose powers have just gotten a big boost," I said. "And perhaps the Sythsaurians as well."

Agata's eyes widened. "If we can sense them…"

I reached for my pack and weapons. "They know we're here."

No one had asked me what the Heartstones had done to me, which was good because I wasn't about to tell them— especially Agata.

Generally, it's not good to have your team be afraid of being anywhere near you, especially when you were about to make a run for it across the floor of a monster nursery.

I'd cornered the market on self-fear all by myself.

At one point, I'd been in an umi'atsu bond with Raine Benares—and the Saghred.

And I was pretty sure that I was in one again.

This time with Agata Azul.

An umi'atsu was a bond forged between two powerful mages—usually goblin mages—binding them first through their magic, then joining their hearing, sight, and finally their minds and souls. After that, an umi'atsu bond could be broken only by death. It was a magical marriage of sorts, until death do you part and all that. In fact, we goblins considered it even more legally binding than a regular marriage.

An umi'atsu bond could be begun by the two mages involved in the bond. Stopping it once it progressed past the first two stages was only possible by death, or the intervention of a mage who specialized in umi'atsu bonds.

My mentor A'Zahra Nuru was one of only two such specialists still living. She was presently in Regor, covering for me as chief mage until my return. The other was in Mermeia.

So, if this was an umi'atsu bond, Agata and I had a very big problem.

The umi'atsu bond between me and Raine had been initiated by the Saghred. Our bond was severed by my temporary death. Had it lasted much longer, I would have been able to use the Saghred just as easily as Raine. I was—and still am—a dark mage, a practitioner of black magic. Like a recovering addict, I experience a daily struggle to keep from surrendering to the dark side of my magical nature. So when you think about it that way, by killing me, Raine had saved all of us.

It'd been a hell of a painful way to get a divorce.

In the instant I put my hands on Agata Azul's arms, I had somehow triggered a bond between us.

I didn't know for certain that it was an umi'atsu, but it felt suspiciously like what I had experienced with Raine. I had known her for years before it had happened. I'd only known Agata for a little more than a month. Perhaps it was our magic that called out to each other. Perhaps it was something more. Whatever had happened, Agata hadn't realized it yet. Locking in on the Heart's position had taken precedence over any uneasiness she may have been feeling. Or if she was aware of what had happened between us, she was pushing it aside and doing her job, like the disciplined and dedicated professional she was.

We had both been under the influence of the Heartstones in the geode. And when I'd touched her, Agata had still been connected with the Heart of Nidaar itself.

I didn't know what the Heart was up to, if anything. The Saghred had turned out to be sentient. We didn't know much at all about the Heart. I did know that I had no intention nor desire to cause earthquakes and giant waves, but given enough time, the dark side of my nature could twist me into thinking that was a good or even great idea. It could come in handy on a battlefield or at a Khrynsani headquarters. I could level the playing field. Literally. Destroy our enemies in an instant by having the ground open and swallow them.

See what I mean? Destructive, yet simple, and oh so successful. All the makings of a great idea.

I felt a laugh bubbling up that might have been a little on the hysterical side. With two umi'atsu bonds within months of each other, at least no one could say I had commitment issues.

I really needed to stop seeing women who were in relationships with stones of power.

Jash and Malik led the way out of the geode, stopping just short of the entrance into the monster nursery.

Malik was using his enhanced cloaking ability to hide both himself and Jash from detection while Jash got a fix on the geode being used by our enemies and determined the fastest route to a narrow tunnel in the north corner of the cavern that Agata said led into the center of the mountain, where the city of Nidaar and the Heart waited.

"What kind of goblins would build a city surrounded by giant goblin-eating dragon things?" Phaelan whispered to Elsu.

"The kind who like their privacy," she shot back.

The elf snorted. "And going through life as a potential main course."

We had one goal with a two-fold problem. Cross the cavern/monster nursery without being eaten by the beasts or slaughtered by the Khrynsani and Sythsaurians who were somewhere in the general vicinity. In a perfect world, we would be able tiptoe quietly from the geode which was Point A to the tunnel Point B and not be noticed by anyone or anything.

Our world was not perfect now, nor did I expect it to become so in our foreseeable—and possibly very brief—future.

We also had the additional problem of blood. Phaelan was wearing some of his, and there was no covering up the scent. I didn't know if there was any difference in smelling prey that still had its blood on the inside as opposed to prey that had been perforated by claws, but I was willing to bet that with Phaelan in our midst, we'd just gone from merely appetizing to downright irresistible. Yet, in our midst was exactly where Phaelan was going to stay. The elf had said he could run, but until I saw it for myself, I wouldn't believe it, and there was no way I was taking the risk of losing Phaelan Benares because I outran him, leaving him for the monsters to eat.

As if in response to my pessimistic thoughts, five small reptilian heads popped up above the expanse of eggs and began calling for their mother. Loudly.

A roar answered them from a side tunnel, and the owner of that roar was closing fast.

20

There are times when, as a leader, you must stick to a carefully considered and predetermined plan without wavering.

And then there was now.

"Run!"

My team didn't need to be told twice.

True to his word, Phaelan nearly outpaced all of us. It was even more impressive considering that I had never run so fast in my life. Any worry at being somehow contaminated by the geode's Heartstones vanished in the sheer exhilaration of running.

There were now multiple roars behind us, and the rhythmic shaking of the cavern floor said loud and clear that we were being pursued, and that what was pursuing us was horrifyingly large.

I wasn't about to turn around to find out. The rest of my team was in front of me, so the only person I had to be concerned about was me. My primitive instincts yelled for me to zigzag, and as I did, a pair of massive jaws snapped the air in the space I'd just occupied, motivating me to an even greater burst of speed.

The tunnel wasn't large enough for all of us to enter at the same time. That was fine, since we didn't all arrive at the same time. I was the last one through, and again, jaws slammed shut just as I'd cleared the threshold. The floor shook and I was knocked from my feet as the beast slammed into the cavern wall outside at top speed.

The wall held.

The beast screamed in frustration and rage.

We were all alive and in one piece.

Sometimes the flawless execution of a brilliant plan wasn't all it was cracked up to be. Once again, improvisation saved the day—and kept me from becoming baby food.

I whooped. I couldn't help it.

"Tamnais Nathrach, you are a difficult man to find."

The sibilant voice came from behind me, from behind us all.

It should have been dark behind us where the tunnel opened into a cave. But now there was light, plenty of it. Enough for me to see what we had run into.

Enough to know that lizard men preferred light.

And enough to learn the reason Jash hadn't sounded the alarm: a curved blade held tight against his throat.

There were ten Khrynsani and four Sythsaurians. Yet it appeared that the Sythsaurians were in charge.

This was not good.

Even worse was that I sensed next to nothing from three of the lizard men—and nothing at all from the one who had addressed me in flawless Goblin.

This was definitely not good.

The Sythsaurian was easily a head taller than me. His eyes gleamed a dark gold in the light cast by the flickering Heartstones covering the cave's walls and ceiling. He wore leather armor that fit like a second skin, leaving only his head exposed. It was hairless, with mottled green skin and a pebbled texture. He slowly smiled, revealing teeth the size of my own, but each ending in a triangular point.

His perusal of my team came to rest on Phaelan.

"And what is this pale creature called?" he asked.

"An elf," a Khrynsani spat in derision.

"Should I be insulted?" Phaelan asked no one in particular.

"You might want to wait until the odds are better," Malik told him.

"That will not be happening," the Sythsaurian said mildly.

"You underestimate what we consider better odds," I said.

While the Syth had been studying Phaelan, I'd caught Jash's eye and had seen the barest upward tilt of his lips in response to my unspoken question.

He was ready when I was.

I wasn't ready until I had more information.

Jash was the only one of my team being restrained—either physically or magically. While everyone—us and them—had lethal magic ready to let fly, we had a bit of a standoff. Neither the Syth leader nor I had given the signal to unleash hell on the other, and judging from the Syth's demeanor and questions, he was just as curious about us as we were about them.

When confronted with a new enemy who isn't actively trying to kill you, it's best to gather as much information on them as possible.

Then you destroy them.

That was how we did things in the goblin court, though I suspected in this instance I might want to alter my approach.

"Tamnais Nathrach, you are a difficult man to find," the Sythsaurian repeated. "Yet here we are, together at last." He half turned to address someone behind him. "You were correct in your assessment. He has presented me with as close to a challenge as I have yet experienced on this world."

Sandrina Ghalfari stepped out from behind the big Sythsaurian.

I smiled, showing as many teeth as the Sythsaurian had, though only two of mine were fangs.

Sandrina had a cold, dark beauty that shone to its full advantage against the Heartstones' gleaming translucence. My team and I were covered in sand and dust, but Sandrina, her Khrynsani, and the Sythsaurians were clean and perfectly groomed, as if they had spent their time somewhere other than these caves.

Sandrina also appeared suspiciously rested and confident. "Are you imagining that you will finish what you started that night in the Khrynsani temple, Tamnais?"

"My imagination has nothing to do with it. I'm merely pre-enjoying a coming event."

"Your confidence is premature, and misplaced."

"As always, Sandrina, we disagree."

She saw Talon and smiled. "I see you brought your mongrel. Were you afraid he wouldn't live one day at court without your protection?"

I was prepared to restrain Talon if necessary. It wasn't necessary. He stood straight and still by my side, temper not only held in check, but a hint of a smile curling his lips and a glint in his eyes.

A dangerous glint, but perfectly controlled.

I felt a surge of reassurance—and pride.

Indigo took his cue from Talon. The little firedrake bristled, raising the armored ridge down his back, and gave a long, sulfur-scented hiss.

"I fear nothing concerning my son," I said.

Talon's smile broadened into a wicked grin.

My wicked grin.

Pride came again, and hot on its heels was concern. I knew what that grin meant when I was wearing it.

Talon was up to something. More accurately, he was up to no good.

His power wasn't building.

It was already there. Ready to release, but held in perfect check.

I knew it, but Sandrina didn't appear to have a clue. Or if she did, she dismissed his skills as beneath her own. She would realize her mistake when Talon unleashed on her.

"Have you spoken to your son recently?" I asked her.

"Of course not."

"Naturally, going to Hell would be beneath you."

"My son is dead. You killed him."

"Now Sandrina, you know that's not true. If you believed that, why did you steal his corpse from the Guardians?"

That got the attention of the Khrynsani with her, at least half of whom were members of Sarad's inner circle, judging from the ornateness of their black robes.

"You must not have shared that bit of information with your son's closest friends."

"It's a lie."

"Are you accusing me, or reassuring them?"

"Yes."

"I have witnesses—and an empty glass coffin in the Guardian's citadel to prove it."

"*They* stole his body. They would think nothing of desecrating my son's remains."

I shook my head. "Sarad and I have spoken on several occasions, very recently. Not in person, but spoken nonetheless. Considering his location and circumstances, he's quite happy and well adjusted. He even has a new lady friend. Have you met Bricarda? She's working with your Sythsaurian allies, and according to Sarad, her visitations have made his imprisonment infinitely more pleasurable." I paused, enjoying this more than I thought I would. "He was most curious as to why you stole his body. We initially believed the trails left in the dust on his coffin's lid were your tears. Sarad laughed and asked me, was I sure it wasn't spit?"

The Khrynsani mage closest to Sandrina grinned in a flash of fangs.

Looked like Sarad had shared his feelings about his dear mother with at least one of his friends.

"Lady Ghalfari," the Khrynsani said, "You assured me that—"

"My son is dead, or as good as," she snapped back.

"Someone sounds defensive," I noted. "And disappointed. I got every impression that Sarad was biding his time and close to negotiating his release."

Sandrina's lips tightened.

"In fact, he seemed to be increasingly eager to do so once he learned of your grave robbing. He was most concerned about it—and you. Perhaps he is merely a good son who wishes to reassure his beloved mother that he is alive and well."

Sandrina raised her chin. "If he is alive, then I will welcome him with open arms."

I gave her a sly smile. "With a poisoned blade hidden in each hand. Sarad would be wise to avoid such an embrace. Then again, I suspect that is why he has survived for so long."

"Yes, I am very proud of him. Sarad is my son. All he inherited from his father was his name. If I could have created him alone, I would have. Your son, on the other hand, is the sum of *both* of his parents."

Damn.

"You never knew your elven mother, did you?" she quickly asked Talon.

Talon didn't respond.

And I waited a beat too long.

Her words came in a rush. "I didn't know her, but I knew of her. A splendid family, such power, such willingness to use it. Silvanus is a respected and revered name among elven magi. Though now it is reviled, thanks to the ineptitude and fatal flaws of Carnades Silvanus. Or as you should know him, *Uncle* Carnades."

I sensed Talon stiffen beside me, but other than that, he made no move.

"That information was not difficult to obtain," Sandrina continued, slowing now, enjoying herself. "Your father knows. He has always known who your mother's family was."

"And I promised I would tell you after this mission, that it was time for you to know." I kept my voice calm. "I have never lied to you." If I didn't allow Sandrina's words to affect me, perhaps I could will Talon to do the same. I wasn't going to hold my breath, but I could hope with every fiber of my being.

"Are you not concerned you may possess the same flaws?" she sweetly asked Talon.

I drew breath to respond, as Talon did the same.

Part of me wanted to stop him, to explain, right here and now; but I knew stopping him from speaking was the last thing I should do.

Instead I held my silence and allowed my son, my adult son, to speak for himself.

"As Sarad is wholly your son," he said, "so I am my father's—and my mother's. I did not know her name or that of her family, but my father has assured me that she was a fine and noble woman. I believe in and trust him—and only him."

I couldn't breathe. Not with apprehension, but with wonder and pride.

Dasant made a show of sniffing. "Is anyone else tearing up here? Or is it just me?" He put an arm around Talon's shoulders and pulled him close. "Is this a great kid, or what?"

I knew what Dasant was doing—getting Talon close enough to protect him if he was momentarily unable to do it himself.

As soon as Dasant made his move, Jash had cleared his throat, enough to be heard, not enough to cut his own throat.

He was ready.

So was I.

21

The key to getting the draw on mages at or near your own level of skill is not to think about it beforehand. You also can't let it show on your face or even by a twitch of a finger. It's kind of like a card game, except it gets lethal immediately. You don't wait until your opponent cheats before unleashing on him—or in this case, her.

But in a mage duel, as in a high-stakes card game, there is one absolute.

Someone always cheats.

And I have never been more proud that that someone was my son.

Talon's words to Sandrina had the attention of every pair of ears in the cave. He knew that Sandrina would be hanging on every word. Talon was a master spellsinger, and he had laced those words with the setup for a paralysis spell I'd seen him use before to great effect. He had spoken directly to Sandrina and those with her. It didn't matter that the rest of us had heard him as well.

Talon wasn't aiming at us.

It was so subtle that no one, including myself, had sensed it.

I had seen it.

In the eyes of Sandrina Ghalfari, and in the eyes of every Khrynsani with her as their pupils dilated wider with every word Talon spoke.

The four Sythsaurians were wild cards. There was no change in their slit pupils. But taking out every Khrynsani in the cave and leaving us with only four lizard men went a long way toward tilting the odds back in our favor.

If Talon had the power to complete his spell before the Khrynsani could block him...

I was determined to give my son every chance.

We all had shields at full strength, but when your allies and opponents alike were masters of black magic, things were going to get messy.

Jash had shielded Phaelan and taken his stand in front of him. Agata had shields of ample strength. That, plus her knack for unconventional warfare in a cave that for her was covered in ammunition, made me worry less for her safety. I had to worry less, because Sandrina wasn't about to give me a chance to defend anyone except myself.

Talon channeled all of his power into his voice, piercing the chaos with notes ringing with a perfect blend of sharp command and silken seduction. A paralysis spell attacking on dual fronts. It was irresistible.

At least it should have been.

Talon froze the plain-robed Khrynsani, and slowed two of the inner circle. We quickly dispatched them, leaving Sandrina, three master Khrynsani, and four Sythsaurians to contend with.

Eight to eight.

If they had all been Khrynsani, I would've considered that even odds.

They weren't, and it wasn't.

I took a page from Das's book and lashed out in a broad wave, beginning with Sandrina and the Syth leader, and ending with the Sarad's fancy-robed friend. The friend was singed, Sandrina was flung across the cave, and the two-legged lizard just smiled.

That was bad.

What I had thought was just tacky jewelry turned out to be something else entirely. The Sythsaurian was wearing wristbands studded with gems. Now they glowed a nasty shade of green.

I wasn't about to stand there and wait to see what happened. I gathered my will and focused squarely on the Sythsaurian, and a red blaze too bright to look at formed around my hands and ran like wildfire up my arms. When facing an opponent who's probably stronger than you are on all levels, don't screw around with what *might* work, just hit the bastard with everything you have.

I did.

He crossed his wrists in front of his face as my best shot consumed him, racing over and around his body…

…and vanished.

Not absorbed into his body, but sucked into his glowing wrist cuffs, and in a blinding blaze sent right back at me.

I barely adjusted my shields in time to avoid being burnt to a crisp by my own magic.

My team was likewise engaged. The lizard leader wasn't the only one with deadly accessories.

I couldn't see Agata.

"Tam, help me!"

The terrified scream came from my right.

Agata was under attack from a Khrynsani and a Sythsaurian. She was bowed into a defensive crouch, eyes wide with terror, her shields gone, empty hands extended to ward off their attack. Her eyes caught mine, wide, pleading for help…

Empty hands? Pleading?

My senses reached out of their own volition, searching for our bond…and found nothing.

An enraged shriek came from behind me.

Now, *that* was Agata.

I snarled and slammed a ball of glowing red rage down on the cowering woman.

At the instant before impact, Agata's panicked face winked out, replaced by Sandrina's features, twisted with raw hatred.

My shot was partially blocked by the Khrynsani who was in on her deception.

The Sythsaurian turned on me, wristbands glowing. His yellow eyes darting to the space directly behind me was all the warning I got.

It wasn't enough.

In the next instant, I felt myself enveloped and lifted off

the ground by a net of green light constructed by what felt like thousands of angry hornets, their vengeance centered on yours truly. My shields didn't help; these things manifested inside my shields. Even my flight leathers were no obstacle to being on the receiving end of pain the likes of which I had rarely encountered. Each pinpoint of sickly green light was a hornet with a stiletto for a stinger.

"He's mine!" I dimly heard Sandrina scream.

I would have gladly surrendered to Sandrina's tender ministrations just to escape the Syth's torture net. I desperately reached beyond my own pain, beyond the net, to what was happening to my team.

Everyone—my team and the surviving Khrynsani, now including Sandrina—was being held to the ground beneath Sythsaurian nets. The Khrynsani had been betrayed by their new allies.

The leader had me, Talon, Agata, and Dasant, and the other three had the rest of my team and the Khrynsani. I moved my head with agonizing slowness to look down at myself. I was no longer suspended in the air, but was on my knees before the Sythsaurian leader.

Then a haze passed before my eyes, and between one blink and the next, Queen Baeseria was standing next to the smiling Sythsaurian, his smile and movements somehow frozen in place.

"Not frozen, but greatly decelerated," Baeseria said. "I have slowed time in this cave. I cannot act on what is happening here, but you are not so constrained."

"Speak for yourself, Your Majesty," I said in my mind, since I think my actual voice was busy screaming.

Her lips briefly curled upward. "Once again you are on your knees. Such obeisance is not necessary."

"Tell him that," I said.

"You have little time left."

Yeah, that's what my screams were telling me.

"He and his kind have gained more power by contact with the crystals."

"So did we."

"Not to the extent that they are able to draw power. It is why they have come here. They have used such crystals before. They think nothing of taking and laying waste to entire worlds to get what they need. Then, like the scavengers they are, they continue on, searching for other worlds, worlds with sources of power to fuel their war machines. As they acquire more resources, they take on more advanced cultures. However, they consider the world of the Seven Kingdoms to be fairly primitive."

"We're primitive? I don't think I like that."

"We're merely a stepping stone. They conquer worlds, taking the inhabitants for food or slaves, leaving no living creature in their destructive wake."

I didn't want to know, but I had to ask. *"Are we food or slaves?"*

"Both. You must stop them."

I think I may have managed to twitch an eyebrow. *"I was trying to do that, before…this."* I still wasn't sure what this was, but I really wanted it to stop. The pain and the screaming. Right now, I think the screaming was worse. It was so close, and so loud.

"If you stop screaming, you will die," Baeseria said.

In that case, it was annoying, but I could put up with it.

"Listen to me," Baeseria said earnestly. "You have it within you not only to resist, but to escape, and to strike back."

That didn't sound right, but it might have been all the screaming. Others were joining in. That didn't improve my concentration.

She grabbed my face between her hands, and pinched my earlobes. Hard. Her eyes bored into mine. "Listen to me!"

I did.

Baeseria vanished, and I was left looking at a sadistic, smiling, green lizard man.

My body drew breath to continue screaming, and in that breath, I felt the stabs of a thousand stiletto-stingered hornets cease their stinging, and I could think.

Better still, I could move.

And I knew how I could escape.

But I didn't do either. Not yet.

The Sythsaurian had been expending a significant amount of power to hold the four of us prisoner, but I somehow knew it wasn't all the power he had at his disposal.

That was more than a little concerning.

Escape now, be concerned later.

The Sythsaurians were killing all of us.

I remained on my knees, hands by my sides. I twisted my wrists, putting the daggers strapped to my forearms in my waiting hands. The Sythsaurian knew who I was. He wouldn't kill me, not yet. Right now, all he wanted was me subdued and captured. He had both. He had lowered the power in his shields just enough.

Confidence can kill.

It can also cripple.

I didn't know if Sythsaurians were anatomically the same as goblins, but they had two legs, legs that looked the same as ours.

I hamstrung him.

A Sythsaurian scream is more like a keening wail, a really high-pitched keening wail. The leader collapsed bleeding to the ground, and I was pretty sure my ears were doing the same thing.

Shouts rang out as armored goblins streamed into the cave—golden-skinned goblins.

Each held what looked like a smaller version of Phaelan's shoulder cannon, except these were powered by a fist-sized Heartstone, blazing with light.

The Sythsaurian leader touched a crystal on his wristband, and his body became undulating waves of light before vanishing right before my eyes.

This wasn't magic. This was something else.

The other Sythsaurians must have done the same. Only my team and the Khrynsani remained in the cave.

One of the Khrynsani made a run for it. A Cha'Nidaar soldier aimed and fired.

A beam of fiery light shot from the weapon and struck the Khrynsani, vaporizing him instantly.

The rest of us put our hands up and didn't move as the Cha'Nidaar soldiers disarmed us all.

I had no idea if they could understand me, but I had to try.

"Take me to your queen," I told the Cha'Nidaar with the most decoration on the chest of his uniform, judging him to be the senior officer.

The officer tilted his head and said a few words. They sounded vaguely familiar, but weren't anything that I could understand.

"Queen Baeseria," I said. "Please take us to her." I gestured to include my team.

I don't think the officer heard anything past Baeseria's name. He blanched nearly platinum, as did those near him.

I didn't think that was a good sign.

The officer said three words in some ancient form of Goblin. I heard the queen's name and a word that was close enough to the modern term that I could understand him.

Now it was my turn to blanch.

He had said: "Baeseria is dead."

22

Our hands were secured behind our backs with manacles fitted with Heartstones that negated magic. I knew they negated magic, because I tried using it to get out of them. Unlike the bonds used in the Seven Kingdoms for restraining mages, these didn't inflict pain if you attempted to use magic. Your magic simply didn't work.

The Cha'Nidaar had taken all of our weapons and had done a depressingly thorough job of it.

The officer had also found and taken the ring and pendant that Agata and I wore.

I tried to reach Queen Baeseria without luck, which made me wonder if the ring had been my link to her, or if that in combination with my magic had enabled me to communicate. Or, what was seeming most likely, that she really was dead and that I was delusional.

Dead.

How could that be? She'd pinched my earlobes, which, aside from an area significantly south from there, were the most sensitive parts of a goblin's body. I'd already been in pain from the Sythsaurian's attentions, but I knew what I'd felt.

Queen Baeseria had spoken to me on three separate occasions.

That she was dead was an unexpected twist, but communicating with the dead was possible. I'd seen it done. What I wouldn't give to have Vidor Kalta here right now to find out exactly what was possible. Though I was certain Vidor wouldn't feel the same way.

The Cha'Nidaar were keeping us separate from the Khrynsani. We were in the front with the Khrynsani behind, with four Cha'Nidaar soldiers between us.

It wasn't nearly enough.

I would never trust any Khrynsani at my back, but especially Sandrina Ghalfari and three members of Sarad's inner circle.

"Tam."

I tensed, thinking it could be Baeseria. Then I tensed further, and added a wince, realizing who was speaking to me mind-to-mind.

Agata.

So much for her not realizing what had happened between us. Though considering that we were manacled and being marched to who knew where, I was grateful to be able to talk to her without anyone else hearing. An umi'atsu was a magical bond. Perhaps magic-blocking manacles only worked against physical manifestations of magic.

I sighed. *"Yes?"*

"You're not surprised that you can hear me."

"Do I detect a faint note of accusation?"

"You do, and there's nothing faint about it. What happened to us?"

"It's complicated."

"If it involves you, how could it be anything else?" She paused. *"I heard you and Baeseria talking."*

Now that was a surprise. *"You heard?"*

"In the cave back there."

"You heard the other two times?"

"No, just this instance."

I hesitated. *"Do you think she's dead?"*

"She could very well be. I mean, if she were still alive, that would make her over a thousand years old."

"I've met two people who were around the same age. One—Rudra Muralin—is dead as of a few months ago, or at least I hope he is. The other—Eamaliel Anguis, Raine's father—is very much alive. Both had extensive exposure to the Saghred. Baeseria could have had the same length of exposure to the Heart. So, yes, her being alive is possible."

"Except the officer said she was dead."

"There is that. We wore Heartstones for over a month, with no effect. Yet thirty minutes in a geode amplified all of our magic."

"Well, I did stop an earthquake," Agata noted. *"I've never been able to do anything like that before. But that doesn't explain Talon being able to help me. He said nothing like that has ever happened to him, either."*

"I've given up trying to explain what Talon can do."

"You haven't found his limits, have you?"

"No, I haven't, and I wish I could."

"The geode doesn't explain why we can mindspeak," Agata said. *"Or whatever this is."*

"Umi'atsu."

"What?" Agata blurted out loud.

Two of the guards behind us prodded us, none too gently, with the barrels of their guns.

I should be grateful Agata didn't have the gun at my back. She would've shot me.

Three guards held their Heartstone-powered guns on us while others removed our manacles and locked us in a cell made entirely of Heartstone. It had the same effect as the manacles: our magic didn't work here.

"And we thought we were going to have trouble finding this stuff," Elsu said, sitting on a Heartstone bench and kicking at the Heartstone floor with the heel of her boot.

"Not only is it everywhere, apparently it's useful for all kinds of things," Malik added. "Amplified power, imprisonment, talking to dead people."

I threw him a look. "Mal."

"My apologies, Tamnais. Merely venting my frustrations. If you say you've spoken to Queen Baeseria, I believe you. I thought every one of those Cha'Nidaar would faint dead away when you told them. There's something afoot. Most people would have simply looked at you like you were crazy. Those men looked afraid." He glanced around at our prison. "Any chance of you pulling some strings with her to get us out of here?"

"I've been trying. Nothing."

"Do you think it's because they took your ring?" Dasant asked.

"I don't know. Every time we've spoken, she initiated it."

"Maybe she doesn't think you're in danger now," Elsu said. "She gave you what you needed to break that Sythsaurian's hold on you... Maybe she thought her work was done."

"Yeah, and that being taken prisoner by her people was a good thing," Jash quipped.

Suddenly my head snapped back from a punch to my jaw. A good one.

Talon.

He had been quiet since our capture. Now I knew why.

He couldn't exactly express himself while we'd been manacled and surrounded by armed guards.

This was the reaction I had expected. Finally, Talon was doing something I understood.

I held up my hand to stop any of my team from interfering. "I deserved that."

"*Why?* Why didn't *you* tell me? Why did I have to hear it from that *bitch*?" Talon's voice rose to a roar, and I endured the onslaught.

He was furious and he had every right to be. Yet he wasn't letting his anger get the better of him. As a spellsinger, he could have made each and every word more painful than that punch. Ronan Cayle had taught him that.

But he didn't.

Talon was angry, hurt, and afraid—afraid of who he was, afraid of what he might do, of what he might become. It was something he felt he had no control over. He needed to take it out on someone, and since I was the one who had fallen in love with a Silvanus and together we had made Talon, I was the only one he could strike out at.

"You're right," I said, my hands at my side and making no effort to defend myself. It wasn't necessary. Talon had done what he'd needed to do physically. Now came the hard part.

My explanation for why I hadn't told him.

And the full story of how it had happened.

23

I was going to tell him, right here and right now, in front of everyone.

Though we were all locked in a cell. It wasn't like I had much of a choice. And being locked in a cell, we had the time.

"I was your age," I began. "Very much like you, in fact."

Dasant barked a laugh. "And *that* is explanation enough."

Talon and I shot him an identical glare.

Dasant took a step back, hands raised. "Just trying to be the diplomat here, lighten the mood."

We continued to glare. Talon added a growl.

"When I was seventeen, your grandparents sent me to D'Mai in Brenir to study with your Aunt Kisa," I said. "You haven't met her yet, but you will. She's your grandfather's sister, and the only Nathrach of her generation with measurable magical skill. She also has some very strong beliefs about when magic should be used, and when it should not be used—and she is *not* shy about sharing her opinions. I had entirely too much magical power and I enjoyed using it. I had fallen in with the wrong people and was becoming increasingly involved in court politics."

"At seventeen?" Talon asked.

"Your father has always been a go-getter," Malik told him. "Pushing the limits, and all that."

"Pushing entirely too many limits," I said. I exhaled slowly. "I toyed with power I had no business having, let alone playing with, and that was exactly what I was doing—playing. I had no concern for the consequences of my actions. Though once I was in D'Mai, most of the time I was a model nephew. Kisa found plenty to keep me busy and out of trouble. Until trouble came to me." I had to pause for a moment before I said, "Her name was Gelsey. She was a spellsinger Kisa had met through a friend, Gelsey's mentor in D'Mai. One day, I heard a laugh coming from Kisa's laboratory. I simply had to see who that laugh, that voice, belonged to."

"And when he did," Jash said, "it was all over."

"You were there?" Talon asked him.

"Believe it or not, your grandmother considered me a 'stabilizing influence' on your father. I don't know how much stabilizing I did, but I was more studious than he was."

"And still is," Elsu muttered.

"There was a lot to learn from an alchemist of Kisa's skill," Jash added. "And knowing what she did about Tam, she made sure to keep us busy. You're not the only one adept at sneaking out of the house at night, Talon."

Malik grinned. "You inherited that trait from your supremely gifted father. With you, we've all enjoyed watching him essentially attempt to parent himself."

I ignored them both. "Kisa knew Gelsey to be serious-minded, so naturally she encouraged us to spend time together. I found out later that Gelsey's family had sent her to D'Mai so they could secretly arrange a marriage for her with a politically powerful elven family. They didn't want her finding out about it until the negotiations had reached the point that she couldn't possibly back out or—"

"They could force her to marry someone she didn't love?" Talon asked in disbelief.

"It's common for nobility, especially with elves, less so with goblins."

"Only highborn elves," Phaelan interjected with satisfaction. "The rest of us marry—or don't marry—who we damned well please."

"Goblin women have a similar attitude," Elsu said with a smile. "They're also more inclined to make those feelings known through blades or poison, or blades *with* poison. If enough suitors don't survive until the wedding, offers for a noble girl's hand in marriage go way down." She leaned in close to Talon. "And if the husband doesn't show his true colors until after the wedding... Well, that's why there always seem to be plenty of young widows at court. Something to know about goblin girls: if they say no, they mean it."

"Duly noted."

"A healthy attitude to have."

"And good advice to give," I told her. "Now, may I continue?"

Elsu inclined her head with a tiny smile. "Please do."

"No one knew that Gelsey was a Silvanus. To hide from any fortune hunters or the many enemies of her family, she used her mother's maiden name while in D'Mai. Even if I had known who her family was, it wouldn't have stopped me. We fell in love and fell hard. We were discreet, so Aunt Kisa didn't know there was anything going on other than harmless flirting. Gelsey's mentor didn't know. Summer ended and I was sent home. Gelsey was to leave a few weeks later, but she discovered that she was pregnant and ran away. I found out all of this months later. Gelsey kept one step ahead of her family by staying with a series of friends she had made without their knowledge. By then the marriage negotiations with the noble elven family had fallen apart, and the Silvanuses learned that Gelsey had had a child—a half-goblin child. She ran, knowing that her brothers would kill her for dishonoring the family name. When her brothers, Carnades among them, tracked her down, Gelsey left you with a friend and continued alone, leading them away from you."

Talon had folded his arms over his stomach, his pale eyes fixed on the far wall. "Why didn't she try to contact you?" he asked softly.

"I don't know. If she had, we would have taken her in, protected her. I would have married her. Your grandparents would have loved to have had her as a daughter-in-law…" I closed my eyes for a moment. "I could have been a true father to you from the beginning, watched you grow, raised you together with your mother. I never would have taken the dark path that I did." My anger grew and I let it. "Her brothers found Gelsey and killed her, then they returned to where she had left you and burned the house to the ground with all inside—except for you. Gelsey's friend must have suspected Carnades and his brothers would return and had gotten you out of the house before they arrived."

"I ran away from the people I was with when I was seven," Talon said in a small voice.

"I looked for you," I told him, nearly choking on the words. "I swear it. The trail ended at the burned house. I was told that everyone inside had died, and any who tried to escape were struck down by the Silvanus brothers waiting outside. In that moment, I vowed revenge, not only for Gelsey, but for the son I had never known."

"So I'm half Silvanus," Talon managed, his voice bitter. "I'm related to *Carnades*."

"No, you're Gelsey's son and mine," I said vehemently, willing him to believe it. "She disavowed her family and her name. You're mine. My son and my heir. You're a Nathrach."

Talon wasn't buying it, at least not all of it, but perhaps it was enough.

He snorted. "I wondered why I was so curious about mirror magic. Somehow I don't think *Uncle* Carnades would have been proud."

I went still. "Curious?"

My son flashed a humorless smile. "You've had your secrets. I've had mine. So, they killed her because of me."

I took a step closer to him, within Talon's striking distance, but I didn't care. "*They* did the killing. Don't you ever blame yourself."

Talon turned to face me. "Carnades killed her, and you knew."

"Yes." There was no room for denial, only the truth.

"And you did nothing. Took no revenge. Carnades murdered my mother and you did nothing."

"I had power when I was your age, but not enough to take on a family of the Silvanus's skill and influence. I swore I would have revenge; but to do that, I believed I needed more than what Kesyn Badru would teach me."

"Black magic."

I nodded tightly. "I found those willing to teach me, and I learned, and I learned well. I planned and I plotted. But to get the vengeance I wanted, I needed more than magical skills; I needed political power. I became a part of the Mal'Salin court and worked my way up, fought and killed my way up, until I was at the right hand of Gilcara Mal'Salin." My words came in a rush of emotions that had been pushed down and held back for far too long. "I played the games of the court and learned to win by any means necessary. Eventually I decided what games would be played, and I made the rules. What began as a desire for revenge grew into a lust for more power. I was at the height of my black magic addiction, but I considered myself at no one's mercy, let alone that of my own magic. As with everything else in my life, I believed that *I* controlled *it,* not the other way around. It ate away at my soul until my own family didn't recognize me. They told me I was out of control, but I didn't believe them. I thought I had perfect control, over myself and anyone I chose. I never forgot Gelsey, but I convinced myself that I needed to be even stronger. As a result, another woman I loved was murdered, and this time I truly had no one to blame but myself."

The room was completely silent.

My friends were silent because they didn't know what to say. I was silent because my throat had constricted around the words that still needed to come out.

I swallowed on a dry mouth. "That was when I hit rock bottom. I sought help, first from A'Zahra Nuru, then I met Mychael Eiliesor. I began a new life for myself on the Isle of Mid and Mermeia." I felt my lips twitch in a tight smile. "While looking for new spellsinging talent for my club in Mid, I heard of a half-elf/half-goblin spellsinger who had recently arrived from Brenir. Against all odds, I hoped." I met my son's eyes. "I went to the club you were performing at… and as soon as I laid eyes on you, I knew you were Gelsey's even before I heard you sing. When you did, I was taken back to that afternoon standing outside of Kisa's lab." I blinked my eyes several times. "I had found my son, and nothing or no one was going to take you away from me. I didn't put aside my desire for revenge, but I swore to be more discreet. To protect you." I took a slow breath; calming myself. "Gelsey was dead. Nothing I could do would bring her back. But I had you, the son I thought I had lost. To take direct action against Carnades would risk exposing you to him and his family. I failed to save your mother. I would not fail to save you. Carnades is dead, and his family remains unaware of your existence."

"So they've gotten away with it."

I smiled. "Revenge doesn't have to be a blade to the heart. Yes, you can take your enemy's life, but their evil works remain behind, continuing to grow and poison the lives of others. The Silvanus family does not value life, even the lives of its members. Carnades was not mourned. His name is cursed for what his failure has done to the family name, the damage to the plans they have nurtured for centuries. Thanks to uncovering Carnades's plot, we now know his family's ultimate goal is no less than to take the elven throne, and from there assure the destruction of the goblin people. Carnades is dead, but his brothers are not. His family is in disgrace, but they still have influence and power. They are every bit as dangerous as the Khrynsani. Until now, I have limited my efforts to undermining their power from behind the scenes. Now they blame Raine for Carnades's death. Raine didn't kill Carnades, Sarad Nukpana did, but with Sarad dead, they place the blame at Raine's feet. They are plotting against her." I smiled, and it felt good. "I am plotting against them. To destroy the Silvanus family is to destroy their chance at ever reaching the pinnacle of ambition and power. After we get home, the time has come to be direct. They need to know who I am—and why I am coming after them."

Talon held my unblinking gaze. He sniffed, then swallowed. "You're close to destroying them?"

"Oh, so close."

A hint of a smile appeared. "Promise?"

"On your mother's precious memory." I put a hand on Talon's shoulder. "You're a man now. You know who your mother was, and what happened to her as a result of loving me and loving you. The Silvanus family thinks you're dead. It is up to you whether to let them know otherwise."

"I think you know my answer."

I pulled Talon close and he let me. "Then let's finish here so we can go home and get to work."

The clear door wavered and vanished into the Heartstone floor.

It wasn't the captain of the guard. From his robes, this visitor could've been a high-ranking member of the court. From his expression, he thought I was something to be scraped off the bottom of his boots.

"Princess Maralah wishes to see you," he told me—in flawless modern Goblin.

24

It was the throne room from my dreams—except without Queen Baeseria.

Another unpleasant surprise awaited me.

Sandrina Ghalfari standing at the foot of the throne dais.

Her hands were manacled, as were mine now. I could hardly blame the Cha'Nidaar for not taking any chances. I sure would have chained Sandrina.

In Rudra Muralin's book, my ancestor had found himself in much the same situation—brought before the throne with a pack of back-stabbing Khrynsani with evil on their minds and in their hearts. At least here it was just Sandrina without her entourage.

It appeared we were to be given the chance to explain ourselves, and what we were doing once again trespassing where we had been told never to return.

I had a good excuse. She was standing right next to me.

Sandrina was more than a master shapeshifter; she was a master liar, adept at what I referred to as "court charm." I had watched her verbally eviscerate her opponents while appearing to be the very model of polite gentility. If any indelicate phrase passed her lips, it was due to the boorish behavior of her opponent. She was the perpetual victim, unjustly vilified, wrongly blamed.

I expected her to pull out all the stops here.

A door opened to the side of the dais, and a troop of guards marched through, escorting the courtier who had brought me here—and a woman I would have instantly recognized, had I not been told she was dead.

If this was Princess Maralah, she was the very image of her mother, or her ancestor, or whoever I had been talking to. She ascended the dais, turned, and sat on her throne, the courtier following to stand only one stair below.

Not a mere courtier then, but a high-ranking official.

The princess was tall and slender, with white hair that fell in a silken wave to her waist. On her head was a simple golden crown set with flickering Heartstones. Her robes were the blue of the sky on the surface, embroidered with delicate vines and leaves of the palest green and what looked like white roses.

All things that no longer grew on Aquas, thanks to the predecessors of the woman standing to my left.

The official had barely said a word to me as he'd brought me here from the dungeon, but I didn't need to speak to a man to know who and what he was—or the danger his presence here boded for my mission.

He had the angular features and high cheekbones of the

old blood goblin families. Like Princess Maralah, his skin was gold and his hair white, but any resemblance either of appearance or intent ended there. His robes were unexpectedly plain for so one so highly ranked, which told me even more.

I had known many of his kind during my time in Queen Gilcara's court. These men and women possessed the hunger for power and control, but they wished to avoid notice while they fed.

The peacocks who displayed their finery, bragged of their influential friends, and curried favor with sweet words were cowards when confronted with their deeds. The ravens kept to the shadows, quietly spreading their poisonous words and plots. They were rarely confronted, and seldom caught, and to do either put a target between your shoulder blades for the rest of your life. They were cunning and cautious—and deadly.

The princess was studying me, her pale eyes going from me to Sandrina and back again, all with no expression and in complete silence.

When she had looked to me, I inclined my head and bowed as I would for any monarch—especially one who held my life and that of my team in her hands.

Sandrina curtsied, but pride did not allow her to lower her eyes until the last moment, and she didn't keep them downcast for long.

I saw where this was going. Sandrina was going to play the wronged woman and appeal to the princess as one woman to another.

Sandrina didn't hesitate. "We have come to stop the Syth-saurians—the lizard men—from taking the Heart of Nidaar from your people. We were—"

I smiled. "The Sythsaurians' staunch allies until they turned on you."

"We were here to stop them," Sandrina said smoothly. "We were doing that from the inside, gaining their trust—"

"And doing an abominable job of it." I turned to Princess Maralah. "Your Highness, I do not want to take or destroy the Heart or your civilization. I merely want to keep it out of the hands of those who would use its power to enslave and destroy." I hesitated. "I believe I have spoken with your mother, the queen. She has come to me in twice in dreams and most recently while I was in the hands of a Sythsaurian."

"I was told of this," Maralah said, in modern Goblin.

Even her voice was nearly identical to her mother's.

"The ravings of a madman," Sandrina spat dismissively.

The princess's voice was as a breeze crossing a glacier. "That should be for me to decide, should it not, Lady Ghalfari?"

"Of course, Your Highness, it is just that Tamnais Nathrach was linked to the Saghred, a great stone of power known to cause mad—"

"My people have heard of this stone," Maralah interrupted. "It is a source of great evil." She glanced down at Sandrina's armor, which bore the Khrynsani serpent emblazoned in red on the chestplate. "And by fault of your predecessors' greed, the indirect cause of the destruction of our land."

"The Saghred has been destroyed," I said.

Her pale eyes narrowed. "When?"

"Two months ago, Your Highness."

She leaned forward. "It was allowed to spread its evil all this time?"

"It was lost for most of that time, taken by a brave

Guardian to keep it out of the hands of those who would abuse its power. The Khrynsani found the person the stone had forcibly taken for its keeper, and took the stone from her, intending—"

"A bond you shared with the Saghred through Raine Benares—" Sandrina added.

"A link that was against my will."

"Spare me your protestations of your purity and innocence, Tamnais. Your magic called to it."

"I've never claimed to be either pure or innocent. And yes, my magic responded to it; but I resisted, as I have resisted since leaving the goblin court—"

"*Forced* to leave, for the murder of your wife."

Fury built in my gut. "You poisoned and murdered my wife to force me out, so you and Sathrik could murder my queen and steal her throne."

"So you failed twice—to save your wife *and* your queen—and now you attempt to cast the blame on others—"

"Silence!" Maralah's voice cracked like a whip. "I will have silence," she continued, her voice quieter, but no less commanding. "Silence and peace."

I bowed my head. "Forgive me, Your Highness. Lady Ghalfari delights in opening old wounds."

"That is becoming quite clear," Maralah murmured thoughtfully.

I raised my head to see the princess's searching gaze locked on Sandrina's frozen and now pale face.

Time to take a big gamble.

"Your Highness, do you possess the same abilities as your mother, the queen?"

"Abilities?"

"Magic. Gifts of the mind. The ability to see into the heart and soul of another, to know if the words they speak are true and their honor is genuine."

"Yes, I can."

"Then I welcome you using your gift to know the honor of my intentions."

"Your Highness, I must protest." The official's voice was low and smooth, the voice of a man used to getting his way.

Maralah frowned. "On what grounds, Advisor Karnia?"

"Tamnais Nathrach is a powerful practitioner of magic. To put yourself—"

"Should not I be the one who decides where I do and do not put myself?"

"Of course, Your Highness. I did not mean to imply otherwise. I am simply concerned that—"

"I will discover the truth, Advisor Karnia?" she injected mildly. "The truth must always be known, regardless of any risk, real or imagined." Maralah turned her attention to Sandrina. "Lady Ghalfari, do you likewise welcome my examination?"

"Of course."

Sandrina had hesitated just enough to tell me she didn't welcome this at all. In fact, her mind was presently racing to come up with a way out. A meld the depth of what Maralah was about to do would bare Sandrina in the most intimate way possible. While Sandrina Ghalfari was lovely to look at, her soul was rotten to the core, her motivations self-serving, her concerns for herself alone.

I knew what I was, and I wasn't ashamed of it. It was what I had done since my time as Gilcara's enforcer that would redeem me in Maralah's eyes.

Or not.

There was nothing I could do to change her mind once she had seen what was inside of me. I could only hope that she would understand the failings of a mere mortal, the continuing efforts of a man trying to do the right thing.

Maralah came down the dais stairs with measured steps, never taking her eyes from mine.

Perhaps sensing Sandrina's desire to escape from what was to come, or fearing any attempt by me to harm their princess, two of the guards moved closer, stopping about five feet behind us.

I wholeheartedly approved.

History does indeed repeat itself.

Ten centuries ago, Kansbar Nathrach stood in this same room and subjected himself to a mind link with Baeseria, queen of the Cha'Nidaar. Now his descendant stood ready to do the same with her daughter.

I hoped the meeting of minds turned out as well for me as it had for my ancestor.

As I had with Agata when she had asked to do the same as a condition for joining the expedition to Nidaar, I opened my mind completely as Maralah placed her hands on either side of my head. Her eyes widened slightly at my show of complete trust.

We didn't have time for anything else.

Princess Maralah wasn't selective in her review of my memories. Her mind flew across the entirety of my life, seeing all the people and events who had made me the mage now standing before her, my eyes on hers. She saw all that happened with the Saghred—from the beginning to the night in the Khrynsani temple when the Saghred was destroyed. The night Sarad Nukpana—with his mother as the power behind the throne—came close to wresting the goblin kingdom from its rightful heirs. She saw that I used black magic to summon a demon, but it was the only way I had to stop Sarad Nukpana from fulfilling what he—and his mother—saw as his destiny. Maralah did not stop there. She continued to our reason for being here—to thwart Sandrina's plot to seize the power denied her by allying herself with the Sythsaurians and taking the Heart, and after that the Seven Kingdoms.

She released me and I staggered with the suddenness of it.

A guard behind me grabbed my arm, keeping me on my feet.

"Thank you," I told him when I could speak.

I had no concept of the time that had passed; but from past experience, I knew it to have been less than a minute.

Sandrina Ghalfari's expression was carefully neutral, but I knew better. In the time Maralah had come down from her throne and had linked her mind with mine, Sandrina had come up with a plan.

"Your Highness," I said, without taking my eyes from Sandrina. "You might want to reconsider linking with her. It would be dangerous for you."

Sandrina smiled. "Have you filled Her Highness's head with more lies, Tamnais?"

"There are no lies in mind links, Sandrina. Only the truth."

"As you remember it. As I said, Your Highness, Tamnais was bonded with the Saghred. His memories cannot be trusted."

"I will leave it up to Princess Maralah to determine who is trustworthy."

The princess crossed the floor to where Sandrina waited, her pale eyes glimmering with a metallic tint. "I do not need to touch you to know the truth of your words. Your eyes are the window to your soul. They will show me all I need to know."

It was over in an instant.

Sandrina's knees buckled and she fell to the floor, the guard behind her not quite fast enough to catch her.

I don't think he tried very hard.

"Return Lady Ghalfari to the prison level," she told the guard. "See to it that she is given a cell separate from her companions—in keeping with her station. Advisor Karnia?"

He bowed stiffly, his displeasure evident. "Your Highness?"

"I no longer require your presence. I am quite safe with Chancellor Nathrach. You are dismissed."

25

Princess Maralah kept her back to me until Karnia was gone, and Sandrina had been escorted out with no less than a dozen armed guards.

The princess turned to me, her pale eyes sparkling. "I have discovered that plots are difficult to hatch when the head of the serpent is separated from the body."

I assumed she was referring to Sandrina, not Karnia, but I wasn't going to ask. I smiled and bowed. "You are as wise as your royal mother, Your Highness."

"I have survived the centuries by being nothing less, Chancellor Nathrach." She gestured to one of the four remaining guards, who quickly unlocked my manacles.

I wanted to rub my wrists, but refrained from doing so. The Cha'Nidaar princess had just imprisoned my enemy and freed me. I wasn't about to be rude and imply I had suffered any kind of ill treatment.

Maralah noticed. "My apologies for any discomfort or indignity suffered by either yourself or your companions."

"Do not concern yourself, Your Highness. We understand completely."

She reached into her robes and brought out Kansbar's ring. She gave it to me. "I believe this is yours."

"Thank you, Your Highness, but it is mine only by discovery. Your mother gave it to my ancestor, Kansbar Nathrach."

"I know." She smiled, a woman with a secret to tell. "I was there when she gave it to him." She drew out the necklace with its Heartstone pendant. "And this belongs to you as well, though I believe you entrusted it to the gem mage in your company."

I accepted the necklace with a small bow. "I have, Your Highness. If you do not mind me asking, how are you able to speak our language? When we were captured, I could barely understand the officer in charge. But when Advisor Karnia brought me from my cell, he spoke to me in modern Goblin."

"We learned much from the visit of your ancestor and even the Khrynsani. We recorded the words of Kansbar and the Khrynsani when they were in Nidaar all those years ago, studied it, and learned the language." She smiled. "The better to know our occasional adversaries—or new friends, in the case of you and your companions. Many large problems are caused by small miscommunications." She paused for a beat. "Speaking of the benefits of honest communication, what are your plans now that we have the Khrynsani serpents behind bars?"

"Excuse me, Your—"

"Your plans, Chancellor Nathrach. You came here to secure the Heart from the Khrynsani and the Sythsaurians, who have disappeared."

"Sandrina and those with her were but one group of Khrynsani and Sythsaurians. We have encountered others."

"And what was the fate of these others?"

"We dispatched a few, but the majority were killed by the beasts we have found in the tunnels."

"Ah, the dakkonan. An annoyance, but they do serve their purpose in protecting our borders."

"Kansbar told of giant centipedes, but made no mention of—"

"The dakkonan were not here when he was. The earthquake caused by the Khrynsani awakening the Heart opened the deepest reaches of our caves, releasing the dakkonan from where they lived. Some of our people think it is Hell. Some days, I'm inclined to agree. The dakkonan ate what few animals survived the quakes."

"Then what do they eat now?"

"The occasional trespassing Khrynsani, and other creatures that were released along with them."

"There's more out there?"

"Oh yes, and in some ways worse than the dakkonan."

"Then we're grateful that we haven't met them." I paused uneasily. "Your Highness, your mother told me of the Sythsaurians' intent for our world. The Heart is a great source of power for them, one they will not easily abandon. I've never seen or heard of the type of magic they use. They vanished in an instant. Do you have wards that can keep them from reappearing in your city—or palace—just as easily?"

"We have the means to know when they appear, which is how we knew that you and your companions were under attack. Unfortunately, we do not have the ability to restrict their movements. My people have encountered the Sythsaurians before. We believe they use a sort of portal that is only occasionally aligned with our world." The princess indicated the weapons slung across her guards' shoulders. "We acquired a few of their weapons, and have duplicated them with a few of our own modifications."

"I've seen them fired. They are most…efficient."

"That they are, Chancellor Nathrach. So you see, we are far from helpless."

"I did not intend to suggest that you were, Your Highness. We are concerned that the Khrynsani have told the Sythsaurians our weaknesses. Considering how advanced they are, our weaknesses are considerable. We do not wish to be conquered and enslaved, or slaughtered."

"The Sythsaurians are capable of doing that with or without the Heart."

"I believe that. But if they do defeat us, and leave a force here with the Khrynsani to rule, the peoples of the Seven Kingdoms will wish they were dead." I realized something and barked a laugh.

"What is so amusing?"

"We came here to help your people, if they still existed. And here I am, asking for your assistance."

"Do not discount yourselves or your abilities, Chancellor Nathrach. What the Sythsaurians have—and we have appropriated from them—is no greater than your magic, merely different." She smiled, again a woman with a secret. "Have no doubt, we will prevail. We always have. Our resistance began when we left Rheskilia for this land. Did you know that the Khrynsani was once an academic order, studying and learning how the forces of magic worked?"

I nodded once. "I did. Learning wasn't enough. It never is."

"Members of the order began delving into the darker magics to increase their strength and gain new abilities. They did not care where that power came from. Some began consorting with demons and other dark forces. Others sought objects with which to augment their magical arsenals. I say arsenals, because that was their goal, to become living, breathing weapons. Kaali Nidaar, my grandmother, was an explorer at heart and had found ancient scrolls that described a stone of fire, a source of power that never died. The leader of the Khrynsani order at that time demanded that all research and knowledge be turned over to him. He said it was for the greater good of the order, that all knowledge should be shared. Some did as told, bringing their research before the Khrynsani council, giving it freely to benefit all. These men and women entered the high council's chamber and were never seen again."

"I had heard that in its beginnings, the Khrynsani had included women as members," I said. "As they became more militaristic—and paranoid, ruthless, and quite frankly, insane—women were excluded from membership."

Maralah smiled, genuine and warm. "Women like my grandmother probably washed their hands of the lot of them. She told her family, students, and those of similar mind that some powers were too great to fall into anyone's hands, and set sail for Aquas to find the Heart, and to secure it from the Khrynsani or anyone like them. We believe what happened to our east coast is but a fraction of what the Heart is capable of."

I watched her face closely. "Your mother warned me to stay away. Do you know why?"

"Perhaps. Our people were once as you are now: silver skin, dark hair, dark eyes. Exposure to the Heart has changed us. When we arrived and found the Heart and the crystals, we sensed their power and used it to light our city. We saw the physical changes that began to happen to us, but accompanied as they were by increases in magical power, intellectual ability, and even physical strength, we dismissed any thought that this could possibly be dangerous."

We had been inside the geode for less than an hour and our skin had become luminescent, our powers increased.

If the Khrynsani took control of the Heart...

"Exposure also affected our judgment as to how it could possibly be bad."

"It sounds like black magic," I noted.

Maralah nodded once. "The temptations and false confidence are the same."

I knew firsthand how seductive contact with stones of power could be. The Heart might not devour souls, but that didn't mean it couldn't enslave just like black magic.

Jash, Elsu, Mal, and Das were all recovering black magic addicts.

Talon was my son.

We were all vulnerable.

Resistance involved more than control of your magic—you had to control yourself. You had to keep your emotions in check, not letting any use of your magic arise from a desire to do harm to another. To lose control of your emotions was to lose control of yourself. It became a downward spiral from there. It would turn you, taking you one piece at a time, feeding on all in you that is good, eating away at it until there is nothing left.

"After a few years in Nidaar," the princess was saying, "we began to notice that we did not age, and that the wombs of women of childbearing age no longer quickened with life. My mother dispatched a small colony to the surface to see if distance from the Heart's influence would restore the semblance of a normal life to us. There was no change, regardless of how far the abroad the colony traveled. After three years, they returned to us unchanged.

"There are not as many of my people as there used to be." Maralah went silent for a time, and I sensed strong emotions warring inside her. "People say that they would like to live forever, to never grow old, never die. Those people do not know what they ask for. I have lived nearly eleven hundred years, Chancellor Nathrach. While it is not yet forever, it is a very long time. The Cha'Nidaar become fewer in number with every passing year as my people take their own lives." Her shoulders sagged slightly as if accepting a heavier burden. "Long ago, I was angry at them for their weakness. Now I almost admire their strength."

This woman had met me less than an hour ago, and was baring her soul. Though it was true she had just witnessed my entire life through my memories. Very few knew me as Maralah of the Cha'Nidaar now did.

I felt my throat constrict as I spoke. "Perhaps your people need to get farther away from the Heart. You could go farther into Aquas's interior—or return home to Rheskilia."

"I have a duty to my people, my mother, and the Heart of

Nidaar," she said simply. "I will never abandon any of them." Her chin came up. "You said that my mother has spoken to you?"

"Yes. Though until the most recent instance, that conversation has been in dreams." I told her what the queen had said to me.

When I had finished, Princess Maralah's expression remained impassive, though I detected a flicker of pain, of grief, in her eyes.

She turned and walked slowly toward the doors. "Follow me."

The princess led me down several halls and staircases, all going deeper into the mountain. We were accompanied by the four guards—two men and two women who I assumed were her personal bodyguards.

Kansbar's account of Nidaar had been one of a thriving city and people.

That was not what I saw.

Granted, we did not go out into the city itself, but I would not have referred to any part of the royal palace as thriving, by any stretch of the imagination.

What I saw looked more like a people in the final stages of a siege.

The people I saw were either stoic and resolved to endure, or waiting for a death that would come only at their own hand.

I would not leave them here. I had no idea how I would do it, the same as I had no idea how to destroy or deactivate the Heart, but I would think of a way. Regardless of what happened to the Heart, I would not sail back to Regor and leave even one of the Cha'Nidaar behind who wanted to leave.

"How many remain, Your Highness?" I kept my voice low and my words for her ears only.

"Less than a hundred."

I said no more, but began devising a plan.

As we descended deeper into the mountain, the temperature remained constant, and our path was lit the entire way by Heartstone sconces.

Eventually we entered a circular room with a vaulted ceiling, supported by five columns of solid Heartstone that stretched from floor to ceiling, each blazing with golden light. On the far side of the room was a simple door, but what lay beyond it must have been treasured beyond measure. A dozen guards, armed and armored for battle, were spaced around the room against the walls, standing at attention.

Two guards posted on either side of the entry respectfully stood aside for their princess to pass, but blocked my access.

"He comes with me," she told them.

"But...Your Highness," said the guard stationed in front of the door itself, "Advisor Karnia ordered that—"

The princess gave him a hard stare. "We go to see my mother, the queen, who despite all, still rules here, does she not? She has spoken to this one, and has bid him come to her. Would you deny the will of your queen and sovereign over a mere advisor whose loyalty I have every reason to doubt? He stands on the verge of treason. Do you stand with him—or with your queen?"

The guard bowed his head. "I serve the queen, Your Highness."

"There are many who are confused now, Colonel Akhai." Maralah's voice lost its edge. "You have always served my mother with the utmost loyalty and reverence, and I believe in your heart you still do. My anger was not for you."

The colonel kept his head down for a moment longer, then slowly raised it to meet his princess's eyes. "Thank you, Your Highness. I did not mean to imply that your words would not reflect your royal mother, my queen's, wishes."

"It is my wish that we not be disturbed," Maralah said. "See to it that no one enters behind us."

The colonel snapped to attention, fist against his heart, and the guard instantly followed suit. "So you command, so it shall be done." He opened the door and stood aside while we entered.

Then he closed it behind us, sliding all of the locks back into place.

I looked ahead and saw what was there.

We were in a tomb.

26

Baeseria, queen of the Cha'Nidaar, royal defender of the Heart of Nidaar, was dead.

She lay on a simple, raised bier that was entirely encased in a tomb of what appeared to be translucent Heartstone, its flames flickering steadily around the base of the bier.

The floor, walls, and ceiling were Heartstone crystals.

We were in another geode.

I didn't want to ask, but I had to. "Is she—"

Maralah slowly shook her head. "She sleeps, but it is the sleep of the dead, a sleep from which she will never awaken."

"What happened?" I asked quietly.

"She sacrificed herself to save our people and protect the Heart."

"What you said back there, Your Highness. Your mother did not bid me come to her."

"A small matter to ease the colonel's conscience. My mother has spoken to you. She would want you to be brought to her."

"Not even a hundred of your people remain," I said, "yet a dozen armed men guard your mother. Has there been any attempt...to gain entry?" I nearly said "on her life," and was glad I'd caught myself in time.

"There have been Khrynsani and Sythsaurian sightings in the outer caves, and then our patrols found you and your companions. I ordered the extra guard on my mother's resting place." Maralah's eyes went distant, her lips tightening into a frown. "The precaution is necessary considering my mother's connection to the Heart—her bond, if you will. Even before she placed herself in this state, my mother did not need to lay hands on the Heart to activate and use it. She could speak to it and it would respond to her regardless of distance."

My gut tightened at what that implied. There were getting to be entirely too many similarities between the Saghred and the Heart.

"A wise precaution," I said carefully.

I slowly walked forward until I was gazing down at the Nidaarian queen. She was just as I remembered from my dreams. Ageless, with luminous golden skin, long hair the color and texture of the whitest silk draped over robes of the same color embroidered with a leaf and vine pattern—nearly identical to the robes her daughter wore. They looked more like sisters than mother and daughter.

"How long has she been like this?" I whispered.

"Since a few days after sending your ancestor away. She spent hours in the chamber with the Heart, calming and communing with it. It was after that she made her decision. We spent little time attempting to dissuade her." The princess's lips curled in a sad smile. "We knew it was the right thing to do, the only thing that would truly ensure that what had happened would not happen again."

"When our ships were offshore, the Heart—"

"Had already begun to stir. We know not why. Nothing had changed that we were aware of. We are sincerely sorry for the lives that were lost, but know that it was not of our doing, or of my mother's doing."

"Our gem mage believes the Heart did not act alone, that someone was behind the attack, and I agree."

"That would be impossible," Maralah said flatly. "Only a few of my people remain who are capable of targeting the Heart."

"Who?"

"Advisor Karnia and two of our engineers."

"Where were they when the attack occurred?"

"I was in a meeting with the engineers. Advisor Karnia was in his office."

"Were there witnesses to Karnia's whereabouts?"

"No, there were not. However, there is only one way into the Heart's chamber, and that is through this room."

I scrutinized the walls surrounding us. If there was another way in, I couldn't detect it. "I'll take your word for it."

Maralah's lips curled in a half smile. "I trust you with much, Tamnais Nathrach. I trust next to no one with the safety of my mother and the Heart of Nidaar."

"Understood. No offense taken."

"There's only one way into this room as well, and that is past Colonel Akhai and his guards. He assured me that no one attempted to enter, that day or any other."

"There must be another way in."

"In the past, there were other ways. But in the interests of security, they have all been barricaded from the inside."

"Who was in charge of barricading them?"

"Our chief engineer." She paused. "Who, sadly, has since taken his own life."

"Who did he report to?"

"Advisor Karnia."

"Are you sure it was suicide? Begging your forgiveness, Your Highness, but this advisor of yours does not appear to be acting in the best interests of your people. He is—"

Maralah waved a small hand dismissively. "I have long known of Advisor Karnia's intentions. He has even gone so far as to approach me with a petition of marriage."

"That sounds familiar," I said, thinking of Sarad's pursuit of Agata. "This Karnia sounds like your people's version of Sarad Nukpana, whom you may recall from my memories."

"Ah yes, Lady Ghalfari's son."

"The very one. Before he tried to steal the goblin throne, he attempted to talk our team's gem mage into marrying him to help him find the Heart."

"I take it your gem mage turned him down."

"Many times."

"A wise woman. Has he given up?"

"Probably not. We thought he was dead, but he's merely stuck in the Lower Hells at the moment, so that's an extra obstacle in his way."

"Once Karnia realized that I would never accept him, he began attempts to subvert those close to me."

"Forgive my bluntness, Your Highness," I began, "but why haven't you…"

"Banished, imprisoned, or even killed him, Chancellor Nathrach? All tempting solutions, but none are an option."

"May I ask why?"

"Karnia is the last of his line, as well. He is the only survivor of the guards stationed in the Heart's chamber during the events of nine hundred years ago."

"Kansbar's account said there were no survivors."

"Karnia was not in the chamber that morning."

"That's highly suspicious."

"Yes, it was. The guards were masters of gem and earth magic. Their presence helped keep the Heart from fully awakening and destroying us all."

"Based on our recent experience, the Heart is only napping."

"Which concerns us greatly. No one has been in the chamber since my mother placed herself here as an eternal guardian to keep anyone from activating and taking control of it. As long as she lives and remains so encased and bonded to the Heart, Karnia is denied access to it."

"Then why does he need to marry you?"

"One, to legitimize himself in the eyes of our people, but mainly to stand where you are standing. No one is allowed in here with my mother except myself and Colonel Akhai."

"As long as the Heart exists, the queen remains in a state between life and death—and you and your people live forever."

"Not forever. However, as long as we are in close proximity to the Heart of Nidaar, yes, we continue to live."

"And if something were to happen to the Heart…if it were to be taken or destroyed?"

"We know not, Chancellor Nathrach. Before she bonded herself to the Heart, my mother and our engineers attempted to destroy it. All they succeeded in doing was releasing more creatures from the caves beneath the Heart's chamber. As to the possibility of it being taken, it is an enormous stone that would easily fill the throne room and beyond. It is embedded in the mountain itself, so I do not see how that can be done. But if it were, perhaps we would age instantly and die, since it was the Heart that has sustained us all this time. Or perhaps we would become mortal, and age as it is normal for goblins to do. If my mother had known how long we would continue to exist in this way…and make no mistake, what we do is not living…if she had known we would continue in this way, I believe she would not have done what she did."

"Have you tried to awaken her?" I asked.

"The case containing her body is sealed, and her connection to the Heart is complete and absolute. I have spent many hours sitting here with my mother in an attempt to reach her. It has been in vain. She has spoken to no one until she reached out to you. We assumed she had passed beyond the point of being able to communicate, that perhaps she had drifted into that land beyond life. I am grateful and glad that we were wrong, and that she has spoken to you, but we all wonder why now and why you?"

"I imagine the guards who brought us into the city wondered much the same thing," I said. "I asked to be taken to Queen Baeseria, and I got quite the reaction."

"No doubt."

"Perhaps your mother reached out to me because I am an outsider, and a descendant of Kansbar. Perhaps sensing my arrival here—with the ring and necklace she gave him—sparked a renewed awareness in her. I'm sure she didn't mean to hurt you by remaining silent. Maybe it was not her choice."

Maralah nodded once. "It could be as you say. Regardless of why it has happened, I am grateful that you have come and that you have arrived safely. I know my mother desires to end this for herself, for me, and for our people. Our people feel as if they are prisoners in their own city. The Heart and our sense of duty to it hold us captive from within, and the creatures freed from the depths by the continuing quakes are like our guards." She swallowed. "We exist, balanced on a blade's edge, between life and death, salvation and damnation, unable to alter our lot to attain one over the other. In finding the Heart, all we discovered was a quicker path to our own destruction." She took a trembling breath. "Chancellor Nathrach, we are cursed beyond our ability to bear."

I took both of Maralah's hands in mine. "I swear on my honor, my family, and my people, that I will do all that I am able to accomplish that her will is done and your people are freed."

27

I was reunited with my team in the guest wing of the palace, not a dungeon cell.

Bedrooms radiated off of a central sitting room filled with plush couches and chairs that begged to be fallen onto. However, like the rest of the palace, everything had the appearance of disuse, and this room looked as though it had been cleaned only very recently. The air was still heavy with the mustiness that came from being closed off. I imagined the Cha'Nidaar didn't have many guests.

Dasant had already answered the siren call of one of the couches and was face down on it, snoring.

The others were sitting around a table, plates filled with…

"Am I delirious…or do I smell beef?" My mouth suddenly watered so much I had to swallow once to finish my question. "And it's not drugged, right?"

"Please, Tamnais," Malik said, "do give me more credit than that." He grinned. "I used Dasant as a taster."

"What?"

"Just kidding. He was the first one out here, had filled a plate to absurd levels, and had a fork halfway to his mouth when I stopped him. I checked everything. No drugs, no poison, nothing but the most sublime meal I have had since setting sail on our little excursion."

"As the captain of said excursion fleet's flagship," Phaelan said, slurring and fumbling over the alliteration, "I take offense at that." The elf had his recently healed foot up on a cushion, and it was obvious he'd had more than one glass of wine.

Malik snorted. "My dear captain, all you're offended by is that the wine has nearly run out, mostly by your own imbibing. I like seafood as much as the next man, but sometimes nothing except a fine steak will suffice."

"That can't be beef," I said. "Where would they have—"

"Better than beef," Malik replied with relish. "Roast beast. We are eating that which tried to eat us. The irony isn't all that's delicious."

"Dakkonan," I corrected him.

"Pardon?"

"The beast in question is called a dakkonan. It's another thing to thank the Khrynsani for. They lived in the levels under the city, but when the Khrynsani destroyed the east coast, they also cracked open this subterranean world where the dakkonan, and so I am told, even worse creatures now roam free. The Cha'Nidaar use them as perimeter guards."

"Worse, as in larger?"

"The princess didn't go into specifics."

Elsu smiled. "So you've been with this Princess Maralah all this time?"

"And an extremely unpleasant few minutes with Sandrina Ghalfari." I went to the sideboard to pour a glass of wine, suddenly needing one very badly. "And I have seen Queen Baeseria."

That quieted the table, but Dasant snored on.

"I think we'd like you to elaborate," Jash said quietly.

"Have you checked the room for listening courtiers or devices?" I asked.

Malik, Jash, and Elsu gave me identical looks.

"Of course you did," I told him, "but I had to ask. It's my job."

"And rest assured we have done ours," Malik said.

I told them everything that passed between me and the Cha'Nidaar princess—and of making the acquaintance of the unpleasant Advisor Karnia. I finished with the condition of Queen Baeseria.

Talon had been feeding Indigo bits of dakkonan. "The queen has been asleep all this time?" he asked in disbelief.

"Yes."

"Just to keep the Heart from going on another rampage?"

"The princess didn't phrase it quite like that, but yes."

Jash looked horrified. "And no one here ages because of the Heart."

Phaelan pushed his wine away. "And no babies because nothing below the belt works anymore. Just because I didn't glow in that crystal cave thing back there doesn't mean the Heart isn't shriveling me as we speak. Tam, we need to get this job done and get out of here."

"I fully intend to."

Malik crossed his arms and sat back in his chair, his sharp eyes searching my face. "And you, my noble friend, fully intend to take as many of the Cha'Nidaar back with us as possible."

"If they no longer need to protect the Heart, there's no reason for them to stay here," I told him. "They would be free to go further inland, though having been trapped in these caves for centuries, they don't know what would await them there. Or they could return with us. We could resettle them wherever they desire. I don't intend to force my will on any of them, but I am determined to give them a choice beyond endurance or suicide. They were once our own people, and now there are fewer than a hundred. If they had remained in Rheskilia, the Khrynsani would have killed them. In that, they are very much like ourselves."

Malik held up a mollifying hand. "I never said I disagree with your intent or sentiment, but this is a substantial departure from our 'blow it up and get out' plan."

Agata had been silent until now. "Tam, you said Baeseria is 'bonded' to the Heart."

"Correct."

"The bonding, the extended lifespan, the unsuccessful attempt to destroy it—"

"I know. It sounds way too much like the Saghred for my comfort."

"Not only that, but if the Heart did act on its own as Maralah believes, then it is likely sentient as well. Even if there was a way to destroy it, that option has been taken off the table."

"Agreed." I sat in the closest chair. "I've been thinking."

Elsu winced. "Good rarely comes from that. It usually involves us running for our lives."

I leaned forward, elbows on my knees. "If we can't destroy the Heart and we can't take it with us, the only choice I see us having is to bury the thing."

"Bury?" Talon asked. "If it's that big, how—"

"The city is between the summit of the mountain and the Heart chamber below."

Phaelan slowly sat up straighter, getting where I was going, and no longer worrying about his fully functioning body parts. The pirate captain knew he was about to earn his keep.

"Are you talking about bringing a mountain down on top of the Heart?" he asked, eyes sparkling.

"Yes, I am."

Phaelan positively beamed.

"Oh, Bane is going to hate that he missed this," Jash muttered.

Phaelan was instantly on his feet, pacing and thinking. "I'll tell him every detail when we get back. This almost makes the risk of shriveled parts worth it."

"I'm not sure it can be done—" I began.

"Oh, it can be done," the elf pirate assured me. "I'll need a detailed map of the city to locate the load-bearing places and any vulnerable spots."

"Uh, Tam, have you told Princess Maralah you plan to destroy her city?" Elsu asked.

"Not yet, but she knows I intend to do everything I can to free her people and disable the Heart, and I can't think of another way to do both. We can't leave the Heart unguarded, and if we can't destroy it, we need to ensure no one can get to it." I turned to Agata. "I'll need your help with the Heart—and Queen Baeseria."

"I was wondering when you'd get to the part where we didn't leave her behind," she said.

"Now's the time, and you're the lady who can do it," I told her. "The Cha'Nidaar couldn't sever the bond between their queen and the Heart. I'm hoping that with your connection to the Heart you can do it."

Agata smiled very slightly. "Hmm, the need to sever an unbreakable magical bond," she mused. "Where have I encountered that before?"

I eyed her, which only made her smile wider.

"There's also the problem of the Heart striking out," I continued. "Either at us or Phaelan and the city engineers— or both. You talked the Heart into not killing us at sea; I'm counting on you being able to do that again. The rock might be protective or even possessive of Baeseria since she's been bonded to it for so long. The rock doesn't know us; it knows you."

"Not very well," Agata said, "but I'll do everything I can to convince it that we mean Baeseria no harm."

Jash snorted. "We don't mean the *queen* any harm, but we're talking about burying the Heart, taking away its best friend, *and* all its worshipers. That's bound to piss it off."

"That's where Agata's convincing comes in," I told him.

"Sounds more like strong-arm and body-slam," Agata said. "Talon, I might need an extra strong arm."

My son's eyes brightened. "At your service, my lady."

"I haven't met Maralah yet," Elsu said, "but she sounds

practical-minded. I think she'll go along with your plan." She flashed a quick grin. "I especially like that she didn't buy Sandrina's twisted tales, and knew what she was with one glance. A smart young lady."

"Actually she's not so young," I said. "She was there when her mother gave Kansbar the ring and pendant." I fumbled around in a pocket for the necklace, and returned it to Agata. "You'll be needing this. Her Highness will take us to the Heart in the morning, which is apparently five hours from now."

Agata blinked in amazement. "Just like that?"

"Just like that."

Malik saluted me with his wineglass. "Never underestimate Tamnais's ability to coax a beautiful woman into doing nearly anything. She is beautiful, isn't she? And charming and brilliant and brave?"

I chose not to answer.

A very slow smile crept over Malik's lips. "I'll take that as a yes to all of the above."

Phaelan had his pack on a nearby table, inventorying the contents with far too much zeal. "I'll need to go with you."

Oh joy.

He noticed my lack of enthusiasm. "Hey, the Heart's a target just as much as the city is. The job is to bury the thing. I have to know how big it is. I'll also need to know the rock composition of the mountain on top of the city. The harder the rock, the more boom needed in the city to bring it down."

"I'm sure Maralah's engineers can provide you with all the information you need."

"Speaking of coaxing," Malik continued, "your nose may not have noticed because of the scent of delectable roast beast—I'm sorry, 'roast dakkonan' simply doesn't have the same flair—but we have all bathed. Unfortunately, our armor is still filthy, but at least we're clean beneath it all. May I suggest you take the opportunity to do the same."

I felt a smile tug at one side of my mouth. "Are you saying I stink?"

"I'm sure you do, Tamnais, but this past month, my nose has been traumatized beyond its ability to function. I can only hope that once we return home it will recover."

Phaelan glanced uneasily at the front of his trousers. "*Fully* recover."

"The water is hot and comes out of metal pipes running through the walls," Jash said, delighted.

"No buckets?" I asked. "No fire?"

"No and no," Jash replied.

"That's an offer I can't and won't refuse."

Malik took my now empty plate. "May I make another suggestion?"

"Would my saying no stop you?"

"Has it ever? We have five hours until the princess calls for us. We will keep watch while you get some sleep. And since you have your ring back, hopefully you can have a lovely chat with her mother about blowing up her city."

28

My clothes and armor were piled on the floor by the tub.

I told myself that I'd clean my armor as well as I could once I got out of the bath. The problem was, I didn't foresee me getting out of this tub. Ever.

The last proper bath I'd had was the night before we'd set sail. That had been over a month ago. While I could do what I had to for as long as I had to, there were limits. Until now, I hadn't had a choice. Now I had, and like my team, I'd taken full advantage.

A hot meal and a hot bath.

There was a bed a few steps away, but I didn't think I could make it that far.

Hopefully, if I fell asleep in the tub, I'd wake up before I drowned. Though if trouble did come to our suite, I'd be naked and in a bathtub. I'd fought naked before and had absolutely zero modesty, but I'd rather be armed and armored, and if I slept that way while sprawled across a bed, I'd at least stand a chance at survival.

"I hate being disciplined," I muttered.

In the end, I had to force myself to get out of the tub. Once I'd partially dressed, I washed the dust off my armor and flight jacket as best as I could. I armored up and cleaned my weapons before allowing myself the luxury of a bed. I knew I'd be needing them again before this was all over.

I lay back across the bed, and couldn't stop a groan from escaping as I sank into the soft mattress. The blankets were far too fine for a goblin in still-dirty armor, but I stretched out on top, facing the door, blades within easy reach, and within moments was asleep.

Almost instantly, Queen Baeseria of the Cha'Nidaar was in my bedroom, sitting in a chair next to the tub.

I was too exhausted to be surprised, and apparently that exhaustion extended to being unable to get off of the bed to greet the queen properly.

"You came twice to my throne room," she said. "It is only right that I repay the courtesy."

I managed to pull myself up to sit back on the pillows. Barely. "I wouldn't exactly call this proper, Your Majesty, but it is your palace, so it is your choice." I paused awkwardly. "Your daughter took me to see you."

"I know. You must forgive me for not having risen to greet you." She gave me a bleak smile. "Physical movement is beyond me now."

"I'm feeling much the same way at the moment. I am dreaming again, correct?"

"That is correct."

I huffed a laugh. "You know you're tired when you can't even stand up in your own dream."

I wasn't sure how to begin. How do you tell a queen who is so devoted to her people that she would put herself into a centuries-long sleep to protect them that her beloved subjects were killing themselves rather than continue to live with no hope of their situation changing? They had no escape from the city they built with their own hands, a city that had become their prison. They could never grow old, never hear the laughter of their children. They were trapped in an endless cycle where the only escape was death at their own hands.

"Several things weigh heavily on your heart, Tamnais. One of them is your son."

"How do—"

"I have touched you, seen into your thoughts, your memories. Even though it was in a dream, that doesn't make it any less real. I know of your fears for your son. I know what it is to have concern for a child. To protect the Heart, I had to leave Maralah, trust her to care for and guide our people. Children resent being defined by their parents. Yet they fear who they may become as individuals. Sometimes it is easier to blame the parent for their own shortcomings, whether real, imagined—or deeply feared."

"Talon's fears may be all too real," I told her. "That's my fear."

"He is a powerful mage."

"Yes."

"He fears that power."

"We both do."

"You fear what he will do with it."

It wasn't a question.

It was a statement of fact.

"Am I that obvious?"

"Any parent who loves their child does not bother to hide their concern. It is born out of our desire to protect our young." She paused. "Especially if that fear is from themselves. His fear is even stronger."

"I know."

"And as is the way of the young, they will deny that they fear anything. To admit fear is to relinquish control. Talon desperately wants to be in control of his power, but with much of his power still unrevealed, his fears are renewed and intensified every day. It is unrelenting. He does not know if he will help—or harm."

"My former teacher and I are instructing him. We're there to help. I brought them both to Aquas so we could continue to teach, even though I know the danger."

"That is his second fear. That one day he will be alone again, with only himself to rely on. But at the same time, he is torn. It is the way of young men, that they step away from their elders, to prove themselves, to gain the respect and admiration of their family, their people. Normally, a young man has had the support and care of his clan from the time he was born. Then it is a natural progression for him to want to cut those ties, to become independent, to grow into his own man."

"Talon never had that," I murmured.

"No, he did not. And it is for that reason that he is now torn. He has both the desire to step away and be a man, and the need to remain close to learn to manage his growing power, to become the kind of mage he desperately wants to be." She paused. "To become a man and a mage that his father—whom he loves and admires above all others—will be proud of. That is his greatest desire—to be worthy of your respect and admiration, to make you proud of him."

"I am."

Baeseria shook her head. "He strives to earn your regard and admiration as a man, one mage of great power to another."

"But he's—"

"Not a child any longer. He knows this, and he needs you to acknowledge this, while still reassuring him that he will continue to have your support and teaching as he travels this difficult path to power, so that one day, he could become your equal. That is his greatest desire."

Again there was silence between us, but it was the comfortable quiet that came from being with a friend.

"How much do you hear in your sleep, Your Majesty? How aware are you of what is happening in your palace, your city?"

"I feel the hum of activity around me much as a bee in a hive."

"A queen bee who is cared for by her subjects—"

"A queen who is unable to leave the hive. The comparison is even more accurate than I imagined."

"Your daughter misses you."

"She is a strong leader."

"Stronger than you know." I hesitated, unsure of how broach the subject. "Why haven't you spoken to her?"

Baeseria stared at me for a long moment, her eyes bright and hard. "Don't you think I have tried?"

I briefly bowed my head. "Of course, you did. Forgive me for implying otherwise, Your Majesty."

"I do not know why I have been unable to speak with Maralah as I do with you. I have no way of knowing if the Heart is responsible, or if it is a natural consequence of my state." The queen actually huffed a laugh. "Natural. Nothing about my state is natural." She stared blankly at the far wall. "I cannot sense the passing of time, which is a blessing. Otherwise I surely would have gone mad. Years feel as minutes. Centuries as hours. Perhaps that perception of time was the Heart's gift to me."

I had no words.

Baeseria's eyes flicked back to mine. "Tell me the truth of how my daughter and our people fare."

I didn't mince words, telling her what I had seen and what Maralah and her people had endured since she had bonded herself to the Heart to protect them, but instead had consigned them to a life that had become a lingering death.

When Baeseria spoke, her voice was quiet and unflinching. "I had to bond myself to the Heart to prevent its use by anyone. I knew it would only be a matter of time until the Sythsaurians returned or the Khrynsani were successful in finding Nidaar and again infiltrating the Heart's chamber. The Heart is connected to the very roots of the world. Its influence runs deep. It is like a tumor in a body that I have kept from awakening and destroying that body. The body is our world, Tamnais. What would you have had me do?"

"You did the right thing, Your Majesty. Never doubt that. And no one could ever doubt the love you have for your people, the enormity of what you sacrificed to protect them—to protect all of us. Your daughter said you tried to destroy the Heart after you sent Kansbar away."

"Yes. All our efforts accomplished was to open more paths to the underworld and allow more creatures out of nightmare to infest our city."

"We believe we have a solution," I said quietly. "A way to seal the underworld and the Heart, to entomb them all. But first, I want to free you from your sleep and take you with us."

"Take?"

I told her the plan: taking her and her people to the surface, explosives in the city bringing the mountain down on top of the Heart, sealing it away forever, or at least for a very long time.

"My bond to the Heart is complete, Tamnais. It cannot be broken."

I got off the bed, went and knelt at her feet. "I believe our gem mage can help. It was she who calmed the Heart when it attacked our fleet with giant waves. I believe she can find a way to safely separate you and the Heart."

Baeseria shook her head sadly. "Our engineers told me that even when the Khrynsani turned half of our continent into a wasteland, only a fraction of the Heart's power had been released. Their calculations indicated that if the full power of the Heart was ever unleashed, it could easily split our world, causing massive earthquakes that would crack it like an egg. I was left with no choice but to preserve the lives of not only my people, but all people, as best as I could. Take my daughter and my people, Tamnais, and leave this place. Leave me. To attempt to free me from my bond could do more damage than the Khrynsani ever dreamed."

"Your daughter and your people would never leave you, Baeseria, and neither will I, and neither will my companions. The Khrynsani temple lies in ruins, the few that are left are being hunted down. The new goblin king and queen are good and compassionate people, I am their chancellor, and until they have a child of their own, I am their heir. It is the beginning of a new age. Please let me take you home. Let me try."

"My people have guarded the Heart for over a thousand years," Baeseria said. "Finding it and keeping it safe was our uniting purpose in coming to Aquas. It is not a responsibility that can be easily relinquished."

"The Heart will only be buried, not destroyed," I told her. "There will be a need to watch over this mountain, or what will remain of it. I cannot think of more faithful guards than your people—those that wish to remain. Garrisons can be built that are close enough to guard, but far enough away so that those posted there won't be affected by the Heart. They can still guard, but they can also have a life beyond these caves."

Baeseria's eyes glistened with unshed tears.

"Yes, Tamnais. It is time. Take my people home, those who wish to go. And if you can do so without endangering them, you may carry me home, as well."

29

If you can't destroy the Heart, destroy the mountain around it.

Sounded simple enough.

However, it had been my experience that when a plan sounded simple, there were endless ways it could go wrong.

Fatally wrong.

I didn't see this plan being an exception, since Phaelan Benares would be the one doing the destroying, but Bane trusted him, so I needed to.

My job was to tell the princess of the Cha'Nidaar, a people who had faithfully guarded said Heart for well over a thousand years, that we needed to blow up her city.

When I left my bedroom for the central sitting room, the Cha'Nidaar had once again brought food. Dasant had still been asleep, but the instant the covers were removed from the dishes, he stirred and sat up, eyes still closed.

"It's alive," Elsu noted dryly.

"That's debatable," Malik said, a serving fork poised over a platter of roast beast, perusing the selection—and scanning for unwelcome additives.

"Where are Talon and Indy?" I asked.

"Napping," Elsu replied.

"Princess Maralah wishes to see you and meet your companions when you have finished dining," one of the servers told me. "Will half an hour be sufficient?"

"That will be plenty of time," I told him. "Thank you again for your gracious hospitality."

"Stop it," Malik snapped as soon as the door closed.

I turned to see Dasant with a fork full of eggs half way to his mouth. Eggs that, like the meat, were probably also courtesy of the dakkonan.

The big goblin lowered his fork with a grumble. "Be quick about it. My stomach doesn't have all day."

"Excuse me for trying to ensure that after that bite you'll still have a stomach."

"But they like us."

"The princess likes us," Malik corrected him. "That sentiment does not extend to all of the Cha'Nidaar. While you were asleep, other players have come onto the stage."

"Again?"

"Again, and always. We're goblins. There will always be people who want us dead, and those people will usually be other goblins. This instance is no different."

Malik completed his scan of the food and determined it once again to be drug- and poison-free.

I brought Dasant up to speed on our situation.

"Did you have a chat with Her Majesty?" Malik asked when I'd finished.

"I did. She is agreeable to our plan to bury the Heart, and to take her people, her daughter—and herself—out of here. Which brings up another problem to add to our growing list. Elsu, I didn't see any way into the queen's…"

"Coffin?" she said helpfully. "Hey, I'm just calling it what it is."

"She's not dead."

"It doesn't make a box she sealed herself into any less of a coffin."

"When I saw it, I didn't see any kind of lid or a way to shift it off its base, so we may need your unique skills to cut a way in."

Elsu flashed a grin and inclined her head. "At your command."

"Maralah has offered to take me to see the Heart. I don't believe she will have a problem with Agata coming along, but I don't want to go trooping in there with all of us. The Cha'Nidaar won't like it; the Heart is sacred to them. Most importantly, the Heart might not like it. We don't want to do anything to possibly set it off."

"You talk about it as if it's alive," Dasant said.

"If you'd ever met the Saghred, you'd know it was alive and had all the bad qualities that go with it. It was manipulative, seductive, desperate, vindictive, and more."

Agata nodded. "Not all stones that are capable of using or bestowing power can reach out beyond their confines to influence individuals or events. In fact, few can. Unfortunately, those that do possess extreme power and will use it by any and all means possible to preserve themselves."

"Survival at all costs," Malik noted. "I can understand that."

"Since the Heart doesn't need souls to survive," I said, "I had assumed that it wouldn't attempt to influence those who got close to it. That may be a dangerous assumption. So we'll be taking only those who need to see it. Phaelan, you're one of them."

Phaelan froze. "What?"

Malik grinned. "My, your bomb-building enthusiasm vanished quickly. It's just a rock, my dear captain. To it, you're a gnat. It won't notice you."

"My job is to blow up the mountain and city above the Heart. There's no reason for me to pay the thing a visit."

Malik rolled his eyes. "I repeat, the rock won't notice you."

"What if it does? The Saghred noticed Raine."

"Your legendary cousin is not a null. You are. I doubt if the Heart could care less. Am I right, Magus Azul?"

"Probably."

"See? *Probably* is a long way from *definitely*." Phaelan pushed his plate away, his appetite apparently having vanished along with his enthusiasm.

"Phaelan, you'll be fine," I told him. "You need to see the ceiling above the Heart. Your job is to bury it. You need to see the room it's in to ensure that it'll be done."

Phaelan did a full-body shudder. "I'll go, but I won't like it."

Malik hid a smile behind his glass. "No one expects you to."

"We don't know for certain that the Heart possesses the awareness necessary to act intentionally," Agata said. "Many of the lesser stones of power can cause sickness, delirium, even death by mere proximity. I didn't sense any such danger from my contacts with the Heart. However, I have never encountered anything like it. I don't believe anyone has."

"Except the Khrynsani who have been here before," Jash said. "I still believe they or the Sythsaurians know things about the Heart that we don't."

"Yes," I agreed. "However, people tried to destroy the Saghred for hundreds of years. Raine figured out how to do it, and she did it."

Phaelan chuckled, apparently having regained his confidence. "Anything can be destroyed—or buried. You just need to know where to stick the explosives. After all, Raine is my cousin. My family excels at making things go boom."

"Which brings up a problem," Jash said. "Bane could set charges and trigger detonations remotely—with magic. Phaelan's a null."

"That's not a problem," I told him. "Phaelan can set the charges, and you can trigger the detonations through him."

At that, Phaelan and Jash froze, then slowly turned toward each other.

"You don't mean…" Jash started.

"I most certainly do. Extreme situations call for extreme measures."

"I don't know what either one of you is talking about," Phaelan said, "but I know I don't like it."

"You won't feel a thing," Malik assured him. "It's Jash who has to rummage around inside of your head. All you have to do is visualize the charges; Jash will take it from there."

"We'll do a test first," I said, "but I'm confident it'll work. Elsu will be Jash's backup, but he's the most qualified."

Phaelan looked horrified. "To do what?"

"Create a brief link between your minds."

If anything, Phaelan's horror increased. "A *what* with my *where*? Oh, hell no."

Malik just looked at him. "Then it appears we came here for nothing."

Phaelan blanched further. "You're serious!"

I sat in the chair next to him. "Phaelan, listen to me. It's very simple. Bane would visualize the charges and could remotely detonate them with his mind, magic if you will. Jash or Elsu can do that, but it will have to be through you."

"Why can't he go with me, watch me make the bombs and set the charges, and then do the same thing without involving me?"

"To do that, Jash would have to assemble the bombs himself." I paused, letting the implications sink in. "I don't think anyone wants that."

Malik laughed. "To quote the captain: 'Oh, hell no.'"

"Physical contact with the materials is necessary," Elsu told Phaelan.

The elf sat on the edge of his chair, talking fast. "Okay, okay. What if I make the bombs, then Jash can hold them after I make them? Ergo, physical contact."

"It's the making of the bombs that forges the link," I said. "The thinking plus the handling. The knowledge of how this, this, and that come together to go boom, if you will."

Phaelan's head sagged, hopefully in defeat, because we really didn't have time for this.

"Crap," he muttered.

Victory.

Reluctantly given, but I'd take it.

30

Now came the hard part, or at least the diplomatically delicate one.

"It might be best if I tell Maralah our plan without all of you here," I said. "It might be a bit much."

"Just so you understand that not being in the room doesn't mean we won't be listening," Malik said.

"You're goblins—and a pirate. I'd expect nothing less. In fact, I would be disappointed if you didn't hear every word we said."

"Just call when you're ready," Agata said.

"How about if I call loudly, or better yet, knock? Let's at least give the illusion that you're not all eavesdropping."

When Maralah arrived, I was the only one in the room.

I told her that while I had slept, her mother had visited me.

"I had planned to tell you what she said, but I think it would be better if you heard it for yourself. Again, I welcome you using your gift."

"Thank you. Again, your trust honors me."

"It is you and your mother who have honored me. Would you prefer to stand or sit?"

"Sitting would be nice," Maralah said. "Since your arrival, I have done far too little of it."

We sat on a small sofa, and I closed my eyes and bowed my head.

The princess placed her cool hands on my temples.

And for the first time in almost a millennium, Maralah of the Cha'Nidaar heard her mother speak at length, about the plan to free her people—and of the concerns and fears of a parent for a child. I knew that Baeseria hadn't only been speaking of Talon.

When Maralah released me, I opened my eyes and raised my head. The Cha'Nidaar princess was smiling, complete with dimples, her eyes sparkling with unshed tears.

"You have given me a gift beyond price," she said.

"I'm glad I was able to share it." I paused. "How do you feel about our plan?" I asked quietly.

I didn't say anything about her mother having approved it. Maralah had just heard that for herself. But it was she who had been leading her people all this time. She was in charge. This was her call.

"I will put the plan before my people, and strongly encourage them to accept it."

I blinked. "Strongly encourage?"

"Chancellor Nathrach, this is a decision my people must

make for themselves. We have defended the Heart from outside invaders before. Yes, I could command them to obey, but Nidaar is more than their home; protecting the Heart is their sworn duty. It is the reason our people left Rheskilia so many centuries ago—to keep anyone from accessing power of this magnitude."

"And burying the Heart would do this," I assured her. "Didn't you say that a colony left the city for three years?"

"Yes."

"And they suffered no ill effects from being away from the Heart?"

"We could leave, but where would we go?"

"You can come home with us."

"This is the only home most of my people have ever known."

"And now you have the means to leave. We will take you. Do your people have a way out, other than the way we came in? A way that doesn't involve running through a gauntlet of dakkonan?"

"We have an evacuation route out of the city and away from this mountain, should the Heart ever fully awaken. I have seen to it that we have yearly drills. Every citizen even keeps a bag packed with necessities should we need to evacuate quickly. They are divided into groups with their neighbors and each chooses a leader." She smiled with pride. "It is a good system."

"It certainly sounds like it. I'm impressed."

"As to the route, there's a tunnel that runs from our mountain north to the next mountain in the range. From there are multiple ways to the surface. The western side of that mountain offers shelter." Maralah paused. "I believe when my people know the facts, they will agree with me that it is time to leave, but I want to give them that opportunity."

"How long will it take to evacuate the city?" I asked.

"While they could leave from where they were, I would prefer that they be able to return home and retrieve their supply bags. In our drills, they have done this and been ready to leave in forty minutes. From the evacuation gathering point to the surface takes two hours at a brisk pace." Maralah paused, concern creasing her brow. "Are you certain we will be welcome in Regor?"

"As I told your mother, Chigaru and Mirabai, our new young king and queen, would welcome you."

"You say that with confidence."

"I can do so because the night the Saghred was destroyed and Sarad Nukpana was carried to the Lower Hells, our young monarchs, with my assistance and that of Imala Kalis—the director of goblin intelligence, who will welcome you like a sister—cleaned house."

"Cleaned house?"

"We rid the court of all Khrynsani sympathizers. Those who remain want to put everything the Khrynsani believed in and stood for behind them. You would not have to remain in the capital. We could resettle you anywhere in Rheskilia that you would like." I grinned. "We even have an alliance with the elves."

"I had heard there was an elf among your companions. I thought my men must have been mistaken."

"No mistake. Our fleet is half elf and half goblin. In fact, the elf he saw is the captain of the fleet's flagship."

"I've never even seen an elf, let alone met one."

"I'll introduce you in a few minutes. Phaelan's our team's demolitions expert."

"And the captain of a great ship?"

"Who loves nothing more than blowing things up."

"Things have changed. I think I would like to see this new world; and if my people see this as a means to free them from their obligation, I believe they would be eager to leave. My people are explorers at heart. The desire for discovery is what brought them here from Rheskilia. Now, after over a thousand years, going home could be their new adventure. I think it will be helpful to hear from you how Regor has changed, and to assure my people that they would truly have a home to return to."

"I would be honored to address your people on behalf of our new king and queen." I stood. "If you are ready, I would like to introduce you to my companions."

Talon and Indigo were barely awake when I asked my team to join us.

That changed for Talon the instant he laid eyes on Princess Maralah.

His greeting was coherent enough, though that was probably due to still being half asleep, but after that, all Talon could do was stare.

I didn't know if it was Maralah's exotic appearance, her beauty, or both, but Talon appeared to be smitten. I think Agata had just been supplanted.

Fickleness, thy name is youth.

Malik and Jash didn't do so much as an eye roll, but I

knew they would have plenty to say as soon as Maralah left. Some observations were too good to resist.

Maralah's eyes kept darting to Phaelan. I couldn't tell if the interest was because she'd never seen an elf before, or was it something more?

We had an ancient civilization—small though it was—to convince to leave their city, then hopefully an evacuation to oversee and a city to destroy. Getting us and the Cha'Nidaar clear of the mountain was our only goal. Any personal interactions could and would wait.

"Your Highness, have any other Khrynsani or Sythsaurians been captured?" Malik asked her.

"Just you and your companions—and Lady Ghalfari and her three Khrynsani, who remain in our dungeons."

My team and I exchanged concerned glances.

"That's highly suspicious," Elsu said. "Are the caves and tunnels outside the city patrolled?"

"They are," Maralah replied.

"And they have seen nothing."

"No."

"Tam, we could hope," Elsu said, "but I don't think the dakkonan have been that thorough."

I nodded. "Agreed. But there are only eight of us, and we each have jobs to do. There's no time to go looking for trouble. If it's there, it'll find us. All we can do is get this done as fast as we can and keep our eyes and ears open. Your Highness, how long will it take for your people to gather in the throne room?"

"I can have all of them there within the hour."

"Good. I take it that will be minus your mother's guards?"

"Yes, they are loyal to me and my mother. I will inform them of the final decision."

"Do you think they will be in favor?"

"They will go wherever my mother goes. If that is across the sea to Regor, then they will go there also. I must warn you about Advisor Karnia. Some of our people are loyal to him. When your ancestor was with us, he led those in favor of killing Kansbar instead of allowing him to leave. He believed it was too dangerous for anyone to come here and be allowed to return to Rheskilia. It would be a trail back to us. He was right. Not that Kansbar should be killed, but that the Khrynsani would find their way back to us."

"Kansbar didn't tell anyone," I said. "You know this. Not of his own free will. He was tortured by Khrynsani interrogators, his memories laid bare, filleted like a fish, his mind destroyed."

"I know this. I saw the contents of the book in your memories. But now that you have come, Karnia says it is a sign that one Nathrach left us, but two have returned—at the same time that the Khrynsani again come searching for us and bring the Sythsaurians to our gates. He believes that you led them here."

"We followed them, Your Highness."

"I believe you, but that does not change the facts that once again, there are Nathrachs and Khrynsani in our city. He argues that we must not fail to act this time. We must leave no one to return to tell of us, our city, and the Heart."

"You must admit, Tamnais, killing us all is a logical and tidy solution," Malik said. "Were I in his place, I'd do the same."

"Advisor Karnia is not an evil man," Maralah said. "Protecting the Heart is his duty, and he will do all that he feels he must to faithfully execute that duty."

I snorted. "Including coercing you into a marriage you do not want to gain access to the Heart and your mother's tomb."

"He and his followers believe that offense is a stronger defense. Karnia advocates judicious use of the Heart to keep anyone from getting close to our mountain."

"Regardless of how many more monsters it could release into the city or what damage it could do not only to this continent, but the rest of our world."

"Karnia claims he can control the Heart. I know he is wrong. The two of us have a standoff."

"That sounds all too familiar, Your Highness," I told her. "Many ambitious men and women throughout our history thought they could control the Saghred. It didn't go well for any of them, or the millions of people who died in the wars to secure it, or were sacrificed to feed it. Those already possessing vast power believe that they and they alone can control any power regardless of the magnitude. They have all been wrong, dead wrong. And because of their arrogance, people died. We cannot allow that to happen here."

"Rest assured, Chancellor Nathrach, I will not."

"Excellent. I need for you to set up a meeting with your top city engineers and Captain Benares as soon as possible."

"Consider it done. There are four of them, and they are the younger generation, so while they did not oversee the building of the city themselves, they know every inch of it." Her lips twitched at the corners. "Unlike some of my people, I think you will find them most agreeable to your plan."

31

"I thought I'd leave Jash and Elsu with you as intermediaries,"
I told Phaelan, as one of Maralah's trusted courtiers took
us down palace back hallways to a quickly arranged and
clandestine meeting with the city's engineers.

"I can be diplomatic."

"I believe Raine once said that Benares diplomacy
means firing cannon shot across a bow rather than through a
waterline."

"Yeah. So? We're not at sea."

"These are goblins from over a thousand years ago. If
you're not familiar with ancient elven military history, our
peoples were hell-bent on wiping out each other during that
period."

"That's been true several times, but I do see what you
mean."

"In addition," Elsu noted, "some of these people may have never even seen an elf before. Especially if they were born here before the…um, Great Gelding."

Phaelan gave her a flat look. "You had to bring that up, didn't you?"

"Of course I did." Elsu's eyes glittered. "Jash, you were right, teasing Phaelan *is* a source of endless amusement."

Jash slapped Phaelan on the shoulder. "And once again, you're the sole ambassador for your people. Make 'em proud."

The elf pirate's eyes went a little wide in realization. "Oh crap."

I glanced from Elsu to Jash, starting to have serious doubts about my choice of elf chaperones.

That Nidaar's city engineers were agreeable to our plan was a vast understatement.

"They're just like you," Jash told Phaelan in as close to amazement—and concern bordering on fear—as I'd ever seen from him. "I know we want these people to cooperate, but this is scary."

Yes, these three men and one woman were responsible for the city's structural upkeep, and were only one or two generations removed from those who had designed and overseen the building of Nidaar. But this city had become their prison, so I really shouldn't have been surprised that they were unanimous in their desire to blow it up and bury the Heart. In fact, they had been quite industrious over the years in assembling the means to do just that.

Phaelan had made some new friends.

Not only were they playing nicely, they were even sharing their toys.

The engineers had done all the calculations of how much explosive material they'd need to bring the mountain down on top of the city and collapse both to bury the Heart. They had built the devices, and knew exactly where they needed to place the charges. Unfortunately, they told us, they lacked sufficient explosive power to get the job done.

Phaelan just smiled and unpacked his case of cylinders packed with Nebian black powder.

Nebian black powder had been around nearly as long as the Nebians themselves, so the Cha'Nidaar engineers knew precisely what it was and what it could do.

It wasn't an exaggeration to say that the engineers were giddy with delight, and that they and Phaelan were well on their way to becoming friends for life.

Bane was going to be so disappointed he missed this.

"Princess Maralah said that the Cha'Nidaar could be ready to evacuate in forty minutes," I said to the chief engineer, whose name was Esha. "And it would take another two hours after that to reach the surface."

"Sounds about right." Then the Cha'Nidaar engineer chuckled. "Though they can move faster than that if they've got a pack of dakkonan at their heels."

"Couldn't we all?" Jash muttered.

"Now that you have sufficient explosives," I continued, "how long will it take to assemble and place the bombs throughout the city?"

"All we need to do is add the Nebian black powder," Esha said. "Will Captain Benares be staying with us?"

"He will, and so will Jash and Elsu."

Esha nodded in approval. "Good. There will be six bombs. It will take two of us to place each one. We can work quickly, but with Nebian powder, we wouldn't want to work too quickly. A mistake would be bad."

"So, with each team placing two bombs, from the time I walk out that door until the bombs are in place, *and* you're all safely away and ready to detonate, how long?" I asked.

"Without any unexpected delays…" Esha did some calculations in his head. "We could be on the surface when the rest of our people are. Possibly before."

I did some math of my own and frowned. "That doesn't add up."

Esha grinned impishly. "That's because our way out is faster. Only one can go at a time, but when we go, we go fast." The engineer winked. "Another invention we have prepared for when this day came."

Phaelan's answering grin was fierce and oh so happy. "Blowing up a city *and* getting the hell out faster than anyone else. I love this plan!"

The courtier escorted me back to our quarters, where I collected Agata, Dasant, Malik, and Talon with Indigo, and together we were escorted to the throne room. Since we weren't sure if we'd be coming back, we had our packs with us. Our weapons had never left us.

I brought them up to speed on the plan and its timeline.

Agata walked by my side. "It's about three hours from when Maralah orders the evacuation to when the bombs can be detonated." She paused. "That is, if she can convince them to go. That leaves out one very important variable."

"Yeah, I know. The unknown is how long will it take for us to free and awaken Baeseria."

"The lady doesn't have to be awake," Malik noted. "Break her out of that coffin now, worry about her being conscious later."

Agata and I exchanged a glance. Our overriding worry was that the Heart would try to stop us from freeing Baeseria, and bring the mountain down on all of us, no explosives needed.

The courtier showed us to an anteroom. Maralah was waiting for us.

Her Highness was not amused.

"Karnia has requested to speak with you before I address my people," she said. "I refused. I do not see the purpose in it. He spews hatred and will do naught but blame you for that which was not of your doing. It is a waste of time, time we do not have."

"I take it you told him our plan and he didn't like it." I didn't phrase it as a question. I didn't need to.

"Not in the least. Especially when I told him that as the ruler of our people, the final decision is mine and mine alone. He then questioned my authority and said that I'm clearly under your black magic influence and thus compromised, am no longer fit to rule."

"Black magic? Could he have been listening to us after you ordered him out of the throne room earlier?"

"That would be impossible. When the doors are closed in this room, it is completely soundproof. And the only others in the room with us were my four personal guards. They have my complete trust."

"Information can be acquired from the mind of another without that person being aware."

Maralah just looked at me, rather like Malik in that respect. "My guards have my trust, but I require more than trust. I mind-gazed them after Karnia made his accusation. They remain as they have ever been. Utterly loyal."

I gave the princess a slow smile. "You are most definitely a goblin, Your Highness. With your guards' loyalty intact, there is only one other way Karnia could have known that I once practiced black magic."

"Dear Sandrina has had a visitor," Malik said smoothly.

Maralah scowled. "I ordered that no one see the prisoners."

"It seems Karnia doesn't believe your orders pertain to him," I said. "With your permission, Your Highness, I would like very much to speak with Advisor Karnia."

"As you wish. The people are gathered outside of the throne room. I met with Karnia there, and I want you to speak with him there as well."

Malik smiled slightly. "A reminder of who sits on the throne. A wise and prudent move, Your Highness."

Maralah inclined her head at the compliment. "I arranged for Karnia to be brought to me alone. My guards are in the throne room with him now. If necessary, he can be taken into custody and removed before the people are allowed in. I will not have him making trouble. The safety and lives of my people depend on it. Would you wait here for a few more minutes? I would like to have a few more words with our esteemed advisor."

I bowed. "Of course, Your Highness."

She left the door ever so slightly ajar.

"If that's not an invitation to listen," I murmured to Malik, "then I don't know what is."

"Great goblin minds, thinking alike and all that."

"Das, would you stay with Talon and Agata?" I asked. "We don't want a crowd at the door."

"Of course."

Talon let out an exasperated sigh. "I never get to have any fun."

"Your time's coming," I told him.

Malik and I went to the door with a silence born of years in the goblin court, where moving without being heard or seen was a matter of survival—political and literal.

I've always preferred to get a look at an adversary before taking them on.

Malik took a look for himself, chuckled silently, and shook his head. He stepped back, gesturing me forward with a flourish.

I looked out into the throne room and my lips twitched in a smile.

Advisor Karnia was exactly as I had seen him the last time we were both here. Severe robes, posture, and expression. I knew that Malik had drawn the same conclusion as I had when I'd first seen the Cha'Nidaar official. We'd dealt with his like many times in the goblin court, and if we survived to return home, we'd be dealing with it again.

Dangerous and determined to carry out his agenda, but shrewd and subtle while he did it.

Karnia took it one step further.

He truly believed in what he did. He was the fanatic, the zealot, who saw himself as the hero of his people, the only one who truly understood the danger they were in, and was convinced that he and he alone could save them, from outsiders or themselves.

I had no doubt that fanaticism had been growing and festering for years, perhaps centuries, to the detriment of his sanity.

I stepped back to where Malik waited.

"That one needs to go away," he whispered without moving his lips. Another skill that came in handy in the goblin court.

"Yes," I agreed, "but no."

That stopped my friend; I knew it would. I bit back a smile.

"He's trouble of the very worst kind," Malik insisted.

"I know."

"We'll be killing him now or later, either way he's just as dead. By doing it now, we make sure he's out of our way."

"Many of the Cha'Nidaar believe him to be their protector, mistaken though they are. And some of those are soldiers. We need their cooperation and help to get these people out of here."

"But we—"

"Mal, how much help will we get if I knife him and say, 'Oh, I'm sorry, but I did this for your own good. Your beloved advisor is a fanatic and quite insane.'"

Footsteps approached the door, heavy and obvious. Someone wanted us to know they were coming.

Malik snickered as he and I quickly stepped back.

It was a young palace guardsman. "Her Highness is ready for you now, Chancellor Nathrach."

"Such a considerate young man," Malik murmured. "I'll be here waiting," he told me. "And watching and listening."

"Always."

32

I walked out onto the throne dais, stopped and bowed deeply to Maralah. "At your service, Your Highness. You wished to see me?"

"I do indeed. May I again present Advisor Karnia, who has requested to speak briefly with you about the dire circumstances in which we find ourselves."

I inclined my head. "Advisor Karnia."

Karnia was standing at the foot of the ten steps leading up to the throne, flanked by two of Maralah's guards. The other two were standing at attention on either side of her throne. There was no one else in the room.

I took one step down from the throne dais, which positioned me below Maralah, but far above Karnia. When I'd first been brought before the Cha'Nidaar princess, I'd been standing on the floor with Karnia one step below Maralah's throne.

Our positions were now reversed.

I saw no reason to avoid the slight. He already hated me, and goblin court etiquette did not require handshakes. Handshakes were traditionally exchanged to indicate that one wasn't armed. And at the goblin court, daggers inside of sleeves, and a fondness for skin-transferable poisons, encouraged courtiers to keep their distance from one another. While I doubted Maralah had allowed her advisor to keep any weapons, I was absolutely bristling with steel. I didn't want to lie by implying that I wasn't armed.

I had no intention of lying. Brutal honesty was called for here.

As Maralah said, we didn't have the time for anything else.

Karnia may not have been armed, but if looks could kill, I would have died the instant I stepped through that door.

Malik was right. A dagger between Karnia's ribs would save us all a lot of trouble.

My hand had been casually resting on the hilt of the dagger at my waist. Of its own accord, my fingers had tightened on the grip.

I reluctantly relaxed them.

Old habits died hard.

Maralah smiled down on her advisor. "Karnia, the last time we were all here together, I don't believe you and our guest were properly introduced. This is Chancellor Tamnais Nathrach, a duke of the imperial goblin court in Regor, and chancellor and chief mage to the goblin king."

I smiled and sighed with exaggerated regret. "Your Highness, as I have sworn to keep no secrets from you, I also have the misfortune to be King Chigaru and Queen Mirabai Mal'Salin's heir until they produce one of their own."

"How trying for you."

"Yes, Your Highness, it is."

"I sincerely hope Chigaru and Mirabai will be blessed soon."

"As do I." I turned my attention back to Karnia. "I understand you wanted to speak with me."

"Yes, I do. Her Highness tells me you have come to destroy the Heart of Nidaar, and having learned that it cannot be destroyed, you propose to destroy our city instead, bringing down the mountain on top of us, to bury the Heart. I'm sure you understand my concern at such drastic measures."

"I assure you, Advisor Karnia, I did not sail halfway around the world merely to inconvenience you. Nor did I come with the intent of rendering the Cha'Nidaar homeless. You may have noticed the arrival of the Khrynsani forces to your land along with their newest allies, the Sythsaurians. I understand that your people have encountered the Sythsaurians before. You know what they both want, yet you scorn our offer of assistance in—"

"Assistance in destroying our very civilization? We did not—"

"I would not call less than a hundred survivors a civilization. What the Cha'Nidaar have built here is nothing short of miraculous, but your people are dying, Karnia. At their own hands. They have given up hope. What I offer is hope, a way your people can leave this place without failing in the sacred duty they have taken upon themselves. You've heard of the Saghred, correct?"

"We have. It is a great evil."

"Yes, it was a great evil. *Was.* It's been destroyed. I am told that's not possible with the Heart, that to destroy it would crack the world, killing us all. The only solution is to bury it, entomb it as it has done to your people. The Khrynsani know of this place, as do the Sythsaurians. Your secret is out."

"Because of your ancestor."

"Who was tortured and killed by the Khrynsani. He never told anyone of the Heart or Nidaar. It was ripped from his mind."

"If we had killed him then, he wouldn't have returned to Regor, and our secret would have remained."

"Yes, your secret would have remained. But for how long? And if not the Khrynsani, then the Sythsaurians, who don't want to kill the Cha'Nidaar. No, you're too valuable to them—as slave labor to dig out the Heart for them. They only want the Heart, and if its removal destroys this world, it is of no matter to them. They have other worlds to go to, worlds they have already conquered. Your people, this city, the Heart—all are known, on this world and beyond. To destroy the Heart would be to destroy the world. Our only hope is to bury it beneath the weight of this city and the mountain above it. It is not the ideal solution, but it is the only one we have now. It will buy us something we *don't* have, which is time."

I slowly walked down the stairs to where Karnia stood, speaking as I did. "Your sacred duty is to prevent its use—by anyone. Isn't that what you want, Karnia? Or do you desire something else? Something more, perhaps?"

"What are you insinuating?"

"I insinuate nothing. I question your motives and actions, directly and openly, here in this place before your princess and ruler. What do you question, Karnia? Her Highness's fitness to rule? That is a serious accusation, treasonous even. But a more interesting accusation is that I have influenced her thoughts and actions by means of black magic. Where would you have heard that I was capable of this?"

I now stood in front of Karnia, within stabbing distance for either one of us. "Who would have told you that I once practiced the dark arts? Which is true, by the way. I do not deny it. I was Queen Gilcara Mal'Salin's chief mage and magical enforcer for many years." I gave him a fang-filled smile. "And I was good at it." I dropped my voice to a menacing purr. "What did you and Sandrina Ghalfari discuss when you visited her in her cell? Or did your conversations begin earlier? You defy the will of a queen who sacrificed herself to protect you, and now you defy her daughter, your ruler, whose word is law and decisions are final. She does not have a chief mage. I am offering my services here and now. Do you require a demonstration, Advisor Karnia?"

33

Karnia didn't require a demonstration. I was disappointed.

And highly suspicious.

That suspicion increased tenfold when he not only apologized to Princess Maralah, but to me as well, going so far as to welcome me as an honored guest.

That sealed it.

In goblin court parlance, that translated to, "You'll be dead before sunrise. Enjoy the few remaining hours of your life."

I graciously thanked Karnia for his apology in the true spirit in which it was given.

Translation: Bring it.

Karnia was escorted out of the throne room under guard, to be taken to his home and put under house arrest once there. Maralah wanted to speak to her people before she brought me in. I returned to the anteroom to wait.

"A nice touch with the heir bit," Malik said.

"Since Maralah was giving Karnia the full litany of my titles, I thought I'd add that to let him know precisely who he was going to try to have killed. Sandrina might not have shared that part with him."

"I told you we should have slipped a knife in his ribs."

"Yes, that would have rid us of Karnia, but ruined any chance of gaining the Cha'Nidaar's trust."

"Tamnais, please, I'm a professional. They never would have found his body." Malik flashed a cheerful grin. "Do you think he's going to try to kill you?"

"I'd be disappointed if he didn't."

"When he tries, may I kill him?"

"We'll see."

"Talon's right. You're no fun."

"Fun's not in my job description."

The Cha'Nidaar were a beautiful people, and disturbingly, none of them looked over the age of forty.

Close to eighty of them had gathered in the throne room at Maralah's request. The rest were soldiers on duty throughout the city, including guarding the dungeon and Baeseria's tomb. And I could hardly forget those escorting Advisor Karnia home.

Each one carried a duffel bag. The evacuation bags Maralah had mentioned.

She had ordered her people to come prepared. Smart lady. In having to bring their bags with them, the people were already thinking about what they would be doing in the next few hours. Some kept them slung over their shoulders, others had dropped them to the floor at their feet.

Malik, Agata, Dasant, and Talon with Indigo had joined me in the throne room.

The people listened attentively and respectfully as their princess stood before them and told them the situation and the plan. There was no panic when she mentioned the Khrynsani and Sythsaurians, merely resignation and acceptance along the lines of "Here we go again."

They were a people who didn't panic easily. Good. Hopefully that wouldn't be tested.

Maralah got to the part about them leaving the city within the hour. Then she told them about returning to Rheskilia, being free to settle wherever they wanted, how the Khrynsani were out of power and being hunted down, their temple destroyed.

That part earned the princess some applause. Again, there were no questions, no disagreements. No problems.

I let out a breath I hadn't been aware I was holding.

When I did, I felt a vibration beneath my feet.

I shot a glance at the others. They were standing straight and still.

"So it's not just me," I said. "Is it the—"

Agata was nodding. "Heart. Yes, I believe it is." She put her hand over the Heartstone pendant. "I even feel it here in—"

The floor lurched, sending us all sprawling.

The door to the throne dais swung all the way open, slamming against the wall.

Inside the throne room, some of the Cha'Nidaar had actually managed to stay on their feet. Maralah was one of them, though she'd had her throne to grab on to. To the Cha'Nidaar's credit, still no one panicked. No doubt they were used to floors and ground that moved beneath them, whether due to Heart-spawned quakes or rampaging beast feet.

Shouts and the sound of the Cha'Nidaar soldier's guns erupted from just outside the throne room.

"The city is under attack!" came a shout from the hall beyond our anteroom door.

Malik shielded. "I got that impression."

Agata pulled her pendant from beneath her armor. The little slice of Heartstone was glowing fiercely. "Whoever they are, they've reached the Heart."

And I got more than the impression that someone was Advisor Karnia.

"Das, do you have your spy gem?" I asked.

He quickly fumbled around in one of his pockets. "Yes."

"Go with the Cha'Nidaar to the surface and call Calik. If there are Khrynsani or lizard men waiting for us outside, those people will need protecting. We also might need pickup. Talon, go with him."

"No. Agata might need me, remember? And I need to help. Don't send me away." He took a breath and let it out unsteadily. "I'll do whatever you say—except leave you."

I nodded once tightly, past a tightness in my chest. I ran in the direction of the throne room.

"So I can tell Calik," Dasant called after me, "where should I tell him you've gone?"

"Hopefully to save the world."

I went to where Maralah was giving orders to a group of ten men and women. Fortunately, none of her guards tried to stop me.

"Das will go with you and your people to the surface," I said quickly. "There should be protection waiting for you. He'll give you the details."

Her pale eyes were cold with fury as she flipped open a shallow compartment on a gold wrist cuff she wore, exposing several flat jewels. She pressed and held what looked like a ruby. Instantly red lights began flashing from all the light sconces.

"He can give these squad leaders the details," she snapped. "I'm going with you."

"Your people need you."

"My *mother* needs me! You'll never get to her or the Heart without me."

I didn't like it, but she was right.

"Let's go."

As we ran, Maralah shouted to her soldiers to fall back to the evacuation route and cover the people's escape. Within minutes, we had one of the city's corridors to ourselves.

"Mal, call Jash and see where they are on placing those charges. Then bring him up to speed and tell them where we're going."

Malik wore his spy gem on a chain around his neck inside a protective silver globe. "Done, done, and done."

A young soldier ran toward us, battered and bloody. "Highness, I was sent to tell…the prisoners…"

I swore. "Escaped."

He nodded once, panting.

Maralah put a hand on his shoulder. "You did what you could."

"I was told…to stay with you."

"I am protected. Evacuate the city. Protect the people."

"But, Your—"

"That's a command."

"Yes, Ma'am." The soldier ran in the direction we'd come from, though it was more of a lurch.

Malik stared after him in disbelief. "The boy doesn't look like he could protect a—"

The princess scowled. "I sent him away so he'll survive."

Once again, Maralah led me down staircases that took us all deeper into the mountain. The difference now being that the sconces that lit our way were all flashing red—and we were running.

When we entered—or attempted to enter—the vaulted antechamber to the queen's tomb, Colonel Akhai didn't look surprised to see us. His eyes narrowed and his stance widened.

This was not good.

He barked a command and his men drew crystal-powered guns. I didn't know what was going on here, but if they opened up on us, we'd be vaporized.

I tried to step in front of Maralah, but she wasn't having it. She was livid.

"Colonel Akhai, what is the meaning of this?"

"The princess and Advisor Karnia warned me you had escaped and would try enter, Lady Ghalfari. You and your accomplices are under arrest."

"*What?* I am your prin—"

I knew. I knew what Sandrina had done.

So did Malik. "Well played, Sandi," he murmured.

I grabbed Maralah's arm, holding her back. "It was Sandrina. She's a shapeshifter."

She shook me off, crossing to the colonel in long, angry strides. "I ordered you never to allow him near my mother, *your queen!*"

Suddenly, Colonel Akhai wasn't so confident. "She said the Khrynsani were attacking. Only because of the emergency was she allowing the advisor inside."

Maralah's hand lashed out. Instead of a slap I'd half expected, she firmly clasped the side of Akhai's head. The mind gaze was immediate, except Maralah wasn't searching Akhai's memories.

She was allowing Akhai into hers. Though "allowing" might have been a bit mild. The Cha'Nidaar ruler forced the colonel to look, to know who she was.

When she released him, he all but fell to his knees. To his credit, he recovered quickly, his pale eyes blazing in rage— not at Maralah, but at the woman who had tricked him into betraying his sacred trust.

"Sandi's in trouble," Malik whispered in a sing-song voice.

34

Now I understood the source of Sandrina's smug satisfaction in the throne room when we'd been brought before Maralah. She was able to watch and listen to the Cha'Nidaar princess unimpeded, memorizing her mannerisms and speech patterns, all to gain access to the queen's tomb—with the one man who could activate the Heart for her.

My team and I had arrived in Nidaar after flying across hundreds of miles of desert and trudging through monster-infested caverns. Sandrina, her Khrynsani, and the Sythsaurians with them had been clean and rested when we'd encountered them. They'd probably arrived in the city via the lizard men's portals or teleportation devices. So, Sandrina could have been here days before us or even longer. Plenty of time to have met and made a deal with Advisor Karnia.

I was gathering my magic, letting my anger grow, feeding the anticipation of finally getting my hands on Sandrina Ghalfari. So close now. She'd escaped that night in the Khrynsani temple. She wouldn't get away this time.

Colonel Akhai couldn't unlock and get that door open fast enough.

I felt it before I could see it, a prickling between my shoulder blades and down my spine, like a charge in the air just before a lightning strike.

We were under a mountain. This was no lightning strike.

It was the approach of millions of hornets.

Sythsaurians, coming from the tunnels behind us.

I spun, grabbing Maralah and shifting the full power of my magic to my shields, pushing it out in an arch to cover my team and Colonel Akhai, who was working on the last lock.

The Cha'Nidaar guards opened up on the Sythsaurians, vaporizing five of them before they could launch those green nets of pain and death.

The lizard men kept coming.

Looked like Sandrina hadn't invited them to her party.

Sythsaurians didn't take rejection well at all.

The colonel wrenched the door open, leveling his gun inside the tomb. It was empty, except for Baeseria's coffin.

The queen was still inside.

My eyes darted around the room. "Where are they?"

"Already in the chamber with the Heart," Maralah snapped.

"I failed you and my queen," Akhai said quickly. "Allow me the honor of defending the door to the tomb. The Sythsaurians will not pass."

More lizard men arrived—and defense turned into a suicide mission.

Colonel Akhai knew it. He bared his fangs in anticipation of the battle to come.

Maralah gripped his shoulder. "Our people will know of your sacrifice and that of your men. Your names will be raised up and join those of our heroes."

Akhai gave a quick nod of gratitude, then those sharp eyes were on mine. "Save her, Nathrach."

The meaning of his words was clear. His tone said that if I failed, he would hunt me down in the afterlife and make me pay and pay again.

"I will. Your sacrifice will not be in vain. I swear it."

Agata, Malik, and Talon with Indigo clinging to his shoulder passed through along with Maralah. Akhai closed the tomb door behind us and threw all the locks back into place.

We were sealed inside Queen Baeseria's tomb with only one way out—through the tomb and into the Heart chamber itself.

I ran to the queen's coffin, Maralah right behind me. "Mal, did Jash say when the bombs would be ready?"

"They were placing the final three when I called."

"Check again."

Malik went to the far side of the room to contact Jash.

I had been here before; Agata, Talon, and Malik had not.

"She's alive in there?" Talon whispered in horror before he could stop himself. "Sorry, Your Highness, I didn't—"

Maralah waved away the comment. "It has sickened me since the day she sealed herself inside to save us."

Agata's eyes darted across and around the coffin. "How does it open?"

"It doesn't," Maralah said. "At least not that we've been able to find. She and the Heart did it together. Our strongest guards and most powerful mages have tried to move it to no avail. It is sealed."

"Did you try hitting it?" Talon asked. "*Really* hard?"

"She and the Heart did this together. It could strike back to defend her—"

"What if we hit it while thinking nice thoughts?"

I knelt at the foot of the bier, running my hands around where the base of the coffin met the Heartstone crystal bier. The plan had been to rescue the queen, then get out of the city. Now we had to stop whatever Sandrina and Karnia were at this moment putting into motion.

"Maralah, where's the door to the Heart chamber?" I asked quickly.

She jerked her head to the left toward a small section of wall, never taking her eyes from her mother's face. "There's a crystal that's darker than the others. Push down on it. The door will open."

I jumped to my feet and ran to where Maralah said the door was located. If there was a crystal that was darker than the others, I couldn't find it.

Malik appeared at my side, his voice low, his words quick. "Jash said the bombs are ready and they're running like hell to their exit point. They need another ten minutes to get there and get clear. I called Das. He said to tell the princess they just passed the stone—"

"Stone falls," said Maralah from behind me.

"Yes," Malik said. "What does that mean?"

"It means the bombs can be detonated any time. My people are now in the interior of the next mountain. A targeted explosion in the city won't hurt them now. They are safe."

We had ten minutes.

Malik was standing behind Maralah. His eyes darted to the coffin and he shook his head.

No words were needed.

If we couldn't free Baeseria within the next minute or two, we would have to leave her for now. Sandrina had Karnia to activate the Heart for her. We had to stop them.

"There's a seam here," Talon said, gripping the coffin's edges toward the base. "Dad, Mal, help me move this."

Malik went to foot of the coffin with Talon. I joined Maralah at the head.

"Shift to the left," Talon told us. "Now!"

We put all our strength against the moving the coffin's base even a fraction.

Nothing.

The ground was shaking in waves, going from throw-you-to-the-floor to tremors and back again.

"I won't leave her," Maralah said. "Go and stop Karnia."

"We're not leaving either one of you," I snapped, desperately trying to think of a solution.

"The fate of this world is more important." Maralah was resigned, like her colonel. "Don't sacrifice millions for us."

She was right. I despised logic.

"I'm not giving up and neither are you."

"Tam…" It was Agata. She was listening, though not to us. "Do you hear that?"

A sound was gradually rising up all around us, a soft thump as the barest touch on a muffled drum, in time with the Heart's tremors.

No, not from *around* us.

From inside Baeseria's crystal coffin.

The flames around the base of her eternal bed began to flicker in time with it. Two beats, then a pause, then two beats, repeated, growing stronger.

Beats.

Heartbeats.

Baeseria's heart.

Maralah darted around both of us and seized the top edges of the coffin above Baeseria's shoulders. "You did this, Mother! You can undo it!" She gripped the edges of the coffin lid until the stone cut into her palms. "Mother! Wake up!"

Heartstone crystals began falling from the ceiling, shattering on impact against the coffin.

Baeseria remained still and tranquil.

"The Heart is destroying the city!" Maralah screamed the words with her voice, her thoughts, and her soul.

The princess's hands were flat against the top of her mother's coffin, on either side of her face, willing, begging the queen to hear her.

The heartbeats grew stronger.

Baeseria's eyes opened.

The queen raised her hands until they pressed against the sheet of Heartstone that was all that separated her from Maralah.

Mother and daughter, palm to palm. Maralah's tears fell freely, dropping to the stone between their hands.

The stone shimmered between them…

…and disappeared.

With a joyous cry, Maralah threw herself into her mother's arms, and for the first time in nine centuries, mother and daughter embraced.

The ground gave a violent shake, throwing me to my knees beside Baeseria's bier.

The queen was sitting up, smiling down at me. "Once again, you ignored my orders."

"But I—"

Her smile broadened. "I told you kneeling wasn't necessary."

The geode shuddered around us, sending more crystals crashing down.

The queen's eyes widened at the destruction taking place and she struggled to get to her feet. "What is ha—"

I swept Baeseria into my arms. "Karnia activated the Heart."

"How could…but I control—"

"Not right now. And it doesn't feel like Karnia's controlling it, either." I dodged more falling chunks of Heartstone, holding Baeseria close against my body. "You're welcome to try to talk to it. I couldn't find the dark crystal," I told Maralah.

The princess actually grinned, the weight of the ages lifted from her with her mother's awakening. "If it were easy, anyone could do it." She dashed across the room to right where I'd been standing and pushed down on one of the crystals there.

The wall opened.

Malik, Talon, and Agata powered up. I did the same.

"I've waited too long for this," Malik said with a vicious smile. "Let's crash Sandrina's party."

35

"I don't think we're walking out of here with this in our pocket," Malik said.

My friend had always been a master of the understatement.

The door in Baeseria's tomb had opened into a short tunnel, which led to a wonder. We were concealed in a niche, but it allowed us to see out into the enormous cavern.

I simply stared in awe. Maralah was right. The Heart was bigger than her throne room.

The Heart of Nidaar was roughly cylindrical in shape. I say roughly, because crystals the length of sentry dragons had grown out of the main stone and attached to the walls of the surrounding cavern, rather like support beams in a building. The Heart was embedded in a base of gleaming obsidian, like a setting supporting a precious gem. A precious gem filled with millions of flickering flames. The walls were also obsidian, studded with crystals that had sprouted from the beams, a breathtaking backdrop that reminded me of a star-filled night sky.

There was one manmade element. Rising up from the cavern floor was metal scaffolding that supported a catwalk encircling the entire Heart.

Most of us were agog at the Heart; Talon was transfixed by the obsidian gleaming like black mirrors around its base.

The awakening Heart was threatening to shake apart the city above us, but as soon as we stepped into the cavern, the quakes and vibrations ceased. It was like being in the eye of a hurricane.

There appeared to be no Khrynsani or Sythsaurian guards. I didn't believe for one instant we would be so lucky as to face Sandrina and Karnia in here alone, but that was what it looked like.

Looks were always deceiving.

Maybe they had activated the Heart and fled. Regardless, we had to stop whatever they had set into motion and get out.

I put my lips next to Maralah's ear. "Is there another way out?"

The princess pointed to the far side of the Heart's chamber. Naturally.

Malik signaled to me that he should go first to ensure the path was clear.

I nodded and held up two fingers. He had two minutes.

Malik could get inside a beehive, steal all the honeycombs, and get out without the bees being any the wiser. He cloaked and disappeared. Completely. It was as if he'd ceased to exist.

"What's Karnia doing?" I asked Agata.

"I don't know yet. He's still increasing the Heart's power. As soon as I know, I'll tell you."

Two minutes passed, and Malik wasn't back.

And suddenly, we were no longer alone.

Khrynsani armed with Sythsaurian guns shimmered into being not ten feet away—and those guns were aimed directly at us.

How in the hell?

Gleaming on their right wrists were the cuffs the Sythsaurians had used to teleport their way out of being captured by the Cha'Nidaar—and that had encased us all in those green nets.

An alliance with lizard men had its privileges.

Sandrina walked into view from the far side of the Heart. "Bravo, Tamnais. I told Karnia we didn't need to bother extracting the queen from her crystal box. I assured him that you, in your seemingly endless resourcefulness, would take care of it for us. Now that Baeseria is awake, we can complete our work here and leave. With her, we will be able to use the Heart from anywhere."

The Khrynsani prodded us all out into the center of the cavern.

Advisor Karnia was on the catwalk, slowly sidestepping his way around the Heart, hands moving over the stone, his touch triggering gouts of flame just beneath the surface. His concentration on the Heart was complete. I doubt he even knew we were there.

Agata had backed up a few steps. The two Khrynsani guarding her thought she was backing away from them in fear. The gem mage was simply maneuvering to put unlimited ammunition at her fingertips—a small pile of fallen Heartstone crystals. All she needed now was an opportunity.

"Put me down, Tamnais," Baeseria said. "I can stand on my own."

The anger in her voice wasn't directed at me, but I still did as told.

"We had planned to use Nidaar as our base for the invasion," Sandrina said to the queen, "but Karnia tells me that bombs have been planted throughout your beautiful city."

"I know of this," Baeseria said. "I approved it."

"Losing the city isn't a problem now that we have you," Sandrina continued. "My son knew it wasn't necessary to have the Saghred physically in his possession, if he had Raine Benares. He could use the Saghred through Raine, which is exactly what we plan to do here. We can't remove the Heart from the mountain, but with the aid of the Sythsaurians' marvelous devices, we can quickly remove you."

I refused to be baited. I also refused to let anyone remove Baeseria from my side. The Khrynsani surrounding us appeared to be in no hurry to try. Nor had they disarmed us, which was more than odd, not that I was about to complain. Perhaps they didn't think they needed to, since they were armed with their new allies' weapons.

"You speak of the Sythsaurians as if they have any intention of keeping their end of whatever devil's bargain you've made with them," I said.

"You say that like we have any intention of keeping ours. You know me so much better than that."

"If you'll recall, they abandoned you at the first sign of trouble."

Sandrina shrugged. "I didn't take it personally. I would have done the same in their place. Besides, I needed to be captured, so I could be taken before this enterprising young lady." She looked to Baeseria. "Your daughter has done a splendid job in your absence of keeping everything fully operational."

My mind was racing. If Baeseria was teleported out of here, blowing up the mountain wouldn't stop Sandrina and her lizard allies. Behind me, I actually felt Agata reaching out to the Heart, and for the first time, I was grateful as hell for our umi'atsu bond.

"He doesn't have complete control of it yet," she said in my mind. *"But he will soon. It knows him."* There was a pause, and I could feel Agata's blood run cold. *"Tam, through the Heart, I can see what Karnia is doing. He means to destroy Regor."*

"What? How?"

"There's a fault line in a mountain range beneath the Sea of Kenyon, two hundred miles off Rheskilia's coast. He's aiming the Heart there. The resulting earthquake will send a giant wave that will increase in size and speed as it crosses the sea to Regor. His calculations show that every city on Rheskilia's coast will be destroyed."

"How long do we have to stop him?" I asked.

"Not long. Minutes at the most."

Damn.

"Can you slow him down?"

"What do you think *I'm trying to do?"*

Time to buy some time—for Agata *and* Malik. If he wasn't dead, he was up to something.

"Nice trick getting past the queen's guards," I told Sandrina.

"I knew the guards would not hesitate to let their princess see her dear mother, and being in the throne room gave me more than enough time to study her mannerisms and voice." The air in front of Sandrina wavered, and a flawless replica of Maralah stood before us. Ever the showman, Sandrina gave us ample time to admire her handiwork before changing back. "While she linked with you, I memorized her."

The Heartstone in Agata's pendant was blazing red. "Karnia," she shouted, "if you continue what you're doing, you'll bring the mountain down on us all."

"Magus Azul, while your skill in gem magic is impressive, this gentleman has actually used the Heart of Nidaar before." Sandrina grinned at me. "Most recently to prevent your ships from reaching the coast. Did you think there was only one way into this cavern?"

Malik was right. I should've stuck a knife in Karnia when I had the chance.

"He's going to kill us all," Agata said in my mind. *"The Heart is resisting him. That resistance will shake this cavern apart."*

"Before or after it destroys Regor?"

"Unknown. There's so much power…"

"Talon," I said, knowing the guards could hear regardless of how quiet I was, so I didn't bother. "Agata isn't feeling well. Help her."

Agata let out a little gasp and staggered back a step, her hand now against one of the huge Heartstone support beams.

"Nice touch," I told her.

"I wasn't acting," she snapped.

Talon slid his arm around Agata's waist, and I felt her

power increase. I sensed Talon's power through Agata, but that was all. The umi'atsu bond didn't let me into his mind. I tried to share my own power with Agata, but was blocked. By what, I didn't know. Words and sensations could pass between us, but not power.

I had no problem with the cavern, city, and mountain coming down. That was our plan. What wasn't in that plan was us being here when it happened. Ten minutes had passed since Malik had spoken to Jash. Everyone else was safe. We were the only ones who weren't. My spy gem hung on a chain around my neck, I could activate it and contact Jash without touching it or lifting it out of my shirt if I had to, but it might muffle my instructions. A command to blow up a city and mountain—or to give us more time—wasn't something you wanted to have misunderstood.

"The Seven Kingdoms need to know what we are capable of doing should they defy us." Sandrina looked down at me. "It's simple. You killed the Khrynsani and destroyed our temple; I will destroy Regor—and all of its people. The Heart is a precision instrument. Advisor Karnia assures me that the wave resulting from the earthquake he will trigger beneath the Sea of Kenyon will make the one he hit your fleet with appear as a ripple in a pond. You may have been too quick to promise to take the Cha'Nidaar home. Soon, there won't be a home left for them to go to. That show of power should get the Seven Kingdoms' attention."

She paused for a moment. "Though after our demonstration, they should change the name to the Six Kingdoms, since the goblin royal court and government will have ceased to exist, and you will have a front-row seat to their destruction." The smile broadened in delicious satisfaction. "Your family is at your home in Regor, are they not, Tamnais? Perhaps after the Heart has done its work, my allies can arrange for you and your son to visit the ruins."

I lunged for the ladder to the catwalk and got zapped in the back for my trouble. Though from my new vantage point on the ground, I saw Agata use the distraction get her other hand on the massive Heartstone beam, aiming even more of her and Talon's combined power at disrupting Karnia.

And I got my spy gem into my clenched fist.

Maralah helped me back to my feet.

"Advisor Karnia estimates that it will take a little over two hours for the wave to form and reach Rheskilia," Sandrina was saying, "and you have no way to warn them. The Khrynsani will always win, Tamnais. *I* will always win."

The millions of flickering tongues of flame inside the Heart began to coalesce, until the entirety of the Heart's interior pulsed as one.

It was fully awake.

"This is not the Heart's will," Baeseria said, her eyes distant and unfocused. "Karnia is forcing it."

I flashed back to Kansbar's account of what had happened the day the Khrynsani had awakened the Heart. They had aimed the stone outward as a test and had destroyed the east coast of Aquas.

The Heart had struck back and destroyed every living being in its cavern.

We were living beings, but if we didn't get out of here soon, we weren't going to be living for long.

36

The Heart couldn't be moved, but the cavern containing it had no such limitations.

A deep rumble came from below, cracking the rock beneath our feet and running up the wall closest to where we stood, splitting the obsidian slabs.

The Khrynsani continued to stand guard over us, albeit nervously. They didn't need to worry about being buried under untold tons of rubble. All they had to do was teleport out of here when it got too dangerous, a luxury the rest of us didn't have.

The ground lurched violently, throwing us and our Khrynsani guards to the ground.

An invisible force wrenched a Sythsaurian gun from a fallen Khrynsani. Malik uncloaked and vaporized two of the guards before they could bring their weapons around. I attacked the one closest to me and finally got to use my dagger. He'd had two guns and now they were mine. I tossed one to Maralah and we opened fire.

"Look out!" Talon screamed as one of the dragon-sized crystal support beams snapped off from the Heart and crashed toward the floor. I grabbed Maralah and dove out of the way as it hit where we had just been, shattering into lethal shards. I shielded her with my magic and my body. Two Khrynsani were neither fast nor lucky enough and were crushed beneath a column-sized piece. Malik swooped in and collected teleportation cuffs from the arms extending from beneath the rubble.

I spun and scanned the catwalk for Sandrina as another wave of tremors dropped me to my knees.

She was gone, but Karnia was still there. I started to raise the gun, but I couldn't risk missing. I summoned my magic and flipped my right hand palm up to aim a column of red—

"No!" It was Baeseria. "The Heart will fire it back—"

"I'm not aiming at the Heart."

"Karnia is linked to it. To strike him is to strike the Heart."

Dammit.

Waves of quakes struck, one after the other. I struggled to my feet only to be tossed to the floor again, and the queen with me.

Agata and Talon made it over to where we were as I helped Baeseria to her feet.

"I need to get up there," Agata said.

Baeseria disengaged herself from my arms. "I must go with her." She glanced at Talon. "Just the two of us. You are strong, young man, but the Heart does not know you. We are old friends. I will attempt to calm it."

The tremors intensified as we helped Baeseria and Agata to the Heart's obsidian base. The catwalk circled the Heart near its middle, but there were exposed lower sections of the stone that were only a short climb up the blocks and slabs of obsidian.

I didn't know how they planned to stop Karnia. The raw power rolling in waves from the Heart blocked my bond with Agata, but I didn't need to know how they were going to do it. My job was to protect them while they did.

Agata climbed, moving quickly and surely, until she was close enough to the Heart's base to touch it. It had pulsed and brightened over the past minute, charging itself to strike, to channel its energy where Karnia was aiming it. Baeseria moved more slowly, but soon joined Agata at the Heart.

The gem mage and the queen of the Nidaar laid their hands flat against the stone.

No.

Baeseria's word of simple, unwavering defiance echoed in my head.

From above, Karnia jerked violently as if he'd been struck by lightning.

Baeseria reached over and covered one of Agata's hands with her own, joining the gem mage's raw power to her ages-old bond with the Heart.

Now I could feel it.

Through Agata. The Cha'Nidaar queen had given Agata her blessing, and in doing so, told the Heart to obey Agata as it would her.

The two women held fast, oblivious to the chaos around them as they became one with the Heart, fighting Karnia's efforts to force the stone to do his will. He was treating it as though he was flogging an animal with a whip.

And like an abused animal, it turned on him.

His hands were grafted to the Heart. From where I stood, I could smell his flesh being seared, see his blood running bright red down the clear sides of the Heart, the flames beneath the surface lapping hungrily at it, spreading from Karnia's hands, up his arms. Karnia screamed, and kept screaming, even after the Heart's fires had engulfed his entire body. Within moments, all that remained was a blackened and smoking skeleton fused to the Heart's surface.

"Damn," Talon blurted from beside me. "Remind me never to mess with rocks."

Agata and Baeseria were scrambling in a near panic down the obsidian blocks.

"This is not good," Malik said.

The rumbling grew even more violent as the fires beneath the Heart's surface surged into and through the Heartstone beams anchoring it in place against the cavern walls.

Talon managed to stay on his feet. "Karnia's dead. Why is it still—"

"It can't be stopped," Maralah said. "Karnia went too far."

With a cry, Baeseria slipped, barely managing to grab a ledge with one hand. Agata would never reach her in time.

The queen wouldn't survive a fall from that height.

Retrieval spell.

Agata's thought and my impulse were identical.

"I've got her!" I shouted, running to the base of the Heart beneath where the queen dangled.

"Baeseria, I can catch you with magic. Let go!"

To my amazement, she did, almost too quickly for me to react.

To my relief, my magic caught her in midair.

I brought her the rest of the way down as gently as I could, catching her in my arms. I set her on her feet.

Agata nimbly climbed down the rest of the way. She was breathing heavily. "We stopped what Karnia was doing, but we can't shut down the Heart. He pushed it too hard. Those beams go beneath the mountain and beyond."

"To the roots of the world," Baeseria said. "The only way to stop the Heart is to break those beams."

I channeled all my power into my hands.

"Magic will not work," Baeseria said. "It will merely add to the destruction. When the Khrynsani last used the Heart, it only destroyed from here to the coast." She glanced back at the furiously pulsing stone. "This time it is much stronger. It will destroy most of Aquas, and send a wave eastward, a wave perhaps even larger than Karnia intended." The queen of the Cha'Nidaar was calm, the peace that came with the acceptance of one's fate. "These bombs will collapse everything above us, the city and the mountain?"

I swallowed on a dry mouth. "Yes."

"That should sever most, if not all, of the beams."

"Should?"

"Tamnais, we have no other option."

"And we have no escape," Malik said. "The quakes collapsed our way out." He jerked his head in the direction we'd come. "And the way we came in."

Baeseria placed her hand on my arm. "Sometimes the few must die so that the many may live."

We were trapped.

The Heart of Nidaar would be buried, never to be used again—and we would be buried along with it. We had done what needed to be done, and half our team had escaped with the people of Nidaar.

Our mission was successful.

In any mission, sacrifices had to be made, but I didn't want the deaths of the brave people around me to be among them.

Malik smiled and shrugged. "Well, we're damned if we detonate the bombs, but everyone else will be damned if we don't."

I raised the spy gem to my mouth. "Jash, you there?"

"Where the hell have—"

"Are the bombs ready?"

"Yes, where are you?"

"In the Heart chamber." I quickly explained what Sandrina and Karnia had done. "We can't get out. I need you to detonate—"

"What do you mean you can't—"

"We're trapped. You have to detonate. The Heart is about to—"

"Wait!" Talon shouted from a section of obsidian wall. "I need a cloth, something I can polish this with."

This was a smooth, man-sized slab of obsidian. It was covered in dust from the quakes.

Maralah didn't ask any questions. She whipped out a dagger and slit her robe at the base, slicing free a section.

Talon grabbed it and went to work.

A mirror. Talon was making a mirror.

He talked fast as he buffed. "Last year, I found I had a knack for mirror magic and I've been studying with Cuinn Avinel on the sly. You remember Cuinn. The Conclave's mirror expert? Anyway, Professor Avinel said I have a real gift. And because *someone* told me who my mom was…" He shot me a look, never pausing in his buffing. "Now I know why." He stood back and quickly scrutinized his work. "I can link this to the obsidian door in the temple we found back in the canyon. The one I couldn't help but polish when we came in. It'll put us out on the surface and miles away from the mountain."

If it worked.

"Talon, you wanted me to remind you not to mess with rocks," I said.

"This isn't a rock; it's volcanic glass. It's a black mirror. I can do this. It'll work."

Master mirror mages who'd had a lifetime of study and experience would be hard-pressed to do what Talon was about to attempt, and they would have been doing it with mirrors they had made themselves and had worked with for years. Actual mirrors, real mirrors, not slabs of obsidian formed by a volcano ages before.

This wasn't merely difficult. It was impossible.

And we had no choice but to try.

There were three possible outcomes: Talon wouldn't be able to link the mirrors and I'd have Jash detonate the bombs, crushing us all under a mountain of rock. Or the link would partially work and we would end up embedded in the mountain between here and the canyon. Or it would work completely, saving all of us.

Two ways, we die. One way, we live.

Talon's eyes were intent on mine. He was waiting for my order as team leader—and my vote of confidence as his father and a fellow mage.

I gave my son what he needed.

I nodded once. "Get us out of here, Talon." I raised the spy gem. "Jash, we may have a way out. We'll need pickup for six at the canyon temple. Stand by."

There was a moment of silence. I knew Jash had heard me. *"Standing by."*

Talon pried Indigo from his shoulder and handed him to me. The little firedrake shrieked, clearly unhappy.

"I can't do this with you breathing in my ear," Talon told him.

But he could do it with Death breathing down his neck. Opening the mirror meant anchoring the mirror, meaning Talon would be going through last. He wanted me to take Indigo in case he didn't make it through.

Talon stood before the mirror, palms forward and fingers spread toward the gleaming obsidian slab, eyes open and concentration absolute.

Almost instantly, the black mirror began to ripple as it connected to another mirror—hopefully the one in the canyon temple that Talon was imagining in his mind. The ripple turned into a swirl as the connection stabilized, and the mirror was ready.

Damn. He'd done it, and faster than I'd ever seen a mirror linked before.

I stepped forward. "I'll go first to guard our exit. There could be unfriendlies waiting. Mal, I'll need you next as backup, then Agata. Baeseria and Maralah, if you would come after Agata. Talon will follow." I raised the spy gem. "Jash, detonate on my mark—or in two minutes if you don't hear from me."

"Got it."

Talon never looked away from the mirror, but his lips tightened against a surge of emotion.

"I trust you, Talon, but I can't take any chances," I told him.

"I know."

He did. He also knew that I trusted him, one mage to another.

"Ready?" I asked him.

Talon nodded once. "Go."

I went through.

37

I stepped out of the obsidian door Talon had polished only three days before and into the canyon temple, Malik close behind me.

Agata stepped through the mirror, followed by Maralah, who was supporting her mother. After awakening from centuries of sleep, the queen had tried to wrestle a stone of power into submission. I was amazed she could even stand.

I waited.

No Talon.

Agata's hand was on my arm. "Tamnais, we only have a few seconds."

A tremor rained dust down from the ceiling and the floor trembled beneath our feet.

"Come on, boy," Malik urged quietly.

I wanted nothing more than to run back through and get

my son, but mirrors didn't work that way. It would also disrupt Talon's link between the two, trapping him on the other side.

I waited.

An instant later, Talon dove through the door, slammed into me and knocked us both to the ground.

I'd never been so happy to have the wind knocked out of me.

Talon leapt to his feet, arms and fists in the air. "Yes!" He was beaming.

I climbed to my feet, grinning. "Great work, Talon."

"Yes, it was." My cocky son was back.

I raised my spy gem. "Jash, we're out. Tell Calik we need pickup for six in the canyon. Detonate now!"

Instead of Jash, I got a chorus of whooping cheers from the other end.

I assumed that meant my message had been received.

"Pardon the indignity, Your Majesty, but we're in a bit of a rush." I tossed Baeseria over my shoulder.

"We're ready on this end," Jash yelled. *"Detonating in three, two—"*

We were already running.

The instant we cleared the temple doors, a low boom shook the ground and even the air around us. It felt like the whole continent shifted.

I set Baeseria on her feet, but kept my arms around her. "Do you know if the beams—"

The queen nodded, clearly dazed. "I felt them as they broke. The Heart's connections to the land are severed. Your people and mine are safe."

But we weren't.

My eyes panned the sky. No Calik. No dragons.

I needed to be patient, but patience was hard to come by

with the ground shaking beneath our feet and whole sections of the canyon wall starting to come down.

"These are merely aftershocks," Baeseria said.

After what we'd just been through, and had done to get through it, it would seriously suck to be squashed flat in an aftershock.

Talon had Indigo back on his shoulder. "Would we be safer back in the temple?"

That question was answered seconds later as the massive carved doorframe collapsed, filling the doorway that'd been large enough to admit sentry dragons with rubble.

Talon swore. "Never mind."

"Stay in the middle!" I had to shout to be heard over the renewed tremors. I called Jash. "Is Calik airborne? We've got falling rocks down here."

"We're airborne."

We?

"Could you toss up a signal?" Jash asked. *"Everything looks the same from up here."*

I replied by flipping my palms over my head and blasting twin columns of blazing red light into the sky, feeding all my strength into it, and kept it going for nearly a minute.

The ground still shook and rocks continued to fall, but now I heard a new sound, a distant roar that grew louder with every second.

We all froze, eyes wide.

"That's not an aftershock," Agata said.

Maralah blanched. "It's water. The ancient quakes drained all the water to below ground. The Heart…the reservoirs have been breached."

Malik blinked. "Excuse me? *Reservoirs?*"

The Cha'Nidaar people weren't all that'd been set free today.

Talon grabbed Indigo and threw his arm into the air, launching the drake straight up. "Go!"

As the firedrake cleared the top of the canyon, he shot a pillar of fire that was ten times his size. If Calik and the dragons were anywhere nearby, Indigo would be a continuous beacon to our location.

The roar coming from the west grew in volume and intensity. I could visualize a wall of water pushing sections of the canyon in front of it.

All headed toward us.

Another roar split the air—from overhead—as a shadow passed over the canyon, obliterating the sky.

Sapphira.

Two more shadows blocked the sky.

Mithryn and Amaranth.

Malik flung a ring of blue light around us to show our position.

Calik lowered Sapphira into the canyon, turned sideways so her wings could stay fully extended and continue to beat and stay airborne.

Saffie extended her claws and Talon and I pushed Maralah and Baeseria into them. The dragon firmly but gently clutched her passengers and took off, making way for Amaranth—with Dasant in the pilot's saddle.

"Talon, you and Agata next!" I shouted over the approaching wall of water.

Talon didn't argue with me.

He just shoved Malik into Amaranth's waiting claw. Agata was already clutched in the other.

Rocks and debris flew around the turn in the canyon. I stared in awe, but mostly terror as a wall of water and rock, taller than I had ever imagined, extended to the very top of the canyon.

Mithryn was coming down with Jash in the pilot's saddle, but she'd never make it to the bottom in time.

Something was dangling from her feet, secured to her legs.

Ropes.

Talon and I leapt for them and started climbing.

"Go!" I screamed to Jash or Mithryn, whichever one was in charge.

She began her ascent as everything went into slow motion, the speed that said you were about to die. The wall of water picked up the stone doors from the temple as if they were hollow wood and swept them toward us.

We climbed faster.

The water crashed and rushed just beneath our feet as Mithryn fought her way clear of the canyon's rim. The torrent spilled over the rim and raced to fill the surrounding valley.

Ancient lakes and rivers refilling.

Mithryn flew us to a high bluff where the others waited. She dipped to deposit me and Talon on the bluff and then landed behind us with the other two dragons.

"The Cha'Nidaar?" I asked Jash once I'd pulled in enough air to speak.

"Our people are safe." Baeseria said, her arm around her daughter. "Thanks to the bravery of you and your companions."

"Ma'am, we think of it as stubbornness," Jash said. "Our people just don't know when to give up."

I looked around. In the distance, the peak of what was once the mountain containing the city of Nidaar was gone. In its place was a mound only half the height it once was.

"Calik, we'll need to fly over that to make sure the Heart is completely buried. There can't be any kind of opening."

"We'll take care of it once you all have caught your breath."

I gave him a tired grin. "Do we look that bad?"

"You've looked better. I could be more descriptive, but there are ladies present."

The sun had just risen on a new day, and it would shine down on a landscape that had not been seen in over a thousand years.

The waters still churned, but eventually they would fill the dry beds of ancient rivers and the valleys that had once been sparkling lakes—bringing life again to a land that had been barren for far too long.

When the waters settled, Aquas would again be a land of waters, the land Kansbar had seen when he'd arrived on its shores. He was here when it was destroyed.

My son and I were here to see it remade.

Both events had involved violent upheaval, but what we had accomplished had given the Cha'Nidaar a chance at a normal life, and Aquas a chance to be reborn.

Queen Baeseria gazed back at the remains of the mountain, her people's home that had become a prison. "Our burden has been taken from us, but my bond to the Heart remains and my responsibility continues."

"There are two people I would like you to meet," I told her gently. "Raine Benares and her father Eamaliel Anguis—they were bonded to the Saghred. I believe that you and Raine could help each other. Eamaliel's lifespan was greatly increased by contact with the Saghred. He, too, lived a long life burdened with great responsibility. But both have moved on with their lives and are very happy."

"I would like that."

"Then let's all go home."

EPILOGUE

I wasn't surprised.

The Cha'Nidaar had voted to stay on Aquas—at least for now. Troops would be arriving from the mainland to help build and staff a garrison. In addition to requiring the evacuation bags, Maralah had seen to it that her people had stockpiled food and water in the caves of the neighboring mountain.

These were not a people to relinquish their responsibilities lightly.

And neither were we.

That was where we were. On the next mountain over from where the Heart now lay buried beneath the ruins of Nidaar and the mountain that had hidden them both.

Queen Baeseria had been asleep for centuries, and the escape from Nidaar had taken its toll. Our ships' healers felt certain she would fully recover, and that recovery was being greatly accelerated by her reunion with her beloved people.

In addition to the Sythsaurian guns and teleportation/ weapon cuffs we had collected from the Khrynsani, Agata had come out of Nidaar with a bag of Heartstone crystals. The Cha'Nidaar soldiers had their version of the lizard men's guns, and they had stockpiled plenty of extra crystals in the cave holding their emergency supplies. While not powerful on the scale of causing earthquakes and mass destruction, the smaller pieces could power weapons like the guns, and Phaelan theorized that they could be adapted to cannons and was eager to experiment.

There was no sign of Sandrina Ghalfari, the Khrynsani, or the Sythsaurians. I didn't kid myself that it meant anything other than a temporary reprieve. The Khrynsani who had been guarding us had been wearing Sythsaurian teleportation cuffs. If they had each been wearing one, I was certain Sandrina would have been wearing two. While Malik had taken two of the cuffs for study, none of us were in a hurry to activate them and see where they'd take us. We thought they'd be dormant as long as they weren't attached to a wrist, but we'd wrapped them in wards, just in case, until they could be taken to the Isle of Mid for study by Cuinn Avinel or whoever Justinius Valerian thought was best qualified.

Though as it turned out, the cuffs and two of the guns would be taken directly to the Isle of Mid.

By Cuinn Avinel himself via the mirror in his laboratory on the Conclave college's campus.

In theory, mirror travel was possible over any distance.

Talon had found a few obsidian slabs in the caves the

Nidaarians had taken as their temporary home, and had actually succeeded in linking one to Cuinn's mirror. When the professor had been teaching Talon mirror magic, they'd used Cuinn's personal mirror. Talon knew it, and it knew Talon—and recognized him when he attempted to link his obsidian slab to it.

Only written messages were passed at first, until Cuinn was certain that the link was solid and stable.

Getting home again just got a whole lot easier.

As did obtaining supplies and reinforcements for the Cha'Nidaar.

When Cuinn had come through himself and seen the slab of obsidian he had just stepped out of, his eyes went a little wide. Then he was fine with it, impressed even. I was glad. It was one thing to be unique; it was something else entirely to be made to feel like a freak. Just because a skill was different didn't make it freakish, and it appeared the good professor was a firm believer in that. Later, Talon had even told him whose nephew he was. He knew that Cuinn had worked in the same department as Carnades Silvanus, and hadn't liked him in the least. For Talon to share that with Cuinn said a lot about the trust he placed in the professor. I'd only met Cuinn a few months before, but I knew Talon's trust wasn't misplaced. I was grateful he had a mirror teacher of Cuinn's skill to guide him.

We would be needing the professor's help with the Sythsaurians and their portals. Baeseria said they had used portals to gain access to our world. Cuinn had opened the portal to Timurus that had let us view the Sythsaurian armies massing and given us proof that the Khrynsani had allied themselves with them. Hopefully he could find the portal or portals the lizard men were using and slam them shut, barricade them, or whatever you did to a portal to make sure no one ever came through it again.

A day later, Cuinn arranged to have a mirror crated and brought through Talon's obsidian slab. Calik and Saffie flew it to the *Kraken* in a sling clutched in Saffie's claws. Cuinn rode in the passenger saddle, his first trip via sentry dragon. It didn't faze him, though; this was a man who routinely crossed thousands of miles through mirrors without a thought. Having a mirror on the *Kraken* would allow those who had been injured by the wave Karnia had sent to destroy our fleet to be taken to Mid for treatment, and the ships to be reprovisioned for the trip home.

Maralah became fascinated with mirror magic and wanted to learn more, and Talon had been fascinated with the Cha'Nidaar princess from the moment they'd met and was only too glad to teach. My son had always had a thing for older women.

Eamaliel Anguis had come through from Mid just this morning, and I had introduced him to the Cha'Nidaar queen. Baeseria was over fifteen hundred years old, and she took great delight in teasing Eamaliel, who was significantly younger at a mere nine hundred and thirty-four.

Kesyn had come through the new mirror on the *Kraken* to check on both of his students—me and Talon.

I got to have the fun of telling Kesyn what Talon had done with two slabs of polished obsidian miles apart, one on the surface, the other deep in the bowels of a mountain, while the Heart of Nidaar loomed over us trying to lay waste to half the world.

Kesyn was predictably horrified.

"It wasn't like it was the first time I'd ever linked mirrors," Talon told him. "Why are you surprised?"

"I wouldn't call what I'm feeling right now surprise. More like blood-freezing terror."

Talon merely shrugged. "I realized I had a connection to mirrors while in school on Mid. I have a lot of different powers, and since I'm still learning how to control them, the safest thing to do was to talk to an expert."

Kesyn barked a laugh. "*Safest?* Did the boy just say safest?"

I smiled. "Yes, he did, and I couldn't be more proud."

I'd already told Talon how proud I was of him, and how proud his mother would have been. We'd already had several long talks about Gelsey—initiated by Talon. He'd wanted to know more about his mother.

"Cuinn Avinel is the expert on mirrors and portals," Talon was saying. "So, I went to see him. He let me try things to find out what my limits were. Not so safe, but he said it was necessary to avoid accidents later on."

"And let me guess," Kesyn said, "Cuinn couldn't find any limits."

"That's what a lot of my professors said. I don't appear to have any, at least not any I've run into yet."

"Am I the only one who thinks that when the boy finally does run into a limit, there's gonna be a big boom involved?"

"I think that would be a safe assumption," I said.

Kesyn gave an exaggerated—and long-suffering—sigh. "And it's my job to be there when it happens."

I grinned. "That's the job you signed up for. Unless you're having second thoughts?"

"If anyone's qualified to be at ground zero when Talon

finds a limit, it's me. For the sake of the Seven Kingdoms, I'm staying closer than his shadow. You understand that, boy?"

Talon gave his teacher a slow, dangerous smile. "Perfectly, sir."

That smile was mine. Kesyn had seen it before. He'd dealt with the results of it then; he could deal with it now.

I turned away before either could see my own smile.

I think they *both* were in for a rude awakening.

I'd just returned from assessing the damage to the Heart's mountain. Calik and Sapphira had flown me and Agata over to survey Phaelan's handiwork. The collapse had been complete. There was no indentation in the middle of the debris field to indicate that a way still existed to access the Heart. There would probably be more settling, but it appeared that the explosives of Phaelan and his new friends had performed as promised.

I went to find him to tell him what we'd seen.

Phaelan was sitting on a rock overlooking Aquas's newest lake, which was actually more along the size of an inland sea. The sun was beginning to set behind us to the west. The lake had looked like a giant mud puddle in the first few days after the mountain's destruction, but after nearly a week, the waters were beginning to clear.

After the mirror had been taken to the *Kraken,* Phaelan had been back and forth several times. He'd just returned from one such trip.

I sat down next to him. "Magic's not so bad now, is it?"

The elf pirate's teeth flashed in a brief grin. "It has its uses."

"How are your brother and sister?"

"Ready to go home, but willing to wait until they're no longer needed."

"Agata and I just flew over your handiwork."

"And?"

"The collapse appears to be complete. Good work, Captain Benares. By the way, the engineers told me what you did."

"I did a lot of things that day. You'll have to be more specific."

"These things involved you and not one, not two, but three crawlspaces—and one hell of a trip to the surface."

"Oh, those."

"Yes, those."

One of the engineers told me that when the city had first been built over the Heart of Nidaar, they had reinforced the roof of the Heart's cavern to prevent exactly what we had to do—bring the city down on top of the Heart and completely bury it. The workers had used three access tunnels, though calling them tunnels was generous. There was enough room for a man to squirm his way in, then back out the same way. There was no room to turn around, but plenty of ways to get stuck. When the smallest engineer was going to take the bombs inside, they discovered that Karnia had warded the tunnels against entry by any of the Cha'Nidaar or other goblins.

Phaelan wasn't either one.

However, he was claustrophobic, as we had discovered in that chute leading into the Heartstone geode.

Phaelan had barely made it through a thirty-foot-long chute. Esha the engineer told me these access tunnels were a hundred yards long. Each.

Phaelan had planted a bomb—in the dark—in all three, then squirmed out backward the way he'd come in.

Then the elf pirate's Nidaar experience was topped off with his trip out of the mountain to the surface. Esha had told us they had an invention that made it a fast trip.

He wasn't kidding.

It amounted to a metal platform with hand and foot holds just large enough for one person to stand on. It was mounted in an old lava tube that went straight from the city to the surface. It was powered by five Heartstones mounted under the platform.

Phaelan's the trip to the surface—encased in a narrow lava tube—had taken less than a minute.

Esha said the elf had screamed the entire way up.

"I'm impressed," I said quietly. "And grateful to you. You're a good and brave man, Phaelan Benares. Raine said I would be glad that you were with me. She was right."

"You gave me one job, and I was going to do it. Besides, I had to come. Raine would kill me if I let anything happen to you." His jaw tightened. "Have you gotten any updates?"

"Eamaliel said reports would be few and far between. The situation in Pengor's still too unstable to risk sending out a message. He promised that as soon as they heard anything, they would let us know."

Phaelan stood and clasped my shoulder. "That'll have to be good enough." He flashed a roguish grin. "I'm sure they'll be fine. My cousin has a knack for making her enemies regret their actions."

The elf pirate walked back down to the main camp.

Raine and Mychael Eiliesor and others were in Pengor.

The late, not-lamented Carnades Silvanus and his henchman, Taltek Balmorlan, had spent years securing allies—and their money—among some of the most powerful and influential men and women in the elven government, military, and aristocracy. Their goal had been two-fold: the purification of the elven race and the extinction of the goblins. Those efforts had taken a serious hit when Balmorlan and Silvanus had been taken into custody and their plots exposed. Carnades's death at Sarad Nukpana's hands had dealt another blow. But racial hatred ran deep among many powerful high elves: both for elves they saw as inferior due to racial mixing, and any goblin who breathed air. More conspirators had arisen to take the places of those who had been arrested, and Taltek Balmorlan had escaped on his way to his execution. And I had no way of knowing if Sarad Nukpana was still imprisoned in the Lower Hells.

Carnades had sold out his people and the Conclave to Sarad Nukpana and the Khrynsani in exchange for being made king of the elves after Sarad used the Saghred to conquer the Seven Kingdoms. Carnades had provided Sarad with elven and Conclave defenses and military installation locations.

With the destruction of the Saghred, that invasion never came to pass.

But all that knowledge was now in the hands of Sandrina Ghalfari, the remaining Khrynsani—and the Sythsaurians.

The growing new elven conspiracy had gone so far as to accept assistance from their human neighbors—the Nebians, the only kingdom that had refused to sign the pledge to combine armies to fight against the Khrynsani and Sythsaurians.

The Nebians were also the kingdom who had sent ships to destroy our fleet—with Sythsaurian sorcerers on board.

Yes, it was a tangled mess. And it was just going to get worse before it got any better.

If it got any better.

I wanted to be with Raine and Mychael. I wanted to be there when the Silvanus family was destroyed. Most of all, I wanted every Silvanus brother to know precisely who I was to the sister they had murdered.

Agata was making her way up the rocks to where I was sitting.

I didn't hear her. I felt her.

Our bond had become comfortable—and even comforting.

I hadn't experienced either one in far too long. During the last few years, my life had become one death-defying dash after another. The past few days had been almost like a vacation. A guilty vacation. I was needed elsewhere, and here I was, sitting on a rock gazing out at a newborn sea.

And I was going to do it for one more day, guilt be damned.

Without a word, Agata sat next to me.

"You're leaving tomorrow?"

One side of my mouth twitched in a quick grin. "Nothing gets past you with me anymore, does it?"

She leaned in conspiratorially. "It never really did. The umi'atsu merely gives me words to go with what my intuition already knew."

"A'Zahra Nuru might be able to help us break it."

Agata shrugged.

I should have been surprised, but I wasn't. "You don't care if it's broken or not, do you?"

"I'm not exactly detecting any sense of urgency from you."

"There's a reason for that. Even if an umi'atsu can be

broken, it can be dangerous to try. Neither one of us needs to be losing any power."

Agata glanced down at her Heartstone pendant hanging openly outside of her shirt. It was hers now. I'd made her a gift of it. I still wore my ring.

She cradled it in the palm of her hand, the flames inside flickering happily at her touch. "Thanks to spending time in that geode, in the city, and bonding with the Heart itself, I've picked up some extra. And no, I don't want to lose it. I think it'll be needed. Cancel that, I know it'll be needed."

I shifted so that I was facing her. "Agata, your part in this is over. The Heart is beyond reach, its connections to the land severed. Your work is done."

"So, I'm to simply go home, oversee the rebuilding of my house—"

"Which I *am* paying for. If your house being burnt to the ground wasn't due to me being there, it had everything to do with the Khrynsani wanting you to find the Heart for them. I needed you to find the Heart for me, that makes me at the very least indirectly responsible. Talon's linked that black mirror of his to the mirror in my office at home. Barrett says the reconstruction is nearly finished. He's also had your wardrobe replaced. Since your house isn't ready yet, he's put your new clothes in your room in my home."

Agata smiled slightly and raised a brow. "*My* room?"

It was my turn to shrug. "Well, it was the one you stayed in before we left to come here, and it will be yours until your house is ready."

"You know, you have a tendency to take responsibility— or blame—for a lot."

"That's because I've been at fault at lot. Many things would not have happened—and many people would not have died—if not for my actions. I'm dangerous to be around, Agata."

"I've noticed that. But you attract that danger because you resist, you fight those like Sandrina Ghalfari and Sarad Nukpana. You stand up, you fight, and you refuse to let them win."

"And those close to me suffer or die because of it. More than once, those I love have been used against me. I couldn't protect them. Gelsey was killed because of me. I failed to—"

"You didn't fail, because you didn't know. Gelsey was protecting *you*. She *chose* not to contact you. She knew you weren't ready to go up against her family." Her dark eyes were intent on mine. "Tam, you didn't kill Calida."

"My actions—"

Agata shook her head in vehement denial. "No. Your actions wouldn't have affected the outcome. I know what happened. I heard. Sandrina would have killed Calida regardless. She wanted you gone. As long as you were there, Sathrik couldn't begin usurping power from his mother. He couldn't have gotten close enough to have killed her."

"I wouldn't have been chief mage if it hadn't been for the black magic."

"You wouldn't?" She smiled a little. "Be honest with yourself, Tam. The black magic had nothing to do with it. It helped you survive, but you were much more than Gilcara's enforcer. You were her protector. That's why you stayed by her side for so long. She needed you, and you knew you were protecting more than one woman, one queen. You were taking a stand against all that the Khrynsani, Sandrina, and Sarad represented. All that they would do to the goblin people if they ever gained full power. Gilcara's son is equally wise in keeping you by his side." Her smile grew warm. "Chigaru knows what his mother knew, and he chose the best man to be his heir. You were protecting the goblin people, Tam. You still are, and you always will." She paused. "I think Calida was a wise woman, too. She knew why she fell in love with you, because of the kind of man you are. I know who you are. I looked inside of you before I agreed to come here with you."

"You've heard the stories about me."

"I have, and they didn't match the man who was standing in my soon-to-be-destroyed home."

"Sorry about that."

"There you go, taking the blame again. It wasn't your fault. It was yet another in what I suspect is a long line of events you're shouldering the blame for. You can't take the blame for the evil of others."

"But I—"

"Got a little drunk with power? Enjoyed your work? Enjoyed defeating the Khrynsani at every turn? There's nothing wrong—"

"I wouldn't call diving headfirst into black magic *a little drunk*."

She glanced over at Talon, who was laughing at something Phaelan had just said. "I understand your mother described him—and you—as *impulsive, stubborn, arrogant, and believes himself impervious to death*?"

I grinned. "Don't forget *believes himself irresistible to women*."

Agata snorted. "How could I forget that?" Her dark eyes grew solemn. "You were susceptible, Tam. It was unfortunate, but it kept you alive to do what needed to be done. Those who stand up for good often find themselves beset by those who do evil. Have you ever killed innocents?"

"Never."

"Precisely. You killed those who threatened your queen, and the freedom and safety of your people. You may have enjoyed what you were doing at the time, but you acted for the greater good. You're not evil, Tam Nathrach. You never were and you never will be."

"That doesn't change that Calida was murdered because of it."

"She knew the true nature of the man she married. She loved him, married him, and stood by his side. She may not have had magic with which to defend herself, but from what I have heard, she was a woman who knew her own mind. She knew what she wanted. She wanted you."

Agata reached out and touched my hand. The Heartstone in my ring warmed in response—and so did I.

"I don't believe Calida had any regrets." She hesitated, decided something, and raised her hand to brush my face. "You shouldn't have any regrets, either. You need to stop punishing yourself for what is in the past. You have more than paid your self-inflicted penance. I don't think Calida would want you to continue punishing yourself. Do you?"

I shook my head, my cheek brushing against the soft warmth of her hand.

"But Calida didn't deserve to die," I said softly.

"And you *deserve to live*. I did not know her, but I

think she would have wanted that for you. You can't save everyone, Tam. All you can do is your best. Life happens. Death happens. Bad things happen to good people. I have no doubt that you will exact revenge for her and Gelsey, but you can't let this consume you. You are far too important to so many people." She paused, her other hand reaching for mine. "You've become too important to me."

I leaned forward, brushing her lips with mine. "I'm bad to know and dangerous to be around," I whispered against her mouth.

I felt her lips curl into a wicked smile. "Then every day will be a new adventure."

ABOUT THE AUTHOR

Lisa Shearin is the *New York Times* bestselling author of the Raine Benares novels, a comedic fantasy adventure series, as well as the SPI Files novels, an urban fantasy series best described as *Men in Black* with supernaturals instead of aliens. Lisa is a voracious collector of fountain pens, teapots, and teacups, both vintage and modern. She lives on a small farm in North Carolina with her husband, four spoiled-rotten retired racing greyhounds, and enough deer and woodland creatures to fill a Disney movie.

Website: lisashearin.com
Facebook: facebook.com/LisaShearinAuthor
Twitter: @LisaShearin

Made in the USA
Lexington, KY
27 May 2017